TARGET FOR RANSOM

LAURA SCOTT

READSCAPE PUBLISHING, LLC

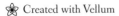

CHAPTER ONE

September 9 – 1:25 p.m. – Washington, DC

"Let me go!" The young dark-haired girl squirmed in her seat, fighting the ropes holding her arms ruthlessly behind her back, her eyes covered by a black blindfold. "Let me go!"

Jordan's gut clenched and bile rose in his throat as the girl repeatedly sobbed, begging to be released. Unable to tear his gaze from the live webcam, he forced himself to think like an agent, concentrating on the pertinent details. The room was dark, windowless, and anonymously bare. It could have been any city in any country across the world. The rope was basic twine, and the chair the girl was sitting in was a cheap card-table type of chair readily available in any store.

"Can't you understand English? Let me go!" Panic mingled with defiance in her tone.

Jordan curled his fingers into helpless fists. What sort of people tormented a child? What did they want? He leaned closer, straining to analyze the situation despite the child's heartrending cries. The girl's young voice sounded American, but he couldn't be certain of her ethnic background without seeing her eyes. What little he could see of her face revealed tan skin. Even though the girl appeared to be alone, he knew she wasn't.

It was a macabre scene, staged solely for his benefit.

"Jordan Rashid, if you want to see your daughter alive, you must follow our instructions exactly." A deep male voice, altered by some sort of mechanical device, came from somewhere beyond the view of the camera. "If you don't obey our instructions, or if you go to the authorities, we will kill her."

"Help me!" the girl shouted, struggling again in earnest. "Please help me. They're going to hurt me!"

A hooded man stepped in front of the camera and slapped the girl sharply, causing her to cry out in pain as her head snapped sideways from the blow. What the— Jordan leaped from his seat, grabbing the computer screen as if he could prevent the next attack.

"Silence, infidel," the man shouted. He let out a stream of instructions in low, rapid Arabic that Jordan tried to understand, then quickly stepped back out of the camera's view and switched to English. "Jordan Rashid, you will receive further instructions within an hour of accessing this website."

The screen went blank. Jordan stood there, his heart hammering in his chest. He couldn't breathe. His vision momentarily blurred. He struggled to focus.

What in the world was going on?

He tunneled his fingers through his hair, pacing the span of his office, trying to block the echo of the young girl's pleading voice. Was this part of the most recent case the FBI had dropped in his lap? The fact that the guy spoke Arabic and the FBI case had ties to ISIS made it likely. He stopped and jotted down the few phrases he'd been able to pick up.

Teach her to obey. Respect authority.

Jordan swallowed hard, trying not to imagine what might be happening in that room off-camera. He stared at the blank computer screen, wishing he could watch the video again. Who was that poor girl? He didn't doubt she was nothing more than an innocent pawn in a deadly game. Whoever she was, those guys had gotten inaccurate information. She couldn't be his daughter. He didn't have a daughter.

He didn't have any children at all.

SEPTEMBER 9 – 1:42 *p.m.* – *Washington, DC*

Diana Phillips sat on the edge of her hotel room bed and stared at the number written on the note. The image swam and she blinked, peering through the exhausted haze blanketing her eyes.

She was to contact Jordan Rashid the moment she arrived in DC. Her daughter's life depended on it.

How had this happened? In one moment her peaceful, ordinary life in Jacksonville, North Carolina, had been shattered. Her daughter had vanished, kidnapped sometime after leaving school and before Diana had come home from work. A hysterical sob welled up in her throat. Bryn. Dear, sweet Bryn. Her daughter had to be alive.

She just had to be.

Diana swallowed a cry, struggling to remain calm. She couldn't fall apart. Bryn was counting on her. Bryn needed her to be strong.

Think. She had to think. If she followed the kidnappers' demands, there was a good chance she'd get Bryn back alive.

She needed to call Jordan. It couldn't be a coincidence the kidnappers had sent her to him. Especially since she hadn't seen Jordan in twelve years. Had, in fact, never told him about his daughter.

He'd be shocked to know Diana was alive, and even more stunned to learn about Bryn. So much had happened back then: their brief, yet passionate love affair and then the cold, hard betrayal he'd accused her of mere hours before the explosion that nearly killed them both.

A wave of helplessness rose in her throat. After everything that had happened, he'd never believe her. How in the world could she make him believe her now when he hadn't before?

She wasn't sure, but she had to figure out something.

Bryn's life depended on it.

With trembling fingers, she punched the numbers into her mobile phone. When Jordan answered, his deep, husky voice caused a riptide of memories. Images she hastily blocked.

She swallowed hard, willing herself to be strong. "Jordan? It's me, Diana Phillips. Don't hang up! I know you think I'm dead, but I'm not. I need to talk to you. I need your help. My daughter needs your help."

"Who is this?" he asked in a sharp tone.

"Diana Phillips," she repeated. What could she say to convince him? Panic lanced her heart, and she gripped the phone tighter. "Jordan, listen to me. I swear I'm telling you the truth. Remember the night we spent together in Paris? We ate dinner at *Les Deux Magots*. It's really me. And my daughter needs your help."

"Are you connected to the kidnapping?" His tone was blunt. "Is that how you got this number?"

He knew about the kidnapping? For some reason that

bit of information struck her as odd. How could he know prior to her call? Confused, she stood and stared out the window of the hotel room. "The kidnappers gave me this number. Please, Jordan. I need to talk to you. In person."

"Fine. I'll be waiting." He disconnected from the line.

Sucking in a harsh breath, she stared at the phone. After everything they'd gone through together twelve years ago, after she mentioned their evening in Paris, the night they'd been intimate, he still didn't believe her. But somehow he knew about the kidnapping.

Whoever had masterminded snatching Bryn had figured out Jordan Rashid was her daughter's biological father.

A cold shiver lifted the hairs on the back of her neck. How could anyone know the truth? She'd never told Jordan. Hadn't dared to break the rules surrounding her placement in witness protection, especially after Bryn was born.

The FBI agent who'd sent her into witness protection knew. But why would he tell anyone? Tony Balcome had handed her off to the US Marshals, and her handler was the only one who knew where she lived.

Bitter guilt coated her tongue. Ever since Bryn had disappeared, twenty-one hours and seventeen minutes—no, eighteen minutes—ago, she'd been trying to figure out what was going on. Twelve years had passed since the explosion had nearly cost her her life, and Jordan's too. Twelve years in witness protection. If this was related to her and Jordan's tangled past, why go after Bryn now, after all this time?

Or was this kidnapping the result of something more recent? A fist of fear knotted in her belly. She couldn't deny having a few secrets, and taking Bryn may be an attempt to get back at her. But if that was the case, why send Diana to

Jordan? How would anyone discovering her secret mission even know about her and Jordan?

No, this might not be her fault. She'd been beating herself up enough, knowing if she hadn't stopped for groceries on the way home from work, Bryn might still be safe and sound.

Was it possible Bryn's kidnapping was related to her mother's brother, Omar Haram Shekau? She didn't see how since Omar was dead. She'd watched Jordan kill him twelve years ago, shortly before the crash and the subsequent explosion. She hadn't been in contact with anyone from her mother's family since going into witness protection.

Not that she'd wanted to. Her family was dead to her.

Except for Bryn.

None of this made any sense. Bryn's kidnapping had to be connected to Jordan. To one of his FBI cases.

It had to be his fault her precious daughter was taken.

Spurred into action by a sudden flash of anger, she swept her purse off the bed and flew toward the door. The note directed her to call Jordan Rashid at his office number. It also gave her the location of his office in the Washington, DC, Piermont Office Building.

She'd find him and demand his help in rescuing Bryn. Bypassing the elevator, she ran down the stairs, tripping and falling heavily against the wall in her exhausted haze.

Muffling a startled cry, she yanked herself upright and pulled herself together. Ignoring the pain of her twisted ankle was easier than losing her mind over Bryn. In the lobby, she found the bellman and requested a cab.

Glancing at the crumpled paper in her hand, he noted her destination. "The Piermont Office Building?" He tipped his hat back and raked a skeptical glance over her.

"You don't need a cab, lady. It's right there, across the street."

It was? She stared. No wonder she'd been directed to this hotel. The coincidence was too much. The extent of their well-organized and carefully planned approach gave the kidnapping a deep, sinister tone.

Bryn. She had to find Bryn. Fresh tears sprung to her eyes, and she dashed them away with an impatient hand. Where was her anger? Being mad was better than weeping. She strode outside and across the street, running on pure adrenaline.

Bryn was in danger. That's all that mattered. She ripped open the door to the office building and glared at the directory, searching for Jordan. Through the process of elimination, she figured out that Security Specialists, Inc. had to be where she'd find Jordan's office.

Twelve years ago, Jordan used to be with the FBI, but it seemed that had changed. She paused outside the doorway to his office, assailed by a towering inferno of doubt. Should she have gone to the authorities? Had she made things worse for Bryn by not going straight to the police? Or to the FBI? What sort of mother was she?

Jordan needed to understand she was telling the truth. And if he didn't believe her, surely he had enough compassion to care about the life of an innocent girl. If he told her to go to the authorities, she would.

At least, so far, she was doing exactly as directed by the kidnappers. She was meeting their demands, hence assuring Bryn's safety. Or so she hoped.

She couldn't afford to consider the alternative.

Yet aside from how Bryn had been dragged into this mess, despite the belief it was all Jordan's fault, she knew he'd also protected her with his life twelve years ago. Surely that meant something.

Deep down, she firmly believed that Jordan offered the best chance at finding her daughter.

He had to believe her.

He had to help her get Bryn back.

SEPTEMBER 9 – 2:00 *p.m.* – *Washington, DC*

Jordan paced the length of his office. The child's kidnapping followed by a call from a woman claiming to be Diana was enough to raise his suspicions tenfold.

How had she known about their night in Paris? And the exclusive restaurant where they'd eaten dinner? And afterward when they'd first made love?

A shiver snaked down his spine, and he thrust the memory away.

The website access had arrived on his personal account, accompanied by an anonymous note. The website address, *Jordanrashidsfuture.com*, was not amusing.

The poor kid. He kept seeing the image of the girl being held against her will. Reliving the moment when the jerk slapped her. What else had they done? There were things much worse than a brutal slap.

He felt sick just thinking about it. She was just a little kid!

The determined rap on his door was a welcome relief, even if it came faster than he'd expected. The woman, whoever she really was, made good time getting here. Bracing himself, he opened the door to let her in.

A slender woman, a good five inches shorter than his six-foot frame, stood across the threshold, her deep brown eyes regarding him warily. She wore a pair of brown slacks and a gold sweater. Her black straight hair was pulled away from her face. She looked older, more mature than the woman he'd once loved, but the uncanny resemblance to Diana Phillips squeezed his heart.

When she reached up and twirled the tiny cross earring in her right ear, the familiar nervous gesture hit him square in the chest, forcing him to take a step backward. She looked similar to Diana, had mannerisms just like Diana, and had known about their night in Paris.

Whoever she was, she'd been well trained. No way did he believe she was the woman he'd lost twelve years ago. But what was the point of this elaborate charade?

No clue.

"Jordan." She didn't quite meet his gaze as she swept past him, entering the room. "How did you know about the kidnapping? Tell me everything."

He closed the door behind her, keeping a safe distance between them, ready for any sort of attack. He didn't trust her but would play along. For now.

For the kid's sake.

"Have a seat," he invited. Regardless of how much she looked like Diana, he figured this had to be a trap. Keeping his hands loose at his sides, he stared at her for a long moment. "I assume it's your daughter I saw on the webcam?"

"Webcam?" She jerked around, the frank hope in her eyes too fevered to fake. "Show me! I want to see Bryn. I need to see my daughter."

Her reaction appeared all too real. Was this woman really Diana? He didn't see how it was possible. Diana was dead. This woman had to be an imposter. He waved a hand at the computer. "The site's already been disconnected. I can tell you that I saw a young girl, about eleven or twelve years old with dark hair, sitting blindfolded in a chair, obviously held against her will."

"Eleven. She's eleven." The woman's hoarse voice was full of such anguish he almost winced. Diana fiddled with her gold cross earring again, then met his gaze. "Bryn will be twelve in May."

Counting backward, he realized he'd lost Diana almost twelve years ago in October. If she had gotten pregnant in Paris and lived, her child would have been born in May.

The connection was unnerving. Was it possible? And if so, how? Regardless, even if this woman was Diana, he couldn't afford to trust her. "I'm sorry."

"She's alive, right?" Diana stepped closer, causing him to take another hasty step back. She followed, closing the gap. "If she's alive, we still have a chance. We can find her!"

This close, she looked far too much like the woman from his past.

The woman he had once loved.

The woman whose obituary still lined the bottom of his desk drawer.

The woman who had betrayed him.

SEPTEMBER 9 – 2:07 *p.m.* – *Washington, DC*

A strained silence fell between them. Jordan finally brought the subject back to the issue at hand. "The kidnappers wanted me to believe the girl was alive, but there are no guarantees." He refused to offer false hope. This Diana-clone needed to be prepared. The way she was acting, it seemed possible the child might really be her daughter. "Start at the beginning. When did you discover she was missing?"

"Yesterday, late afternoon, when I came home from

work." The woman didn't sit but moved back and forth in short agitated movements. "I called all her friends, trying to find out if she went somewhere after school without telling me, but as the hour grew later, I began to panic. I was just about to call the police when an envelope was delivered to me by special courier, giving me these instructions." She pulled the paper out of her pocket and handed it to him.

He took the note, the paper damp and crumpled having been folded and refolded several times, likely clutched in her hands while taking the steps as directed. "You didn't call the police?"

"No." She crossed her arms over her chest, hugging herself. Again, the familiar gesture brought him up short. This is exactly how Diana had looked the night her mother died, stricken with grief, holding herself, yet stoically determined to remain alone.

Back then, he'd taken her into his arms, comforting her. But that wasn't an option now.

Even if this was Diana, he had no proof she wasn't involved in this up to her pretty neck. There were women in the world who wouldn't hesitate to sell their child for an easy buck. He wouldn't have thought Diana was the type to do that, then again, he'd never expected her to betray him either.

"I almost did call the police," she said in a low voice full of uncertainty. "I was so afraid. When I was instructed to call you, I figured I'd wait. You're obviously not with the FBI anymore, but what do you think? Should we call the authorities? Will the kidnappers somehow know if we do?"

He let out a heavy breath, dragging his gaze from the pure anguish etched in her features. Her fear was so real he was having trouble remaining objective.

Call the police? Of course they should call the authorities. And the locals would likely turn right around and call in the Feds and maybe even the CIA once he explained that the guy on the webcam had spoken Arabic. Jordan knew from his time with the Bureau that going to the police was always the best way to ensure getting the hostage back alive.

But this kidnapping wasn't some random, spur-of-the-moment decision. If this woman was Diana Phillips, and she happened to be innocent, this elaborate setup reeked of something big. A master plan. The way they'd taken the girl and sent Diana a precise set of instructions, bringing the child's mother to him, tightened his gut in alarm.

There was far more at stake here than money.

"Jordan, please. I know you don't believe me, but I'm begging you to listen to what I'm going to tell you." She stopped, drew in a deep breath, and let it out again. "I've been in the witness protection program for the past twelve years. Bryn is our daughter. I couldn't risk breaking my cover to find you, until now. Bryn's life is at stake, and that trumps everything. You have to help me."

He didn't say anything, his mind grappling with the possibilities.

"Jordan!" Her dark eyes flashed with anger. "Don't you care about her at all?"

He flinched. "How can I care about a daughter I don't have?"

She stiffened, her chin jerking up defensively. "Bryn is your daughter. Remember the explosion that nearly killed you? Nearly killed us both?"

He gave a small nod. How could he forget the worst night of his life?

"They told me I was unconscious for two days. The FBI was at my bedside when I woke up, and Agent Balcome told me I had to go into witness protection if I wanted to stay alive. I'm sure if you need proof, the FBI can dig it up for you."

He stared at her in surprise. Would his previous employer have done something like this without telling him? Yeah, maybe. Although he didn't understand why.

"I didn't know I was pregnant until I was in the hospital," she continued, glancing away. Because she was lying? He couldn't tell. Twelve years ago, he'd believed Diana's claims about not knowing what her uncle was up to, only to be proven wrong. Ironic to find himself in the same situation again. "When I discovered I was going to have our child, I wanted to find you, but I couldn't break the rules of witness protection."

"Forget the rules," he interjected harshly. "The Diana I knew would have told me."

"And put my daughter's life at risk? No." She spoke the word with emphasis. "Bryn's safety had to come first." Her expression turned grim. "Besides, it was better for you if I stayed away."

Better for him? He fought the insane urge to laugh. Yeah, right. Who was she trying to convince?

"What can I say that will make you believe me? I already mentioned our dinner in Paris. The night Bryn was conceived." Diana's gaze implored him to remember and believe. "My mother is buried in the Prospect Hill Cemetery, under the name of Anna Phillips. But you know her birth name was Zara Haram Shekau. Her brother was Omar Haram Shekau. Omar found and killed my mother, and you killed him."

He stared at her in surprise. Was it possible she was telling the truth? He was afraid to believe.

But he wanted to.

"Fine, whatever." Her tone was curt. "None of that

matters now. I'm here because of Bryn. You don't trust me? Fine, I don't care." Her eyes flashed with anger, and her voice shook. "I swear on my mother's grave Bryn is your daughter. And she's in danger. The kidnappers sent me here for a reason. We have to find her, Jordan. Before it's too late."

He didn't know what to say or what to believe. The information Diana had provided was persuasive. Especially their night in Paris. There was no easy way for anyone to know about that, and crazily enough, he was beginning to believe her.

Still, it wouldn't hurt to check with his old boss at the FBI. Ray Pallone could set him up to talk to Agent Balcome. If Diana Phillips had really been placed in witness protection, someone had better give him some proof.

"It may already be too late," he warned, unwilling to sugarcoat the truth.

"No!" She spun away, but not before he noticed the glimmer of tears. When she stumbled toward a chair, he took a step toward her as if to catch her, but then pulled himself up short. "I don't believe it. I'd know in my heart if Bryn was dead. God wouldn't take her from me. From us. She's alive. We just need to find her."

A lump formed in the back of his throat. What if she was right? What if that girl in the video really was his daughter?

He didn't want to be so gullible, but the tiny seed of hope had been planted in the center of his heart just the same. He capitulated, because really, what choice did he have? "Okay, I'll call my FBI contact. See what I can find out."

"Thank you." Her dark eyes glistened with gratitude.

For a moment, he was reminded of the first night they'd met all those years ago.

The phone on his desk rang, jarringly loud. The screen indicated the number was blocked, but that wasn't surprising. He hit the recording device attached to his phone, then punched the speaker button so Diana could hear the conversation. "Rashid."

"Jordan Rashid?" The voice was distorted by a mechanical device. "I have a very special request for your services. If you wish to see your daughter again, listen very closely to my instructions."

He'd been right all along—this wasn't about money. "I'm listening."

"The Lebanese authorities have arrested a Syrian by the name of Ahmed Mustaf who is currently being held at Camp Bucca. There are plans to move him to a new location within the week. There is a flight to Lebanon leaving tonight. We demand you go directly to Lebanon to release Mustaf from prison prior to his transfer. Once he is safe in our hands, I will arrange for your daughter to be returned home."

A shiver of alarm rippled down his spine. Ahmed Mustaf was at the top of the terrorist most-wanted list; in fact, Mustaf was suspected of supporting a terrorist cell operating here in DC. The same terrorist cell Jordan's FBI contact had recently asked him to infiltrate.

He didn't like the coincidence. Not one bit.

"I want to speak to Bryn, to know she's still alive." He gripped the phone, praying they'd put Bryn on the line just for a moment.

"I will call you back within the half hour with another webcam address where you will be able to see your daughter," the mechanical voice intoned.

"No! A webcam can be fixed. I want to talk to her while she's on camera." There was a long pause. "Do you hear me? I'm not doing anything for you until I know I'm speaking to my daughter and that she's safe."

"A brief communication will be arranged."

"Good." The tightness in his chest eased. His hostage negotiation skills were rusty, but he did his best to pull them from the depths of his memory. "I also want regular communication with Bryn moving forward."

"No. After this, all communication will cease until we know you're in Lebanon." The line went dead.

Jordan looked at Diana's pale face and knew that he'd do what he was told if that meant saving the life of an eleven-year-old girl.

A child who he was beginning to believe may very well be his daughter.

CHAPTER TWO

September 9 – 2:23 p.m. – Baltimore, MD

Bryn tried to control her involuntary shaking. Never in her life had she been so afraid. A blindfold covered her eyes, so she strained to listen. Silence. She sniffed and licked the corner of her mouth, tasting blood. Her cheek throbbed with pain.

She'd been raised to believe in God. Had prayed since these men had taken her. But her faith was wavering.

She'd tried to use the self-defense and Tae Kwon Do punches and kicks her mother had taught her to get away from the men who'd taken her, but they'd held her so tight she couldn't move. Tears pricked her eyes.

A door slammed and she jumped, a whimper escaping from her throat before she could stop it. She tried to relax so the bonds around her wrists wouldn't hurt so much. Swallowing hard, she fought the urge to cry.

She wanted her mom. She really, really wanted her mom.

"He is gone. I untie you."

The woman, the one who identified herself Meira,

spoke in a low, hushed tone. Since this nightmare had begun, the woman who took care of her, who kept those icky smelly men away from her, was the only one she wasn't afraid of.

At least, not yet.

"Th-thank you." Her arms fell loose, the muscles in her shoulders jerking painfully. Meira took one arm and then the other, gently massaging the soreness away. When she finished, Bryn sensed she had moved away.

"I bring food."

Bryn nodded, wishing she dared to yank the blindfold from her eyes. But the first time she'd tried to do that, Meira had shouted at her to stop. Bryn was so afraid the horrible men would come back that she decided it was better to leave the blindfold in place.

At least her wrists were no longer tied to the back of the chair. Sitting in the dark could have been worse. From what she could tell, Meira shared the room with her. If she was hungry, thirsty, or had to go to the bathroom, Meira was there to help, reassuring despite her broken English.

This nightmare would be so much worse without Meira.

"Eat." Meira gently pushed a bowl into her hands.

Bryn had no idea what was in the bowl, but the contents tasted similar to the oatmeal her mother sometimes made. It was blah, but not awful. Carefully using the plastic spoon, she took a bite.

At first Bryn had been afraid to eat, fearing they'd poison her. She and her mom had poisoned some mouse food and left it in the garage to keep the little buggers from building nests in her mom's car engine. She'd mentioned the idea of poison to Meira, but the woman hadn't seemed to understand. Eventually, Bryn had gotten so hungry her stomach had ached, so she'd caved in, eating what they'd given her.

It wasn't Mickey D's, but the thick gloppy stuff hadn't made her sick either.

How long would they keep her? As she ate, questions zipped through her mind. The men wanted something from the guy named Jordan Rashid. They'd claimed he was her father, which only proved they were total wackos. Her mom explained that her dad had died before she was born.

Had they confused her with someone else? She'd only heard one of the men speaking English, the other didn't seem to, so she wouldn't be surprised if they'd messed up and grabbed the wrong kid. Maybe they'd picked her house by mistake. After all, speaking English is different from reading it. Seriously, how smart could they be?

Idiots.

She heard a rustling sound. "Meira?"

"Yes?" The woman came close enough that Bryn could smell the hint of some spice on her skin.

Bryn hesitated, trying to figure out what she could say to convince her captor to help her. She wasn't stupid, she'd read lots of mystery books. There was one by Lois Duncan where these bad guys kidnapped a girl, keeping her in some dark scary basement, promising to let her go when in reality they had planned on killing her.

This was worse than a stupid story. Or a movie on TV. This was real.

Bryn didn't want to die.

"What you need?" Meira asked.

"Do you believe in God?"

There was nothing but silence for a long moment. "Yes, I believe in Allah."

Bryn wasn't sure if Allah was exactly the same as God,

the way she'd been taught, but she found some comfort in the woman's answer.

"Why?" Meira pressed.

"Are you going to let them kill me?" Bryn asked bluntly. Meira didn't answer, and Bryn blindly reached out, groping and swiping at air. "Well? Are you?"

"You will not die." Meira's voice was so quiet Bryn could barely hear her. Was she afraid the men would overhear? "Soon, they will let you go."

Bryn couldn't believe what Meira was saying. Panic twisted her stomach, and she thought she might throw up the gloppy food. Meira seemed nice enough, but she also did whatever those men told her to do. If they said tie Bryn up, she did. When they hit her, Meira didn't stop them.

What else would Meira do?

"Meira, listen to me. We can get out of here," Bryn whispered. "If you and I work together, we can escape. We're still in the United States, right?" Meira didn't answer, so she continued, "Do you know what it's like to live here? You would be free to do whatever you wanted. You wouldn't have to do what those men tell you to do. I promise I can help you."

Silence. Bryn held her breath, wondering what it would take to convince Meira to help her escape. As much as she wanted her mom to come, she didn't think the police would be able to find her. She'd been taken from her house, put in a car, and had driven for what seemed like forever. Who knew what state she was in now? Probably not North Carolina, that's for sure.

Meira was her best chance of getting out of here. She just had to help. Bryn was afraid they didn't have much time.

She needed to escape before the icky men did something worse than slapping her.

SEPTEMBER 9 – 2:49 p.m. – Washington, DC

Too anxious to sit, Diana paced the small confines of Jordan's office, the seconds passing by with infinite slowness as he made the phone call to some guy named Ray Pallone who was fairly high up the chain of command, reporting to the director himself, Clarence Yates. When forced to leave a message with some lackey, Jordan made a second call, demanding to speak to Agent Tony Balcome.

"Unavailable? For how long?" Jordan's gaze locked with hers, the call on speaker so they could both hear.

"That's classified information."

"Put me through to Clarence Yates," Jordan said firmly.

"I'll leave a message with him to call you." The guy on the other end of the phone sounded as if he wouldn't budge.

"Thanks." Jordan disconnected from the call. "That was a dead end."

"Once you get a chance to talk to Tony Balcome, you'll know I'm telling the truth."

Jordan's dark gaze held hers for a long moment, then he made another call, again putting it on speaker. "Hey, Sloan. You know that latest case Yates dropped in my lap? Well, it's already gotten significantly more complicated. I'm going to need some help on this."

"You may want to call Sun Yin, she's a better linguist than I am," Sloan pointed out. "Unfortunately, I'm still tied up with our other case."

Diana didn't care about any other case, all she wanted was to find Bryn. She was about to interrupt when Jordan held up his hand in warning.

"Fine, ask Sun to call me, ASAP. We don't have any time to waste."

"This isn't helping," she pointed out the moment he disconnected from the line. "We can't keep wasting time."

"We need a decent plan," Jordan pointed out in a maddeningly reasonable tone. "Before I fly off to Lebanon, I need to confirm Mustaf is really being held at Camp Bucca."

"Why would they lie?" she demanded harshly. "The more time we waste, the less likely they'll keep Bryn alive."

Jordan scowled, then dropped into the chair behind his desk, his fingers flying over the keyboard. She edged closer, trying to see what he was doing. When he pulled out his passport, she had the insane urge to pluck it from his fingers, dreading the idea of him leaving her.

"There, happy?" He gestured to the screen. "I'm booked on the next flight out of DC to Lebanon just as the kidnappers demanded. Although what I'll be able to accomplish from that point onward is anyone's guess. It's not exactly like I can walk up to the prison and demand they release Mustaf."

"I know." She forced the words past her tight throat. Even if Jordan tried to meet the kidnappers' ransom, there wasn't any guarantee that he'd succeed. In fact, she knew very well the odds were weighted toward a dismal failure.

Her knees went weak, and she staggered around the corner of his desk to drop into the nearest chair. Dear heaven, what would happen if Jordan couldn't free Mustaf? Were they crazy to even try? Maybe they should focus on finding out where the hooded men were holding Bryn.

Jordan's phone rang, and he hit the speaker button again. "Rashid."

"Jordan?" a female's voice shimmered over the line. "I understand you need linguistic assistance?"

"How quickly can you get here?"

"I'm on my way, but traffic is nuts, may take upwards of thirty minutes."

Diana didn't know who Sun Yin was but hoped the woman could help them find Bryn. She wondered if Jordan was involved with someone these days. She'd never come close to marrying, but surely Jordan had moved on. What did it matter? Nothing mattered except her daughter.

I'm coming, Bryn. Be strong, baby, I'm coming.

There was a faint beep indicating a new mail message. She jettisoned out of her seat and scrambled around to see Jordan's computer screen.

The email was from a David Jones, probably a fake account, and the link embedded in the message formed the phrase *Freemustaforshewilldie.com.*

Fear clawed its way up her chest, lodging in her throat. She didn't dare blink as Jordan clicked on the link, connecting to the webcam.

The image wasn't as clear as she would have liked, but she sucked in a ragged breath when she recognized Bryn's faded blue jeans and yellow and blue Minion T-shirt. Her daughter's face was partially covered with a blindfold, and there was a bruise darkening the corner of Bryn's mouth.

Diana reached out, touching Bryn's likeness on the screen as if that would reassure her that her daughter was still alive. She remembered what Jordan had said about a webcam being faked.

No, she refused to believe Bryn might already be dead.

Jordan's phone rang, startlingly loud. Again, he punched the speaker button and hit record.

"Do you see your daughter, Jordan Rashid?" the mechanically distorted voice asked.

"Yes." Jordan's response was clear and strong. "I want to talk to her."

Diana watched as a man with a hood over his face stepped into view. He held a phone near Bryn's mouth. "Speak, infidel."

"Mommy? Are you there?"

She was about to answer when Jordan quickly hit the mute button. "Wait. Tell me something that only Bryn knows."

Diana thought quickly. "Her favorite animal is an elephant. She fell in love with the baby elephants when we visited the zoo."

Jordan released the mute button. "Bryn? Can you hear me?"

"Y-yes. Where's my mom?"

"She's safe, don't worry. Listen, Bryn, I want you to tell me your favorite animal."

"Baby elephants," the girl answered without hesitation.

Diana breathed a sigh of relief. She was about to speak, but once again, Jordan stopped her with a hard shake of his head. "Where did you see the elephants, Bryn?"

"At the Atlanta Zoo."

Diana nodded, indicating that was correct. Not North Carolina, but Atlanta. Surely the kidnappers couldn't know that level of detail.

"That's good, Bryn. I want you to hang in there, okay? We're going to do everything we can to get you home safe."

"I'll try," Bryn said in a trembling voice. "I've been praying for God to help me."

"Enough!" The hooded man took the phone away from Bryn, and she disappeared from view. "We have fulfilled our promise, Jordan Rashid. Now you must fulfill yours. Free Mustaf or the child dies."

In an instant, the image vanished.

"No! Wait!" Sobs racked her body, and she clawed at the laptop computer screen. "I didn't get to talk to her . . ."

"Shh, it's okay." Suddenly Jordan was gathering her into his arms, holding her close. "She's alive, Diana. We'll find her."

Diana buried her face in the crook of his shoulder, her tears soaking his shirt.

Seeing Bryn should have made her feel better, but it didn't. She wanted to touch her daughter, talk to her, reassure her.

If those monsters touched her baby girl—she couldn't bear to finish the thought.

Her life wouldn't be worth living if she lost Bryn.

SEPTEMBER 9 – 3:11 *p.m.* – *Washington, DC*

Jordan had trouble ignoring how right it felt to hold Diana in his arms, as if the twelve years of being apart hadn't happened. For a brief moment he thought about Shari, his deceased wife. Losing two women in his life had been agonizing.

Except Diana wasn't lost, not anymore.

When her shaking sobs had subsided, he gently placed his hands on her shoulders, easing her away. "You need to stay strong. For Bryn's sake."

"I know." She scrubbed her hands over her face, leaving dark smudges of makeup behind. "I just can't stand the thought of them hurting her."

"Don't go there." He knew what she meant—those same visions had haunted him from the moment he'd seen the first webcam image. "Did anything about the room look familiar to you?"

"What?" She frowned, then shook her head. "No. It could be anywhere."

"I believe she's being held somewhere close by, in or near DC," he told her. "My former boss hired my firm to infiltrate a possible terrorist cell here in the city."

"Terrorists?" The word caused the blood to drain from her face. "Oh, Jordan, what if they behead her like they have so many other American hostages?"

He kicked himself for putting that image in her head. Thanks to social media, the terrorists have been able to broadcast their horrific destruction for the entire world to see.

"They haven't killed any children that way," he pointed out.

"Yes, they have," Diana swiftly argued. "They give them backpacks stuffed with bombs and send them into crowded places to die, taking as many innocent lives as possible along with them."

The spark of anger was better than the tears any day, but he still changed tactics. "Yeah, I know, but this is different. They want something from us. From me. Bryn is safe for the next few days, until we can find a way to free Mustaf."

Diana winced. "A terrorist for an eleven-year-old," she muttered. "If Mustaf goes free, he'll go back to killing people."

Yeah, talk about a big problem. He had to be careful how he discussed this with the Bureau. There's no way Yates would let Mustaf go free, not for Bryn.

Not for anything.

He wasn't so sure he could stomach the thought either,

so he needed to come up with a plan. Some other way to find Bryn.

Too bad he no idea where to start.

"Tell me more about this cell you're supposed to infiltrate." Diana's expression was resolute. "Maybe I can work on that while you're in Lebanon."

No way. He managed to bite back the instant refusal before the words could leave his lips. "I've only had two meetings with my contact thus far. And even if you could manage such a feat, they're not going to say anything important in front of a woman," he said, falling back on sheer logic.

"Maybe not, but it's better than sitting here doing nothing. Besides, the other women may talk to me, and I might learn something about where Bryn might be."

He understood her need for action, to do something in hopes of finding her daughter. Their daughter.

If he accepted Diana's story about being placed in witness protection, then it stood to reason that Bryn was in fact his daughter. He wanted to hear from Balcome himself to verify, but despite everything, he believed her. The knowledge of Bryn being his daughter was overwhelming, so he did his best to push it away. He needed to stay focused.

"These guys know that Bryn is our daughter, which means they also know what we look like. There's no way either one of us will get close to their hideout."

The thought of using some sort of disguise niggled the back of his mind. He'd risk it, but how could he manage that if he was stuck in Lebanon?

Not happening.

His phone rang again, and this time he recognized Sun's number. "Rashid."

"I'm less than five minutes away," she announced.

"Thanks. I'll fill you in when you get here." Sun Yin was half Korean but had an affinity for all types of languages, including Arabic and Farsi. Sun was the newest employee of Security Specialists, Inc., and he knew he was fortunate that she'd accepted his job offer, broadening the base of their language skills, not to mention their ability to run covert operations.

Sun knocked sharply on his office door, beating her estimated arrival time by a full two minutes. She entered the room, her petite lithe frame concealing her strength and agility. She carried a black belt in karate, not to mention she was more than capable in other forms of martial arts. Her dark hair was cut bluntly at her chin, and her almond-shaped eyes held a keen intelligence. Not surprising since Sun belonged to the Mensa group while she was barely in her teens.

Sun wasn't just smart, she was beyond brilliant.

"What's going on?" she asked without hesitation.

Jordan gestured toward Diana. "This is Diana Phillips. Her daughter Bryn was kidnapped by Arabic-speaking men who are demanding Mustaf's life in exchange for the child."

Sun scowled. "That's ridiculous. We don't negotiate with terrorists."

"Bryn is Jordan's daughter too," Diana interjected. "And let me assure you, I will do whatever is necessary to keep my daughter safe."

Sun swung around to face him, her expression incredulous. "Is that true? The child is yours?"

"Yes." Stating the word out loud erased the last bit of lingering doubt. Why would Diana lie about something so easily proved with a DNA test? She wouldn't. The timing fit too. As did the information she'd told him, information that no one else could know. At this point, he was beginning to believe her story.

Sun turned to cast a speculative eye on Diana. The familiar stubborn jut of Diana's chin as she returned the stare made him want to smile. "I see."

He doubted it, but it was time to move on. "I'm not happy about freeing Mustaf either. We need to find Bryn, ASAP. I recorded each conversation with the kidnappers. I'm hoping you can find some clue I may have missed."

Sun nodded. "Doubtful, but worth a shot."

How pathetic that he didn't have anything else to go on. With a little less than five hours before his flight left for Lebanon, he needed to create some sort of game plan.

The office went quiet as Sun replayed the messages he'd received from Bryn's kidnappers. She listened to them over and over until he wanted to smash something, then she turned it off.

"The mechanical voice made it difficult to hear the accent, but at one point the guy with the hood on used a specific derogatory word for women that told me he's definitely from Syria."

Not good news or surprising for that matter. Of course, the Syrians wanted to free Mustaf. "Anything else?"

"I heard some sort of foghorn in the background." Sun looked at them and shrugged. "I know that doesn't help much, but she's being held somewhere near the water."

He latched onto the clue like a drowning man clung to a life preserver. "That's a great start, it means they're somewhere near the ocean. I'll start pulling information on property holders along the coast, focusing on shipping and storage areas."

"The coast of which states?" Diana demanded.

Good point. "Maryland and Virginia for starters," he

said, returning to the computer. "We can broaden our search if need be, but I still think they're close to DC."

"Why?" Sun asked. "They could be overseas for all we know."

"Because I'm here," Jordan said, pulling up the information he needed. "Since they chose me to be the one to free Mustaf, they obviously knew where and how to find me."

His phone rang, and he pounced on it, automatically pushing the buttons to both record the call and place it on speaker. "Rashid."

"I hear you need to talk to me." The voice belonged to Clarence Yates, the Deputy Director of the FBI. "What's going on?"

Jordan didn't dare glance at either Sun or Diana. "Thank you for returning my call. I need some intel before I go off-grid to infiltrate the cell."

"Yeah, like what?" Yates asked.

"I understand you've recently arrested Ahmed Mustaf."

Silence. Jordan's mouth went dry as he waited for Yates to confirm or deny the fact. He wanted to ask about Balcome, but Mustaf was his main priority at the moment.

After what seemed like forever, Yates responded, "Yes, but that's classified information! How did you hear about it?"

"Sir, I need you to trust me on this." Jordan didn't like lying to the man who'd saved his and Sloan's hides just a few months ago as they managed to bring down a terrorist attack on POTUS along with thousands of other civilians. "When did you capture him?"

"A little over forty-eight hours ago."

Knowing that Bryn had been kidnapped a day after Mustaf's capture made his head spin. "And he's being held in Camp Bucca?"

"Not for long, he's being transferred here to the US within the next twenty-four hours. The president demanded we bring him here to be interrogated. Why? What's going on, Rashid?"

"Nothing, sir, there's been some chatter, that's all, and I need information in order to infiltrate the cell." Jordan's gaze clashed with Diana's, mirroring the same sense of horror. Mustaf was being brought to the US? Obviously that information hadn't reached Bryn's kidnappers. And what would they do once they learned the truth? Especially since he had no way of reaching out to communicate with them.

One thing was for sure, he couldn't leave for Lebanon. Not with this latest twist. Having Mustaf brought here to US soil would make his job easier, if he actually went through with freeing the murderous terrorist slimebag.

But he didn't like the idea of deviating from the kidnappers' demands. What would happen once they found out he didn't take the flight to Lebanon?

His gut clenched, fearing Bryn would pay the price for the abrupt change in plans.

CHAPTER THREE

September 9 – 4:12 p.m. – Baltimore, MD

Meira straightened, placing a hand in the small of her aching back. Thankfully, the burka she wore helped keep her secret safe.

But for how much longer? Four months? Less? She couldn't bear to think about the consequences.

These men only viewed her as a caregiver for the child, which was good for her safety. But each day she feared one of them may decide to claim her for his own, to be one of his many wives.

Or worse, to use her, then toss her aside. Only they wouldn't get to the point of using her when they saw the evidence of her condition. And she very much feared they would kill her, cutting the baby from her abdomen in the blink of an eye.

We can escape.

The child's words echoed over and over in her mind. The temptation was difficult to ignore, despite the guards posted outside the door. The child didn't realize that Meira was as much of a prisoner as she was. That she'd been taken from her home and brought here without consent.

Without these men knowing of the baby she carried in her womb.

And where was Elam? He'd promised to return, but days had passed without any sign of him. Her husband claimed he was doing good works, but now she couldn't help but wonder. Was he like these men here, willing to do whatever was necessary to make their point for all the world to see? Or had he been discovered and arrested? Or worse, killed?

Either way, Elam had left her vulnerable and alone when these men had come to claim her.

"Meira?" Bryn's frightened voice brought her back to her senses. Elam wasn't coming to her rescue any more than the child's father was.

They were on their own.

"I am here," she assured the girl. "What do you need?"

"I have'ta go to the bathroom."

Meira nodded, untying her hands and then helping Bryn to stand. The girl was growing weak, maybe from a combination of thirst and exhaustion. The guards barely provided enough food for one person to survive, much less two.

Or in her case, two and a half.

The bucket in the corner smelled awful, causing nausea to swirl in her belly, but Bryn didn't say anything as she crouched over the opening to relieve herself.

When Bryn had finished, Meira returned her to the chair.

"Could I lie down for a while?" Bryn asked in a hoarse whisper.

A bare mattress was located on the floor, in the opposite corner of the bucket. "Yes. Come."

Bryn stumbled, leaning heavily on Meira as they made their way across the room. When Bryn's foot touched the mattress, she sank to her knees. "Have you thought about what I said?" she asked in a breathy voice.

Meira didn't want to admit that she'd thought of little else. There was no sense in raising this child's hopes. They were overpowered, two strong men compared to a pregnant woman and a child. They had guns. All Meira had managed to hide was a carefully honed plastic spoon. The last line of defense if one of the men tried to take her against her will. A defiant stroke that she knew full well would end in her immediate death.

And likely that of her unborn child.

"There is no way to escape," she told Bryn. "The door is guarded by a man with a gun. I have seen two men, but there could be others."

"So what?" Bryn's voice was fainter now, as if she were struggling to stay awake. "We can lure him in, hit him over the head, take his gun, shoot the bad guys, and run far, far away . . ." Her voice trailed off.

Meira crouched beside the mattress for a moment, lightly stroking Bryn's arm until the young girl's muscles relaxed in sleep.

Lure the guard into the room? Hit him over the head? Take his gun?

Escape?

She placed a protective hand over her slightly rounded abdomen.

Was she crazy to dream of such a thing?

.   .   .

SEPTEMBER 9 – 4:31 *p.m.* – *Washington, DC*

Diana rubbed her hands over her arms in a vain attempt to warm herself. Ahmed Mustaf was being transported to the United States. That had to be a good thing, right?

So why did she feel like throwing up?

"There are too many possibilities to check out," Sun protested, watching as Jordan worked the keyboard. "Where do we even start?"

"There are a lot, but look at these two." Jordan stabbed his index finger against the screen. "They are both owned by what look like shell corporations."

A flash of hope warmed Diana's soul. Maybe, just maybe they'd find Bryn. "Sounds good to me."

Jordan scribbled something on a slip of paper and handed it to Sun. "They're both in Baltimore. You take this one, I'll head to the other. Call me if you find anything unusual."

Sun nodded, tucking the scrap of paper into the pocket of her jeans. "Keep in touch, Jordan."

He shut the computer and lifted it off the desk. "Wait." Diana stopped him with a hand on his arm. "What if the kidnappers contact us again?"

"I've enabled the call forwarding feature on my phone, sending all calls to my cell." Jordan placed the laptop in a heavy nylon bag. When he finished with that, he opened his desk drawer to remove a gun. The weapon was a sobering reminder of the danger they faced. Freeing Bryn wouldn't be as easy as waltzing up to the men holding her, demanding them to let her go.

She swallowed a knot of fear. "I'm not sure what good a laptop will do us in the car," she said, gesturing to the computer case. "We need internet access."

"It's a satellite computer. It will work anywhere."

Okay, then. She stepped back, momentarily reassured that they were on the right track. Taking action felt better than sitting around doing nothing.

Ironic that she hadn't seen Jordan in twelve years but trusted him implicitly now. Despite everything that had once transpired between them. She'd given him all the inside information she had on her mother's family, but it hadn't been enough. The explosion on the heels of Omar's death had been her mother's family's ultimate retaliation.

She knew he hadn't believed her when she'd mentioned how going into witness protection had been for his own good.

If her mother's family knew about her, they'd unearth every rock on the planet in an attempt to find her and kill her.

Killing Jordan and Bryn would be icing on the cake of revenge.

Jordan tucked the gun into a holster attached to his belt, then ushered her to the underground parking garage. A black SUV was parked in the corner. He tucked the computer case in the back while she slipped into the passenger seat.

When they hit the highway, they were immediately engulfed in a sea of traffic. The crush had only gotten worse, *thank you, rush hour*, she thought impatiently. Diana had forgotten how congested the city was compared to the quiet life she'd made for Bryn in Jacksonville, North Carolina.

"Is it possible this kidnapping is linked to your mother's family?" Jordan asked.

She swallowed the instant denial. "Anything is possible," she admitted. "But you killed Omar twelve years ago, remember? Shortly before the bomb exploded in the back of our car. I've been in hiding ever since."

Jordan met her gaze. "Omar had a son."

There was no point in denying it. "Yes, my cousin, Tariq Omar Haram Shekau." Just saying his name made her feel dirty. She took a deep breath and let it out slowly. "I already considered this angle. Tariq has definitely picked up where his father left off, but if he'd have known I had survived the crash, then why wait until now to find me? The name I'm currently living under is Deborah Martin, and Martin is Bryn's official last name too. It's not as if I'd be that easy to find, the US Marshals did everything possible to erase any hint of my past."

"Well, it's obvious someone knows that you're alive and that Bryn is our daughter."

The way he said *our daughter* made it difficult to breathe. She hadn't thought beyond saving Bryn, but clearly Jordan expected to be a part of their daughter's life moving forward. Instinctively, she wanted to reject the idea, but that wasn't fair. Of course, he deserved to know his daughter, but they lived in different states. The idea of sending Bryn away for extended visits made her stomach ache.

Yet this wasn't the time or the place to worry about how Jordan would fit into their future. Right now, she needed to focus on finding Bryn. The rest could be worked out later.

"Yes, and I can't help but think that the leak came from within the FBI," she responded evenly. "Who else knew they were close to capturing Mustaf in the first place? I don't think the Department of Homeland Security announced their plan to go after him on the evening news."

"Good point," Jordan conceded. "But here's an alternate theory. Your family left you alone until they needed your help, or in this case my help. So they orchestrated this elaborate plan to get us back together to free an international terrorist. Or are you going to deny Omar had ties to Syria even then?"

Shock stole her breath, holding her silent. Dear Lord have mercy, was Jordan right? Was it possible that this was, in fact, all related to her family? Had they known about her, about Bryn all this time?

No. She refused to believe it. If Tariq had known about her, he would have come after her directly to avenge his father's death. Kidnapping Bryn seemed almost too subtle. "FBI Agent Tony Balcome is the only one who knew I survived the crash," she said in a strained tone. "He handed me off to the US Marshals. Everyone else, even you, believed I was dead." But the thought of Agent Balcome niggled at the back of her mind. Where was he now? Why was that classified information?

She didn't know, but Jordan didn't pursue the argument, for which she was grateful. Wasn't it bad enough that her family had ties to terrorism? Her uncle Omar had denounced her mother after she married an American, but that hadn't stopped him from taking hundreds of innocent lives.

Including her father's.

In her case, blood wasn't thicker than water. Dedication to the old ways, the old traditions were all that mattered. In the years that had passed, she'd done her best to make amends, in just a small way. To honor her mother.

If Tariq was involved in this plot to free Mustaf, she'd do everything in her power to help bring him down.

After they'd saved Bryn.

SEPTEMBER 9 – 5:22 p.m. – Baltimore, MD
Jordan had taken a circular route toward Maryland,

keeping a sharp eye on his rearview mirror for any hint of a tail. When he was convinced they hadn't been followed, he turned on the vehicle's GPS to find the warehouse owned by American Lumber, LLC.

American Lumber didn't transport wood or any other type of construction supplies. As far as Jordan could tell, they only existed on paper. There hadn't been time to dig too deeply, plus he didn't much care. He planned to check the place out, and if Bryn wasn't there, move on.

The warehouse in question happened to be located in the midst of the shipping district, making it the perfect hiding spot for holding a young child captive.

The bad news? There were dozens of buildings, and any one of them could be used for criminal activity. He pulled into a parking lot, wondering if he'd made a mistake in narrowing his search to buildings that didn't have clear ownership.

"Well?" Diana asked impatiently. "Why are we just sitting here? Let's go."

Voicing his concerns out loud wouldn't accomplish anything other than scaring Diana, so he pushed open his door and climbed out. The wind was stronger this close to the ocean, and the temperature was a bit chilly, even for September, courtesy of the low dark clouds overhead.

Diana came over to stand beside him, and he wished she'd stay here to wait for him, knowing even as the thought formed that she'd flat-out refuse. Resigned to the inevitable, he dropped to one knee and drew out the snub-nosed revolver he carried in an ankle holster and handed it to her.

"Do you know how to use this?" he asked.

She nodded. "You taught me everything I know about guns."

He had, and he was glad she'd remembered. Just

another piece of the puzzle that made him believe she really was Diana.

"Although, to be honest, it's been a while since I've fired a gun."

"Let's hope we don't need them," Jordan said grimly. "Consider this a recon mission, if we see something suspicious, we'll call for reinforcements. We're not going in there alone, understand?"

For a moment she looked as if she might argue, but then she nodded. "Agree."

He held her gaze until he was satisfied she'd do as he ordered. Unlike the way she'd tended to fight against him in the past. "Stay behind me."

Diana didn't respond, but as he made his way toward the strip of warehouses that were located across the street from the shipping yard, she followed.

The area was busier than he expected for a Friday evening, but various longshoremen and other local workers were clearly packing up to head home.

Jordan stopped alongside the wall of a building that may have once been red but had been weathered pale pink by years of abuse from a combination of saltwater and sun. The entire row of warehouses looked abandoned, but just because there weren't visible signs of activity didn't mean they stood empty.

In fact, he'd bet each and every one of them was chock-full of stuff. Some of it illegal.

He pulled out his phone and glanced at the screen. The structure belonging to American Lumber, LLC was a gray building sandwiched between the pale pink warehouse and the dirty yellow one labeled *Starkey's Shipping*.

"What's wrong?" Diana whispered, her mouth dangerously close to his ear. "Do you see something?"

"No." And that was the problem. Shouldn't there be someone nearby protecting the place? Or at least acting as a lookout? The itch along the back of his neck wouldn't leave him alone.

Diana moved restlessly behind him, and he bit back to urge to snap at her. It wasn't her fault. Your average citizen didn't have experience running covert operations.

After another full five minutes of watching, he decided to head around back. He turned at the same time Diana moved as if to follow him, bumping up against him with a muffled *oomph*.

He lightly grasped her shoulders with his hands. "Sorry."

She stared up at him for several long seconds, searching his gaze for—what? Some indication that what they once felt for each other was still there? Not likely. Ignoring his racing heart, he let her go as if his fingertips were burned, carefully stepping around her.

"This way," he said, edging along the side wall to the narrow dusty alleyway that ran behind the buildings. From this angle, he could see the outline of a door, no doubt the building codes required two exits, but the warped door frame made him think that no one had used it recently.

Disappointment stabbed deep. He didn't like it. The setup just didn't seem right. No way did he believe there was a terrorist cell here holding a child hostage. They were chasing their tails, nothing more. Baltimore was a huge city, who knew how far you could be from the ocean while still hearing the foghorns?

Talk about trying to find a diamond buried in a sandy beach.

Somewhere a door slammed. Diana started badly, grabbing onto the back of his belt. He glanced over his shoulder. "Do you want to wait in the car?" he asked in a low tone.

"I'm fine," she said, although her grip on his belt didn't loosen. "How long are we going to stand here?"

"As long as it takes." He immediately regretted his tone when she pressed her lips together, her dark eyes brimming with unshed tears. "Stay here and cover me while I investigate."

"O-okay." She released her deathlike grip and pressed herself against the warehouse in an effort to stay out of his way.

"Diana—" He stopped, giving himself a mental shake. "Never mind. Just stay alert, okay?"

She nodded. Before he could move, his phone vibrated with an incoming call. His pulse jumped as he recognized Sun's number.

"Find something?" he asked.

"No. This place is completely empty, looks as if it once held big oil drums. There're still a few left in the corner."

Figured. He'd hoped for better news. "Thanks for letting me know."

"Do you want me to keep searching the area?" Sun asked.

"No, why don't you check the next business on the list." Divide and conquer was always the best approach.

"Will do. Let me know if you find something."

"It's not looking good," he admitted before disconnecting from the call.

"Nothing?" Diana asked, her expression forlorn.

"No, but don't give up hope yet." He slid the phone into his front pocket. Jordan slipped around the corner toward the front of the buildings. Moving stealthily, he made his way down past the pink warehouse to the gray building located in the center.

Up close, the large garage door at the front of the building didn't look as dilapidated as he'd expected. In fact, there was a large shiny new padlock preventing entry inside.

Interesting. He checked the rollers along the sides, those appeared to be greased for easy opening, too, not covered in rust. But he still didn't see any guards, although it was possible they might be inside.

Unless there were cameras? Instinctively, he glanced up, searching for a sign of an electronic device. Nothing jumped out at him, but these days a camera could be hidden in a crevice smaller than the tip of his little finger.

After a full minute without hearing a sound, he decided there weren't any cameras, or if there were, they were broken. He lifted the padlock, peering at the opening in the bottom, thinking about the lock-pick tools he carried, but then he realized the door in the back of the building might be easier to get through. He released the lock and hurried over to meet up with Diana.

He'd barely cleared the corner when a loud *ka-boom* erupted from somewhere behind him, sending him flying down onto the pavement. He managed to catch himself before his head hit the ground. Turning to his side, he glanced over his shoulder.

The warehouse was engulfed in flames.

Bryn!

CHAPTER FOUR

September 9 – 5:45 p.m. – Baltimore, MD

"No!" Diana screamed, scrambling up from the pavement, ignoring the zinging pain shooting through her body. "Bryn!"

"Don't, Diana, please. Stay here!" Jordan lunged up to his feet, grabbing onto her with a steel grip. "We don't know for sure that anyone was inside."

She fought to free herself. "But why else would it explode? We need to go and check—"

"No, we need to get out of here." Jordan ruthlessly pulled her through the alley, away from the burning building. "Hurry!"

She didn't want to go, but Jordan wasn't taking no for an answer. The heat of the blaze caused beads of sweat to sting her eyes. Stumbling in his wake, her mind tortured her with images of her daughter lying dead in the midst of a horrific fire.

My sweet baby!

Her stomach rebelled and she gagged, fighting the urge to throw up. Thankfully, she hadn't eaten in hours, so she didn't have anything in her stomach. Instead, she swallowed hard and took several deep breaths.

When Jordan stopped, she slumped against him, her legs shaking with shock and grief.

"Are you okay?"

His gentle tone nearly did her in. She needed his strength more than she realized. "As much as I can be."

"Good, let's go this way." He turned again, heading straight into the throng of pedestrians gathering around and pointing at the black smoke rising above the warehouse fire. She stayed close to his side, her senses assaulted by the screaming sirens as police vehicles and fire trucks threaded their way through traffic.

She stared at the smoke, unable to bear the thought of leaving without knowing the truth. Jordan's arm was anchored around her waist, and his head was turned toward the smoke too. It occurred to her he was trying to blend into the crowd.

She forced herself to think rationally. If by some miracle Bryn hadn't been inside the warehouse, they couldn't afford to be detained for questioning. Jordan was right, they needed to get away from here. She pulled herself together and attempted to mirror the casual yet distressed expression on Jordan's face, as if they were innocent bystanders just like everyone else.

It seemed they walked forever, but it was likely just a mile or so when Jordan angled around the block, heading back in the direction of the warehouse district.

Despite her earlier wishes to see for herself, she slowed her step, dragging her heels. "Wait, Jordan, I don't think it's a good idea to go back there."

"We're not going to stay long, but we need our vehicle and the satellite computer," he said. "We won't be able to get too close anyway, the police will keep everyone at a distance."

Since the computer and Jordan's phone were their only link they had to Bryn's kidnappers, she didn't argue. Moving at a casual pace, they made their way closer. She could see the fire trucks were in place, hoses streaming water onto the building, police cars blocking off the street while the firefighters worked to contain the fire. The parking lot was effectively shut off. There was no way they'd be able to drive out of there anytime soon.

A sense of hopelessness hit hard. "Now what?"

"Stay here, I can at least get the computer."

Letting Jordan go wasn't easy. She watched his dark handsome profile, biting back the urge to beg him to stay. It hit her then just how much she was depending on him to find Bryn.

If their daughter was still alive.

The tightness in her chest returned, making it impossible to breathe. She didn't understand what had caused the explosion, but it seemed crazy that the fire could be linked to the terrorist cell holding Bryn hostage.

But what other explanation was there?

Without Jordan's steadying presence, she found herself sinking further into the depths of despair.

They shouldn't have tried to find Bryn on their own. They should have called the police. The FBI. The NSA. Even the CIA.

All of them and more!

Dear God, help me! Show me the way!

SEPTEMBER 9 – 6:08 p.m. – Baltimore, MD

Jordan ducked low and darted between the vehicles.

Using the confusion around the scene of the explosion to his advantage, he managed to get close to his SUV without attracting any attention.

Once he had the satellite computer case tucked beneath his arm, he looked up at the fire-encased building. The dry tinder burned ferociously, the flames leaping into the sky, smoke billowing out in black clouds. Anyone or anything inside would be completely destroyed.

Not Bryn, he told himself as he zigzagged back to where he'd left Diana. He couldn't believe the terrorists would hurt her, not if they really wanted him to rescue Mustaf.

And what on earth had triggered the explosion? Touching the padlock? Or a secret camera he hadn't seen? The thought made him wince. If there had been a camera, and it was linked to the terrorists, then they'd have a recorded image of his face.

He told himself the camera theory wasn't likely. Still, even the remote possibility was disturbing.

At least the flight to Lebanon hadn't left yet. Once the plane was in the air, and he wasn't on it, he'd have to be doubly careful.

Enough about that now, they needed a lift out of here. He pulled out his phone to call Sun. "How quickly can you get here?"

"Twenty minutes, maybe less." Sun's tone was all business. "I caught a glimpse of the fire from the news app on my phone. Impressive."

"Gotta love technology," he muttered. "We'll be at the coffee shop at the corner of Blakemore and Landry. Pick us up there."

"Will do." Sun disconnected from the line, and he hoped she'd speed if necessary to get there as quickly as possible.

He didn't like the way this situation was unraveling right before their eyes.

"You have the computer," Diana said in relief.

"Yep. Come on." He nudged her toward the coffee shop. "Sun is on her way."

Diana barely acknowledged his words, inwardly focused on their next task, getting to the coffee shop.

The place was packed. Jordan didn't like it. He needed to find a quiet corner where he could turn on the laptop, make sure the kidnappers hadn't sent him another link.

Threading his way through the crowd, he came upon a table just as two teenagers stood. "Thanks," he muttered, quickly sliding the computer case onto one of the empty seats. He pulled out a second chair for Diana, then sat down. He opened the computer, then reached for his wallet.

"Here's some money, will you please get us something to eat and drink?" He thrust a twenty-dollar bill into her hand.

"I'm not hungry," she protested.

"I know." He reached over and lightly touched her arm. "I understand this is difficult, but you need to keep up your strength. Passing out from lack of food won't help Bryn. Besides, we need to buy something to look legit."

"Fine." She rose to her feet and went over to place an order.

The satellite signal took longer to boot up compared to using a Wi-Fi network, but of course his connection was secure whereas the café's was not. When his screen loaded, he held his breath and accessed his email account.

No message or link from the kidnappers. He let out his breath in a rush, the tension easing from his shoulders. Good. That was good.

Wasn't it?

He honestly didn't know. The warehouse blowing up couldn't be a coincidence. He stared at his cell phone, waiting for it to ring.

Nothing.

Diana returned with two bottles of water and two muffins. She picked at hers halfheartedly. "I don't understand," she said, finally breaking the silence. "Why did the warehouse blow up like that?"

He glanced around. No one appeared to be paying them any attention. "I don't know. The only thing that makes sense is that somehow I triggered it to blow."

"But that's just it. Why was it wired with explosives in the first place?"

Jordan swallowed a wave of frustration. "I wish I knew. Nothing about this entire mess makes any sense." He turned his attention to the keyboard and typed in American Lumber, LLC. There was the one building listed as being owned by the corporation. He pulled up the original property listing, scanning the titles.

Freedom Shoppes, Inc. and Justice Textiles, Corp. abruptly jumped out at him. The words American, Freedom, and Justice linked together in his mind. As if they'd been chosen on purpose.

Dread seeped through his gut.

Was it possible all of these properties, and possibly several others, were linked to the terrorist cell?

And if that was the case, there had to be more to this scenario than freeing Mustaf.

Something bigger and much more sinister.

SEPTEMBER 9 – 6:12 p.m. – Baltimore, MD

"Wake up." A soft hand shook her shoulder. With a muffled groan, Bryn rolled over, opening her eyes to the darkness of her blindfold. The band of fabric must have loosened a bit because she could see some light along the bottom of the blindfold. "Meira?"

"It is time to eat."

"Eat?" Bryn struggled upright, tipping her head back in an effort to see below the blindfold. She caught a glimpse of dark cloth and imagined it was Meira's burka. She'd seen many women wearing them in the past. She was about to try once again to convince Meira to escape when she heard the heavy *thunk thunk* of footsteps crossing the room. She wrinkled her nose when she smelled the stinky bad man.

"Are you ready to obey?" His harsh voice sent icy fingers of fear down her back. Obey what? Bryn reached out to grasp Meira's clothing, as if the woman could prevent this man from doing whatever he planned.

"Are you?" he demanded again.

Bryn nodded, ducked her head, and trembled, fearing another smack from his large brutal hand or worse. It never came. After what seemed like eons, the heavy thunk of his footsteps retreated. Still, she couldn't relax until she'd heard a door open and close behind her.

"Time to eat." Meira helped her upright. She gripped Meira's arm tightly, terrified she'd be separated from the woman.

"What did he mean, ready to obey? What's going to happen to me?"

Meira didn't answer. The woman placed the familiar bowl containing the usual gloppy stuff in her hands.

Bryn tipped her head back, attempting to see beneath the blindfold, but Meira tightened her grip on her fingers in warning, so she dropped her chin to her chest, tears squeezing out from beneath her lashes, trailing down her cheeks.

She knew the icky men were still watching. Waiting.

How long before they killed her?

SEPTEMBER 9 – 6:19 p.m. – *Camp Bucca, Lebanon*

The guards were whispering amongst themselves despite being the middle of the night. Mustaf didn't like it. His English was impeccable, but they were speaking too softly and standing too far away for him to make out what they were saying.

He tried not to panic. His loyal followers led by his people would come through for him, of that he had no doubt. Yet the attitude amongst the guards bothered him. Was it possible they knew a rescue attempt was underway?

He didn't see how they could possibly know of his plan. His followers had a man on the inside aiding their cause. Supporting their mission. He'd be rescued before these men knew what had hit them.

Turning over on his pallet, he closed his eyes and attempted to sleep.

But the whispering continued, like tiny lashes assaulting his mind, making it impossible to rest.

Staring through the darkness, he reminded himself that this nightmare would be over soon. He would escape. And he would fulfill his goal of seeking revenge against all of those who made him suffer.

Every last one of them.

SEPTEMBER 9 – 6:22 p.m. – *Baltimore, MD*

Diana startled badly when Jordan's phone rang. The kidnappers?

"It's just Sun," he assured her.

She nodded and pushed aside the remnants of her blueberry muffin, the cloying sweetness turning her stomach. Or maybe it was the not knowing about Bryn that had destroyed her appetite.

"Thanks, Sun." Jordan disconnected from the phone and began packing up the computer. "Our ride is here."

She rose to her feet, following him outside, grateful to once again be doing something constructive rather than sitting around while Bryn was in danger.

Alive. She refused to believe the worst.

Sun wasn't tall, her head barely two inches above the wheel, and Diana rolled her eyes when Jordan indicated he wanted to drive.

Earlier she'd been grateful for his strength, but now she found the macho attitude that had once attracted her more than a little annoying. He'd always insisted on driving during their time together, and that obviously hadn't changed in the years they'd spent apart.

"You're being ridiculous," Sun said. But she obliged him by sliding out from behind the wheel.

"Sue me." Jordan tossed the bulky computer case into the back seat of the four-door sedan before climbing in. Sun ran around to the passenger side door, leaving Diana to sit in the back seat like a little kid.

Not that she cared one way or the other. Jordan and Sun didn't act like a couple, but that didn't mean Jordan didn't have another woman in his life. She'd only broken the rules of witness protection for her daughter's sake. The important thing was to find Bryn.

Jordan pulled seamlessly into traffic, heading back toward the downtown area of Baltimore.

"What's our next move?" she asked. "There must be more warehouses to check out, right?"

Jordan met her gaze in the rearview mirror. "Are you crazy? After what just happened, that's the dead last thing we should do."

The word dead made a muscle twitch near her eye.

Bryn was not dead. Bryn was not dead.

Not. Dead.

"I don't necessarily agree, Jordan," Sun interjected. "The explosion could be related to some other criminal activity, like drugs or guns. Doesn't make a lot of sense for the terrorists to have rigged the place to blow."

"Sure it does," Jordan countered in a grim tone. "Each and every attempt to take American lives is considered a win for them."

"But our mission is to free Mustaf, that's why they kidnapped Bryn. So why risk hurting her in an explosion?" Diana asked.

"Who knows?" Jordan headed for the interstate.

"Come on, Jordan. We need to stay on track here, we need to keep searching for our daughter." Her tone was sharp with exhaustion.

"I'm aware of the fact that we need to find Bryn. But you need to understand this is bigger than Mustaf," Jordan said. "I found more company names that could all be linked to the terrorist cell I'm supposed to be infiltrating."

"Like what?" Sun asked.

"Freedom Shoppes and Justice Textiles are two examples I've found so far. Not all that different from American Lumber, right? Only American Lumber is now nothing more than a pile of ash."

Freedom Shoppes? Justice Textiles? The nausea returned with a vengeance. "Do we know where those places are located?" Diana asked in a hoarse voice. "We could rent a car so we can split up again."

"Not happening. A rental car would leave a paper trace. Besides, we don't even know for sure where these other places are yet. I think it's time to bring my FBI contact in on this." Again, Jordan's gaze clashed with hers in the rearview mirror. "All of this—Mustaf's capture and the demand to free him, Bryn's kidnapping, the warehouse explosion—must be connected."

She didn't want to believe him. "You don't know that for sure."

"Yeah, I do. Factor in the timing and I'd say we absolutely know for sure."

She frowned. "What timing?"

"Don't you realize what the date is?" Jordan asked.

"September ninth." The minute the words left her mouth, she sucked in a harsh breath.

Two days from the anniversary of September 11, the biggest terrorist attack ever on US soil.

Jordan was right. This wasn't just about Bryn.

It was about ISIS supporters making a bold move against the United States of America.

CHAPTER FIVE

September 9 – 6:45 p.m. – Washington, DC

"Try calling Ray Pallone again," Jordan told Sun as he took another turn, determined to avoid any chance of being followed. He planned to head back to his place, a small house sandwiched between two other structures in a long row of suburban properties.

He was banking on the fact that the property being in his grandmother's name, Colleen McCray, would keep it from being connected to him. The men who kidnapped Bryn had obviously found out about his relationship with Diana, but he was hoping their intel was old. He'd only moved into his grandmother's house three months ago, after her death.

Jordan knew his father's name was Ali Rashid, and according to his mother, Ali had died shortly after Jordan's birth. His mother, Maureen Rashid, had died in a car crash shortly after he graduated from high school. He'd never lived with his grandmother, yet she'd always been supportive of him. After his grandmother died, she'd left him the house and her ancient Buick automobile, which was twenty years old but had less than eighty-five thousand miles on it since his grandmother used it only for church and grocery shopping. He'd been debating whether or not to sell the house and the car but hadn't gotten that far. He'd also searched through her things, looking for additional information about his father because his mother and grandmother never talked about him.

Without success.

His jet-black hair and dark skin indicated he looked more like his father than his redheaded Irish mother. And frankly, his paternal heritage was something he'd used to his advantage while working for the Feds. Exactly why they'd asked him to infiltrate the terrorist cell. A possible connection? Doubtful, but no way to know for sure.

"Still no answer from Pallone," Sun said, dragging him from his thoughts.

He sighed heavily. "What is up with these guys? They ask me to infiltrate a terrorist cell, then decide not to answer my calls?"

"Maybe they're trying to protect you," Sun answered logically. "After going undercover, communication can be deadly."

"Yeah, maybe." But he wasn't really buying it. "I need them to know about these other possible shell corporations, so they can start investigating them."

"I'll work on that after dropping you off," Sun offered.

He nodded, knowing Sun's help would be invaluable. "Thanks."

"Speaking of being dropped off, where are we going?" Diana asked. She still looked shell-shocked, strands of her dark hair hanging loose around her face since the explosion at the warehouse.

She was holding up far better than he'd imagined. He'd

only just learned about Bryn, but she'd raised their daughter for the past eleven years. He couldn't imagine anything more difficult than not knowing if your child was alive or dead.

He didn't particularly care for it much either.

"My place, at least for now. We'll need to keep a low profile since I'm supposed to be at the airport boarding a plane for Lebanon."

Diana grimaced. "How long do you think it will take them to figure out you're not on the flight?"

"Not long enough." Maybe if they'd had more time, he could find someone to take his place. Then again, once Mustaf arrived on US soil, certainly the men who had Bryn would figure that out for themselves. He hoped the kidnappers would contact him again—the more communication, the better their chances of uncovering their location.

"Lebanon is seventeen hours ahead of us," Sun said. "Depending on when Mustaf's flight leaves, he'll lose almost a day, which should help give us time to prepare."

"Good point." Pathetic how that thought was the bright spot of their otherwise awful day.

"We need to know exactly where they're taking him," Diana said.

He didn't answer, knowing that Yates wasn't about to open up to him about national security issues. Then again, he had some former friends in high places who may be able to shed a little light on the subject.

"We need more information on Mustaf. There must be a connection between him and the terrorist cell operating here in DC." A connection wouldn't be easy to find, but nothing about this case was simple. He pulled over a few blocks from his grandmother's house and glanced at Sun. "We'll go the rest of the way on foot."

"Do you want to keep the car?" Sun asked. "I can always use the Metro."

"No, I have my grandmother's old Buick if we need wheels." He made a point of driving the vehicle every few days.

Sun shrugged. "Okay."

Jordan got out from behind the wheel, then opened Diana's door and offered his hand. She stared at it for a moment, then accepted his assistance. After securing the computer case, he took Diana's hand and strolled along the sidewalk lining the row of townhouses.

Diana glanced around curiously but didn't say anything when he led the way up the short flight of stairs to the home that once belonged to his grandmother.

"Feel free to freshen up." He set the computer case on the kitchen table. "Bathroom is down the hall."

"Thanks." Her attempt to smile failed miserably, and he wished there was something he could do to make her feel better.

She turned away, then stopped abruptly, her gaze zeroing in on the large framed photograph hanging on the living room wall. The one featuring a close up of Shari, Sloan's sister, and him at their wedding. Shari wore a white dress, a stark contrast to his black tux.

Oh boy. Diana stared at the picture for what seemed like forever while he grappled with what to say. The photograph was almost three years old now, and he'd lost his wife within the first year of their marriage.

"Diana, I . . ."

"Don't!" The word was hoarse with emotion, and she quickly wheeled away, disappearing down the hall. The bathroom door shut firmly behind her.

He stood frozen for a moment before crossing over and

yanking the picture off the wall. Sloan always blamed himself for Shari's death, assuming the Russian mafia had gone after his sister in revenge.

But Jordan knew that wasn't really the case at all. Truthfully, the blame for Shari's death rested squarely on his shoulders. He'd left Shari alone to follow up a bogus lead, and the Russians hadn't waited to take advantage of his stupidity.

For a moment, he stared at Shari's innocent laughing features. A chilling reminder of how he needed to keep his distance from Diana.

Women who got close to him ended up dead.

SEPTEMBER 9 – 7:05 *p.m.* – *Camp Bucca, Lebanon*

"Get up." The guard kicked him in the back as a way to rouse him from sleep. The unexpected pain made him seethe with anger, but he was careful not to let his emotions show.

"What do you want?" Mustaf shielded his eyes from the flashlight trained directly into his eyes. The murdering idiots would pay dearly for this.

"Time to move, dirtbag. Get up or we'll force you to your feet."

For a moment, he imagined taking a long knife and slicing this guard's head off as he'd done so many times before. But he was still outnumbered, and he needed to be patient to allow his people to rescue him. He slowly stood, facing the men who held guns pointed in his direction.

"Tie him up," one of the guards said to another.

Mustaf swallowed the urge to scream with rage as his arms were harshly yanked behind his back and secured with rope that dug deep into his skin.

They would pay for this.

The guns never wavered, and when they'd finished tying him up, someone threw a hood over his face. A sliver of panic dissected the fury. What was going on? Why the sudden desire to move him to a different cell?

He was ushered forward, but instead of being placed in another cage, he was thrust into a vehicle. The sliver of fear grew as he was driven away from the prison that had been his home for just two days.

This wasn't right. He'd heard them talking about moving him later in the week. What had changed?

He listened carefully, but these men didn't talk or whisper. There was nothing but silence.

The vehicle stopped. "Get out. And if you try anything, we'll shoot you in the knee."

Maybe they would, but he doubted it. Still, it didn't pay to try anything now. It was entirely possible this was set up by his man on the inside. That at any moment his followers would come out of hiding to rescue him.

He shuffled slowly, rough hands pushing him forward when he was obviously stalling.

Then suddenly he was lifted up off his feet. He resisted the urge to struggle, waiting for his followers to let him know they'd come for him.

But he was thrown down onto something hard. An engine rumbled, and suddenly he knew he was on a plane.

No! Wait! This wasn't right!

The plane rolled faster and faster until it soared into the air.

Where were his people?

Where were these infidels taking him?

Hope of being rescued shattered like a crystal goblet at his feet.

. . .

SEPTEMBER 9 – 7:12 p.m. – Baltimore, MD

Elam Nagi staggered away from the warehouse district, his ears ringing from the blast. He was fairly certain that he'd given the American enough time to get away, although the timing had been close.

Still, he'd succeeded in destroying the evidence. He knew Meira's life hung in the balance if he didn't do exactly as he was told.

Melting into the crowd, he hid in plain sight, seeing the people around him talking and gesturing but unable to distinguish actual sounds. The microphone in his ear had amplified the intensity of the blast.

Hopefully, his hearing would return, but that wasn't his biggest problem right now. He needed to make sure that he stayed one step ahead, that he had a plausible story to explain the warehouse explosion. At least the place hadn't been used recently.

His phone vibrated in his pocket, but he didn't reach for it. Not yet. Not until he was far enough away from the scene of the fire.

He walked to the closest Metro station and took the next available train, regardless of the destination. His phone continued to vibrate, and it felt as if everyone was staring at him.

Wrapping his arm around a pole, he finally took the phone from his pocket, looking down at the screen with trepidation. The number on the display made him break out in a cold sweat. Had they heard the explosion from their location? Was it already on the news?

His ears were still ringing, so he sent a text.

A L breached. Trigger pulled. Unknown results.

He pushed send, then held his breath, waiting for a response.

Nothing. Not then. Not by the time he reached the next stop.

Elam closed his eyes, sending up a prayer for Meira and the baby.

He'd promised Meira that he would do good works, but that was before he'd been followed home from work and taken against his will. For two weeks now, he'd been doing his best to walk a fine line, working for the men who'd captured him, convincing them he was truly converted while at the same time doing his best to sabotage their efforts.

Yet he knew that his small victories weren't enough. And that if he was forced to choose between two impossible tasks, that he would do whatever was necessary to protect the woman he loved and their unborn child.

Anything.

SEPTEMBER 9 – 7:25 p.m. – Washington, DC

Jordan was married. Was still married or possibly divorced, no way to know for sure.

Diana stood under the steaming shower spray with her hands braced against the cool tile and her knees locked so she wouldn't collapse in a heap.

Married. Married. Married. The word reverberated inside her skull like a ping-pong ball.

No wonder he and Sun hadn't acted like a couple.

And really, why was she so upset? Agent Balcome told her Jordan believed she was dead and so did her mother's family. He'd emphasized how that was better for everyone involved. When she'd discovered she was pregnant, she'd taken the opportunity to start over with a new name. A new career. A new life.

Jordan deserved to do the same. Had she really thought there was even a remote chance of picking up where they'd left off twelve years ago?

Ridiculous fantasy that had no basis in reality.

She'd loved Jordan once, but that was a long time ago. She wasn't the same woman any longer. Still, she grieved for what they'd lost. The hot water from the shower mingled with her tears. She forced herself to use the shampoo, washing away the layer of grime.

When she finished, she thought she'd feel better, but exhaustion weighed her down. Getting dressed seemed an insurmountable task. She drew a comb through her straight dark hair, leaving it to air dry.

Thinking of Bryn, of what her daughter might be going through, provided her the strength she needed to walk back into the kitchen. Her gaze landed on the large space where the framed photo of Jordan and his bride had been. There was a pale square on the wall where the picture had hung, but the image itself was nowhere in sight. She wondered why Jordan had bothered to remove it.

The scent of fried eggs made her stomach twinge with hunger. He turned to look at her, his expression wary. "Will you try to eat something?"

She shrugged and dropped into the closest chair, belatedly noticing that he had the satellite computer set up nearby. "Why not?"

"Good." He slid what looked like omelets onto two plates and carried them over to join her.

They ate in silence for a few moments before he glanced up at her. "Shari was my partner Sloan's younger sister. She was killed nine months after our wedding."

The mouthful of cheese, mushrooms, and egg lodged in her throat. She forced herself to swallow. "I'm sorry for your loss."

He nodded, his expression bleak, but didn't say anything more.

She didn't ask anything either. She didn't want to know how much he'd loved Shari. How happy they'd been together. And yes, that made her a terribly selfish person.

Jordan's love life wasn't any of her business. He could have a new girlfriend by now for all she knew. It didn't matter, but finding Bryn did. She stared at her half-eaten omelet, wondering if the kidnappers had provided her daughter with anything to eat. Or if she had a place to sleep.

Her stomach rolled, and she pushed her plate away. She couldn't take another bite, not when she had no idea what Bryn was going through.

"What's our next step?" She met Jordan's gaze head-on. "I have a right to know. Besides, we don't have much time before the kidnappers realize you're not on that flight to Lebanon."

"I know." Jordan resumed eating, his movements mechanical, giving her the impression he wasn't enjoying the meal but that he was only fueling up to face whatever was to come. "There are several things in the works. I'm hoping Pallone returns my call. If not, we'll see what Sun digs up from her research. I'm also trying to find a connection between Mustaf and the terrorist cell operating here in DC. If all that doesn't work, I'll connect with the man who is suspected of recruiting for the terrorist cell."

"Recruiting how?"

He grimaced. "Supposedly by seeking believers, also known as radicals, to further their cause. The church is one way of finding recruits, if you can believe that."

She didn't like the sound of that. And what would she do while Jordan meets with this so-called recruiter? Besides go out of her mind with fear. "I'm worried about what will happen once the flight leaves for Lebanon," she confessed in a soft voice. "I'm afraid they'll hurt Bryn."

Jordan's eyes darkened, and he reached out to touch her arm. "Let's agree not to think about the worst. Yates mentioned that they were transporting Mustaf here to the US. If the kidnappers call, we can use that information as a way to convince them that I'm on their side, still working on a plan to free Mustaf in exchange for Bryn's life."

His logic eased the tightness in her belly. That could work, providing that kind of information could actually work in their favor.

Provided the kidnappers didn't physically hurt Bryn in retaliation before they had a chance to talk.

CHAPTER SIX

September 9 – 7:38 p.m. – Washington, DC

"Where is Rashid?" It was a struggle to act casual when what he really wanted to do was punch Clarence Yates, hitting him over and over again until he spilled his guts related to the information Rashid may have given him already.

Not yet. Patience. The time isn't right.

"He's undercover." The blasé response made him grind his teeth. "Don't worry, I'm confident he'll figure out the nature of the threat."

He forced himself to take a sip of the awful wine his boss favored. "You have a lot of faith in this former agent of yours, are you sure it's well placed?"

"What makes you ask that? Rashid has proven himself worthy in more ways than one." His boss's smile revealed teeth stained purple by the red wine. He had to swallow the urge to tell his superior how ridiculous he looked.

"Maybe." He shrugged, sipping the bitter sludge while trying hard not to grimace with disgust. Real men drank scotch, not this garbage. "Although I can't help thinking about the sketchy details of the disaster twelve years ago."

Yates waved an impatient hand. "Old news. Besides, he took out Omar Haram Shekau, what more could you ask for? That was a huge boost in our war against terrorism, since we know one of the pilots, the one on the plane headed for DC, was one of Omar's men. And don't forget the coup he and his partner Sloan did for us this past Fourth of July. POTUS is still singing his praises."

His fingers tightened with annoyance, and he let go of the stem of the wine glass, fearing it might shatter beneath the pressure. He and another colleague had both been recruited as a direct result of what had transpired back in July. The multiagency task force was well underway, but he planned to succeed when so many others had failed. Taking a deep breath, he willed himself to remain calm. He couldn't afford to lose his focus. His goal here was to find the details around Rashid's current location and the terrorist group he was to infiltrate.

Knowledge was power. And with power, anything was possible.

SEPTEMBER 9 – 7:45 p.m. – Baltimore, MD

Bryn silently prayed and sobbed as the icky men tied her arms behind her back. She cringed, scared to death they were going hit her again.

Please, God, save me! I want my mommy!

She could smell Meira's familiar spicy scent, but even knowing Meira was near didn't help her relax. She was so mad at the woman for not even trying to escape.

If they waited much longer to run away, she feared it would be too late.

Two men were speaking to each other in a language she recognized as Arabic, even though she didn't understand what they were actually saying. Her mother knew some Arabic, but the only phrase Bryn had learned to say was *I love you*.

Fresh tears rolled down her cheeks. These men didn't love anyone or anything. Except maybe hurting people.

Anger helped get her crying under control. She sniffled loudly, then immediately wished she hadn't when the men abruptly stopped talking. She tensed, anticipating a blow.

The sound of footsteps made her cringe, and it was all she could do not to scream. She heard a door shut and wished she could see if one man left or both of them.

Meira didn't come over to untie her, so Bryn remained still. Waiting. Wondering. Fearing the worst.

After what seemed like a lifetime, the mechanical voice echoed in the room. "Infidel, you will be told when to speak, until then remain silent."

She bobbed her head up and down, having learned the hard way that when he said remain silent, he meant completely quiet. No sound. Her heart raced and she felt short of breath, panic threatening to overwhelm her. With an effort, she tried to slow down her breathing.

Would the man with the mechanical voice allow her to speak to her mom this time? Or to that Jordan guy who they claim was her dad? Had they been able to break Mustaf, whoever he was, out of prison?

Bryn tried not to get her hopes up but found herself praying for rescue anyway.

And if that didn't work, she needed to find a way to convince Meira that the longer they stayed with these men, the more likely they would be killed.

Bryn bit her lower lip hard enough to make it bleed. She

was scared to death, but at the same time, if they were going to kill her anyway, better that it happened when she tried to escape rather than just sitting here waiting for the death strike to come.

SEPTEMBER 9 – 7:48 p.m. – Washington, DC

Jordan's phone rang, the number blocked the same way it had been the other times the kidnappers had contacted him. He quickly answered, putting the phone on speaker. "Rashid."

"Are you on the plane?" the mechanical voice asked.

Jordan looked at Diana's wide eyes, hoping he was making the correct decision. "No, but only because I learned from my sources at the FBI that Mustaf is being transported here to the US as we speak."

There was a long silence as if the news was unexpected. Diana's expression was full of anguish, and he hoped and prayed they would believe him.

"Did you hear me? Mustaf is being transferred here to American soil, which will make my job much easier. I already have an idea of where they may be taking him. This is good news, freeing him from an American prison will be much easier than trying to get him out of Lebanon."

"I will verify your claim," the mechanical voice said. The line went dead.

A long silence stretched between them.

"What if they can't verify the facts?" Diana finally asked, her brow furrowed with worry. "They'll hurt Bryn. And worse, they'll make us watch!"

Jordan reached over to take her hand. "Take a deep breath, I'm sure they will find out the truth. Once they've verified that Mustaf is in fact on his way here, they'll call us back with additional instructions. Bryn will be fine. They won't hurt her as long as we're doing what they ask." He didn't bother to add that once Mustaf was free, they wouldn't have a reason to keep their daughter alive.

Where on earth were they holding her? He thought about the additional companies Sun was checking out. Maybe they'd find Bryn at one of those locations. So far his search on Mustaf hadn't revealed much.

The warehouses were their best bet, but he wasn't keen on setting off another explosion. Especially since he would have no way of knowing if Bryn was there or not.

Now he was the one getting ahead of himself. First, he needed to convince the kidnappers that he was telling the truth about Mustaf. Then, he needed to find a way to follow their instructions while trying to pinpoint Bryn's location.

Last, but still very critical, he needed to figure out what the terrorists had in store for Washington, DC. The Secret Service should be able to keep them from getting too close to the White House, but there were plenty of other monuments to use as a possible target.

Too many.

SEPTEMBER 9 – 7:55 p.m. – Baltimore, MD

Elam's phone vibrated in his pocket. Bitter fear filled his mouth as he pulled out the device and glanced at the message on the screen.

Report to Liberty.

His blood went cold, but he knew better than to disobey a direct order, so he quickly texted back, *Of course.*

Since he was headed in the wrong direction, he got off the Metro at the next stop and boarded the appropriate train that would take him back to the location known as

Liberty. Their main headquarters, which he'd been able to avoid.

Until now.

His mouth was so dry he couldn't swallow. Rigging the padlock to blow had been the right thing to do, certainly the men he worked for would see the explosion as a good thing. They couldn't be angry with him when he had done nothing wrong.

Well, except for allowing the American to get away unscathed, but the men who forced him to do their bidding couldn't possibly know about that.

Could they?

Elam closed his eyes and struggled to remain calm. What if they hurt Meira as a way to punish him? It didn't make sense, though, because it was only through his skills that the men had gotten this far. They needed him. His knowledge. His skill. The dwellings were only structures.

One less building than they had before.

It shouldn't be that much of a big deal.

But he knew only too well there was no logic when it came to these men. The loss of a building may be enough to push them over the edge.

Elam kept his eyes closed and began to pray. Not to Allah, but to the Christian God he'd learned to believe in.

After the past two weeks, he wanted nothing to do with the land of his birth.

SEPTEMBER 9 – 8:10 p.m. – Washington, DC

Diana stared at the computer screen with mixed emotions. On one hand, she desperately wanted to get a glimpse of her daughter, to verify Bryn was alive and well. Yet she dreaded the idea that these men may take their anger out on the little girl, hitting her again, or worse.

She felt glued to her chair, unable to move, uncaring that she was leaving it to Jordan to clear away the remains of their meal.

There was nothing more important than Bryn.

When a message arrived in Jordan's inbox, she twitched and quickly double-clicked on the link. Her shoulders slumped when she realized it was nothing more than a message from Sun.

Nothing to report so far. Still looking.

Diana's stomach tightened with frustration. They needed to find Bryn. Before Mustaf landed on US soil. Before any more warehouses blew up. Before they lost any more time.

Bad enough that there was only thirty-six hours until the anniversary date. Less, if you considered the strike could very well come at midnight.

So many people at risk. So many possibilities. But deep in her bones, she mostly cared about Bryn.

Dear Lord, help me. Show us the way!

The whispered prayer that once brought comfort now felt hollow. Empty.

"Diana, please try to relax. I can feel your tension from here."

It took all her willpower not to snap at him. This whole mess of requiring them to free Mustaf was proof Bryn being in danger was his fault.

Jordan's job, the one he'd taken on for Security Specialists, Inc., had put their daughter's life in danger. Not her secret mission. Her way to honor her mother's memory.

The phone shrilled, making her jump. Before she could

reach for the device, Jordan rushed forward, placing the call on speaker.

"Rashid," he said.

"We have confirmed Mustaf is no longer in Camp Bucca," the mechanical voice intoned. She tried but couldn't detect a hint of emotion from Bryn's captors. "He will be landing on US soil at eight o'clock tomorrow morning. We expect you to bring him to us by eight o'clock that same evening. If you fail to do so, your daughter will die. Do you understand your mission?"

Jordan's gaze locked with hers. "Yes. I understand, but I need to see Bryn. You must prove to me she's still alive."

There was a long pause before the mechanical voice said, "Another link will arrive soon."

"Wait! I want a live feed like last time. I demand proof she's alive, do you hear me?"

"A link will arrive and we will call." The connection went silent.

"She's still alive," Diana whispered. "This must mean our daughter is still alive."

Our daughter. It was the first time Diana had included him, and it was humbling. "I hope so."

The link came from an email labeled *Rashidsmission* that popped up in his mailbox. He clicked on the link, and instantly, an image bloomed on the screen.

As before, Bryn was sitting in a chair, her arms bound behind her back, a blindfold covering her eyes. He strained to listen for the foghorn Sun had heard, but the shrill ring of his phone had him picking up the device.

"Rashid." He covered the microphone and asked Diana, "I need more information only Bryn would know."

"She plays flute for the middle school band," Diana whispered.

"Do you have a question for your daughter?" the mechanical voice asked.

"Yes. Bryn, what activity are you involved with at school?" He purposefully kept his question vague, hoping and praying for more time.

"Answer, infidel," the mechanical voice commanded.

"I, uh, take Tae Kwon Do."

Jordan glanced at Diana who nodded. "Anything else?" he asked.

"I play flute for the band," Bryn responded.

"Enough," the mechanical voice interrupted. "Do you accept your mission?"

Jordan hesitated, then heard it. The low echo of a foghorn off in the distance. He hoped, prayed that meant Bryn was in the same location as before. "Yes, I accept."

"Eight p.m.," the mechanical voice repeated. A second later, the link went blank and the call ended.

SEPTEMBER 9 – 8:11 p.m. – Damascus, Syria

The delay at the airport was irritatingly long. He despised international travel, but this trip had become a necessity. The situation with Mustaf being transported far earlier than planned raised suspicion. Who had done that, and how?

He didn't know and didn't like it.

It was important to return to the United States as soon as possible.

Despite traveling under an alias, he knew he was taking a dangerous risk. He'd changed his features as much as possible, but was it a good enough disguise?

He wouldn't know until it was too late.

Still, he needed to go. To make sure things went

according to plan. Lives needed to be taken to atone for the past.

He would not rest until his will had been done.

SEPTEMBER 9 – 8:12 *p.m.* – *Washington, DC*

Jordan pulled his gaze from Diana's with an effort. Twenty-four hours. They had twenty-four hours to find Mustaf and bring him to Bryn's kidnappers.

Or to find Bryn's location, freeing her from their clutches.

Both seemed impossible tasks.

"She looked okay, didn't she?" Diana's voice was begging for reassurance. "They must not have hurt her, right?"

He strove to sound reassuring. "They won't hurt her until they have what they want, which is Ahmed Mustaf freed from jail."

"How can you be so sure?" Diana pushed away from the table, rising to her feet and pacing in jerky movements across the room.

He wasn't sure of anything. Didn't she realize how much this was killing him? That little girl bound to a chair was his daughter. The daughter he didn't know he had, the one who'd fallen in love with baby elephants at the Atlanta Zoo, taken Tai Kwon Do, and played flute for the middle school band. What else didn't he know about her? He gave himself a mental shake and forced himself to stay focused. "Diana, please. Don't do this. We need to work together."

"Together?" She spun to face him, her features creased in agony. "Remember what happened the last time we worked together? We almost died."

"Yet here we are, despite your betrayal." He'd couldn't hide the bitterness in his tone.

"No." Her denial was swift. "My uncle used my mother to find us. I didn't tell my uncle about you and me. Never! I will place my hand on a Bible and swear that I never betrayed you."

She sounded so certain. What should he believe? "Even if you didn't, I was told you were dead, Diana. *Dead*. Do you have any idea what that was like for me? I still have your obituary in my desk drawer!"

That stopped her short. She gaped at him in surprise. "You do?"

He raked a hand through his thick dark hair, striving for patience. He didn't understand why she was so upset, except for the obvious reason that her stress level over Bryn was pushing her to the brink. "Yes. After I recovered physically from the explosion and resulting crash, I buried myself in my work. I lived on the edge, taking risks for the FBI. Emotionally . . ." He didn't finish. Losing Diana had gutted him. It had been a long time before he'd allowed himself to care about anyone.

He and Sloan had formed a friendship, then had become partners. He'd cared for Shari and married her, knowing he needed to move forward with his life. Move on from the tragedy of losing Diana.

And then Shari had died. Because of him. Because he'd left her alone and vulnerable.

Was he bound to make the same mistake again?

"And what about your . . . wife?" There was a hitch in her voice.

"I cared about Shari very much, but she was my second choice, Diana." He pinned her with his dark gaze. "Second to you. Because I thought you were dead. If I had known you were alive, I would have done everything within my power to find you."

"Even though you thought I betrayed you?"

"Yes. Even then." Or maybe because of that, his motives were still a bit murky.

Their gazes clung and held for a long moment before she broke the connection by looking away.

"So now what?" She hunched her shoulders. "What can we do to find Bryn?"

He blew out a breath. It was a good question. They needed to stay focused on the present, not ruminate on the past. "Did you hear the foghorn in the background?"

Diana's gaze sharpened. "No. Did you?"

"Yes. There is still the possibility they've moved her, but I'm hoping and praying she's in the same place, with the cameras hooked up and ready to go at the push of a button. It's the only thing that makes sense. We need to understand the purpose for blowing up the warehouse in Baltimore."

She blanched. "You mean, someone else could have been inside? Another hostage?"

"Not necessarily another hostage, but the warehouse must have something to do with whatever is going on here. Otherwise, why did it burst into flames?"

"I . . . can't . . . do this." Her voice was a ragged whisper. "I can't function when I think of Bryn being at the mercy of those men. I keep imagining the worst . . ."

"I know." He crossed over to her, lightly resting his hands on her slim shoulders. "But we need to stay focused on finding her, okay?"

She nodded, then rested her forehead on his chest. "I raised her to be strong, Jordan. I didn't tell her about being in witness protection, but I did teach her about always taking safety precautions. I taught her self-defense, Tae

Kwon Do, but most importantly? I taught her to have faith in God. But I can't seem to find solace in my faith at the moment."

He bent and pressed a kiss to the top of her head. "I can tell from the videos that she's smart and spunky. You've taught her well, Diana. She'll be okay, you'll see."

"You can't possibly know that." Her voice was barely a whisper.

True. But frankly, thinking the worst would only paralyze him. And if there was ever a time to trust in God's will, this was it. "I feel certain God is watching over Bryn for us."

"Oh, Jordan. I hope so." Her breathing hitched, and her shoulders began to shake as deep sobs racked her body.

Feeling helpless, Jordan gathered her close, wishing there was something—anything—he could do to make things right.

But he was as much of a victim in this as she and Bryn were. Maybe more. They'd targeted him to pay this ransom.

And he was fairly certain they had no intention of letting him live once he'd succeeded in his so-called mission.

"Shh, it's okay. We're going to be okay." He forced confidence into his tone, ignoring the sinking feeling in his gut.

Diana wrapped her arms around his waist, holding tight. As he cradled her close, it occurred to him that these terrorists had brought the woman he'd loved and a daughter he didn't know back into his life.

And they could just as cruelly take them away, forever.

CHAPTER SEVEN

September 9 – 9:05 p.m. – Washington, DC

Jordan's phone rang, causing Diana to jerk out of his arms. "Bryn?" she asked hoarsely.

He shook his head. "Sun." He answered the phone and placed the call on speaker. "Did you find something?"

"There was one fatality from the warehouse explosion." Sun didn't mince words. "Victim's name is George Larson, and he's homeless, known to sleep in doorways in the warehouse district. His body was found several feet away from the source of the blast, cause of death appears to be a broken neck."

Diana bit her lip, feeling terrible about the man's death while secretly relieved that it wasn't Bryn.

"What about the contents of the warehouse?" Jordan asked.

"No news on that front. They're still attempting to figure out what was inside the building, but honestly, I doubt they'll come up with anything as much of the interior was burned to a crisp."

She met Jordan's resigned gaze, knowing he'd hoped for

more. "Okay, thanks. Anything else on the other warehouses?"

"I might have a line on Justice Textiles, Corp. It's buried in another shell company, incorporated in DC."

A flicker of hope bloomed in her chest. "You think Bryn might be there?"

"Maybe, however, the building isn't anywhere near the water."

And just that quickly the flicker died. "What about the other place? Freedom whatever?"

"Freedom Shoppes doesn't appear to have any structures associated with it as far as I can find. But I'm still looking."

Diana balled her fists in frustration. They were no closer to finding Bryn.

None.

"Thanks, Sun," Jordan said. "Keep us posted with anything else you come up with." He disconnected from the call.

"Maybe the foghorn sound is a trick, something they're using to hide Bryn's location." As soon as the words left her mouth, she realized how paranoid she sounded.

"These guys aren't that good, Diana. Trust me, we'll find her." He gestured to the computer screen. "I haven't found much on Ahmed Mustaf, other than he was born in Syria and will stand trial for numerous terrorist attacks, including the London subway bombings a few years ago."

She remembered hearing about them and did her best to stay focused. "He must be part of ISIS, right?"

"Yeah. I can't help but wonder if there's any connection between your cousin Tariq and Mustaf." Jordan stared at the satellite computer screen.

Her stomach churned at the thought, but she forced

herself to consider all the options. "You mean other than both of them being Syrian-born?"

"Yes." Jordan glanced at her. "I mean, do you really think that kidnapping Bryn was a coincidence? I still can't figure out how they learned she was my daughter."

"Not from me," she protested, her cheeks flushing with anger.

"FBI Agent Tony Balcome?" he pressed.

"Maybe." She thought back. "He came to me in the hospital and arranged for me to be transferred into the care of the US Marshals."

"Is that when you found out you were pregnant?"

She rubbed her temple and nodded. "Yes, that's when I found out, and Agent Balcome was there guarding me when the doctor told me the news. But even if Agent Balcome knew, why suddenly tell someone now, after all this time?"

"Who is the Marshal assigned to you?"

Her gaze locked with his for a long moment. It was ingrained in every fiber of her being not to reveal anything about her past. But they were beyond this, weren't they? The fact that Bryn was in the hands of Syrian terrorists proved that her cover was blown. Her secrets revealed for the entire world to see. "US Marshal Christopher Wallace."

"Never heard of him."

She blew out an exasperated breath. "Why would you? He's my handler, not yours."

"Those are the only two men who should know about Bryn being my daughter, correct?" Jordan asked.

"Yes." She could see where he was going with this. "So one of them leaked the information."

"On purpose or by accident," Jordan agreed.

"The creed of the US Marshals is to die before revealing the identity of those under their protection."

"When is the last time you spoke to Marshal Wallace?"

She slowly shook her head. "I don't know, months probably."

"It may be time for you to call him."

"The kidnappers told me not to tell anyone." The protest was automatic, but now that she thought back to those first few hours after Bryn's disappearance, she understood they must have known about her connection to the US Marshals. She drew in a deep breath and nodded. "Yeah, okay. I'll call him." She reached for his cell phone, but he caught her wrist.

"Wait. You need to use a throwaway phone." He released her and stood, rummaging in the computer bag. He pulled out a small old-fashioned flip phone. "Here."

"You always have disposable phones lying around?"

"Yes." He dropped back into his seat. "I assume you know the number?"

She resisted the urge to roll her eyes. "It's not as if I programmed his information into my smart phone under US Marshal." She willed her fingers not to shake as she entered Chris Wallace's number. The phone didn't ring, the way it normally did, but went directly to a message.

This number is no longer in service.

Click.

Goosebumps rippled up her arms as she stared at Jordan. "I . . . don't understand. It states his number is no longer in service."

Jordan's expression was grim. "Could it be a safety measure? Something the phone does when an unknown number comes through?"

"No. I'm told to change my phone number and carrier every six months, and I always call Chris to let him know."

She'd left Chris messages on occasion in the past, but never once had she gotten this type of recording.

"What happens if Wallace is dead?"

Dead? She shivered. "I assume my case gets assigned to someone else."

"But you haven't heard from anyone else within the US Marshals Service?"

"No." She stared at the flip phone, her stomach curdling with dread. If someone had tortured Chris to the point he broke down and talked, they were all in grave danger.

Not just from the terrorist group who'd kidnapped Bryn, but from her mother's family.

Specifically, her cousin. Tariq Omar Haram Shekau.

SEPTEMBER 9 – 9:22 p.m. – Baltimore, MD

"Meira," Bryn whispered.

"I'm here." Meira's spicy scent grew stronger as the woman moved close to her mattress on the floor.

Bryn tried to think of something, anything that would convince this woman they needed to escape. Soon.

Tonight.

"Rest now, they won't be back for a while," Meira whispered in English.

"We need to escape. Tonight. Before they return." Bryn kept her voice low but urgent. "I can help keep you safe. My mother can help you start over, the way she's helped many others."

Meira put her hand on her stomach, then shook her head. "Too dangerous."

"Staying here is too dangerous. Do you really think they're going to let me live? As soon as what's-his-face has been set free, they'll kill me. And maybe you too."

"No," Meira whispered, but there was a hint of uncertainty in her tone.

"Yes," Bryn insisted, feeling desperate. "You know they will. Deep in your heart, you know they'll kill us both. That's what they do. Don't you see? These men are killers."

There was a pause before Meira said, "I can't leave without my husband, Elam."

Husband? This was the first Bryn had heard about Meira being married. "Are you sure you can trust him?" Bryn knew that many Muslim women were not valued by the men in their family. Often the males in charge would refuse to allow women to work, or teach, or do anything other than obey their husband's every command.

Bryn was so not getting married, ever.

"Yes. He's not like them."

Bryn's hopes faded. If Meira really cared for her husband, then it would be impossible to convince her to escape. She'd be stuck here in this horrible room, with the stupid blindfold over her eyes, until she died.

Uh-uh. No way. Bryn was not going to sit here and wait for the icky men to kill her.

There had to be a way to escape. With or without Meira's help.

There just had to be!

SEPTEMBER 9 – 9:51 p.m. – Washington, DC

His phone rang as he left the restaurant meeting with his boss. The number on the screen indicated it was from one of his men. He frowned. "What?"

"There's a problem."

He scowled, ducking through the doorway and into the dark night. Instead of finding a rideshare, he walked quickly, moving as far from the restaurant as possible. No sense in being there when his boss left. The dinner had been excruciating, but he felt certain his boss remained clueless, which was the most important thing. "What kind of problem?"

"Idiot hikers stumbled across Wallace's body earlier today in the Smoky Mountains. They just pulled him out of the ravine and identified him, his name hit the US Marshal database. It's only a matter of time before someone high up on the totem pole realizes that Diana Phillips has been compromised."

He swore beneath his breath. The Marshal had been dead less than a week; he'd been hoping he'd remain lost for much longer. "Implement Plan B."

"But—" the caller hesitated, then added, "Yes, sir."

He disconnected from the line without saying anything more, then scrolled through his apps to find the rideshare company he preferred. The fact that Wallace's body had been found wasn't the end of the world.

But it was a complication he didn't need at the moment. Especially since he'd wasted several hours with his boss without learning anything new.

It had been all he could do not to reach over to choke the life out of Clarence Yates.

He drew in a deep breath and let it out slowly. Plan B needed to work, at least for the next thirty-six hours. After that, it wouldn't much matter.

Anyone who got in his way would be dead.

And he'd be rich and powerful. Exactly the way he was meant to be.

SEPTEMBER 9 – 10:10 p.m. – Washington, DC

"I think I found Freedom Shoppes."

Sun's statement had Jordan straightening in his chair, his heart thudding with excitement as he spoke with Sun via the phone. "What sort of building is it?"

"A warehouse, just like American Lumber. And it's near the water, not far from downtown Baltimore. I'm heading that way now."

"Wait." He glanced from the phone at Diana who stared at him with desperate hope in her eyes. "Don't go alone, we'll meet you there."

"Are you sure that's a good idea?" Sun asked cautiously. "Why don't you let me check things out first?"

If there was the slightest chance Bryn was being held there, he fully intended to be the one to go in and get her. "I'm sure. Wait for us."

"It's going to take you longer to get there," Sun protested.

"I don't care. Please, Sun. I need you to wait for us." He stood and began packing the satellite computer into its bag.

"Okay, but at some point, you're going to have to trust me, Jordan. You hired me for a reason, didn't you?" Sun's tone was testy through the phone connection.

"I do trust you." He trusted in Sun's Mensa intelligence and her ability to speak in a multitude of languages. He trusted her with his secrets and those of his family. But he couldn't bear to let anyone else put their life on the line to rescue his daughter. "In fact, I'm counting on your smart brain to help us crack this case."

"Fine." Sun's short tone indicated she didn't believe him. "I'll call you when I reach the warehouse."

"See you soon." He disconnected from the call and hefted the computer bag over his shoulder. He jutted his chin toward the doorway connecting the house to the garage. "Let's go."

Diana didn't argue but moved toward the doorway leading to the single car garage. She let out a low moan when she saw the ancient Buick. "Are you kidding? This thing looks as if it will fall apart before we get to Annapolis."

"Doesn't matter what it looks like as long as it runs, right? Besides, it's still registered in my grandmother's name, which might work in our favor." He shoved the computer bag behind the driver's seat and slid in behind the wheel. Diana came around to join him on the passenger side.

"How long will it take us to get there?" Diana asked as they hit the road, leaving his grandmother's house behind.

"This time of night? Around forty minutes." He headed for the interstate, taking the southbound freeway.

"Forty minutes." Diana twisted her fingers in her lap. "Hang on, Bryn. We're coming."

He didn't mention the fact that this lead could turn out to be a bust, just like American Lumber had been. In fact, he'd be shocked if the stupid place wasn't rigged to explode, just like the other warehouse.

All he could do was hope and pray nothing bad happened, especially if Bryn was being held inside.

SEPTEMBER 9 – 10:38 *p.m. – Baltimore, MD*

Elam willed his hands not to shake as he approached Liberty. His mouth was dry with fear, and he couldn't help performing a quick sign of the cross, praying for God to watch over him.

Before he could lift his hand to knock, the door swung open. "Enter," came the terse command.

He bowed his head in a sign of deference and crossed the threshold. He continued to stare at the floor until he was addressed.

"What happened to American Lumber?"

He still didn't look up, partially out of fear—he was unwilling to look directly in the wild evil eyes of the man standing before him and partially because he was expected to show respect for his superiors.

"I happened to notice a couple of people examining the lock on the front of the warehouse." He paused, licked his lips, and forced himself to continue. "When it appeared the structure might be breached, I detonated the device as previously ordered."

There was a long silence, but Elam still didn't look up. He tried to control his breathing and waited.

"There was one fatality, was that the man attempting to enter the building?"

Elam's heart hammered against his ribs. This was it, the moment he'd dreaded. Should he lie? Or tell the truth?

Meira, love of my life, mother of my child. I'm sorry, so sorry.

"Unfortunately, no. The man attempting to enter the building moved too quickly. By the time I detonated the device, he was only thrown to the ground from the blast but not killed."

"*Al'abalah!*" *Idiot!* While he'd braced himself, the blow to his back forced him down to his knees.

Elam swallowed a cry, cowering on the floor at the Master's feet.

A second blow came, and a third. But when it was done, he was still breathing, his hands unmarred.

He was alive.

Long enough to be tortured for another day.

SEPTEMBER 9 – 11:01 *p.m.* – *Baltimore, MD*

"Sun? Where are you?" Jordan held his phone to his ear while sweeping his gaze over the row of warehouses not unlike those in Baltimore.

"Behind you," came her sarcastic reply.

He whirled around, belatedly realizing she'd sneaked up on him. He lowered his phone, tucking it into his pocket. "Have you checked the place out?"

"Yes." Sun glanced between him and Diana. "No lights that I can see through the narrow windows, and no sounds from inside." She paused, and his heart sank.

"Let me guess, there's a brand-new padlock on the front door of the building."

"Yes," Sun confirmed. "It looks just like the one you mentioned at American Lumber."

He let out his breath in a low hiss. "Not good."

"Why?" Diana demanded. "There has to be another way inside."

"Not if it's rigged to blow." Jordan stared at the innocuous building located just across the street. It was so close, yet so far out of reach. In the distance, the sound of a foghorn went off sending chills down his spine.

"We need to find a way to get eyes inside the place," he told Sun. "There must be some sort of nook or cranny we can use to slide a camera in."

"I thought you might suggest that, so I came prepared." Sun gestured for him and Diana to follow as she led the way to her car. "I had time, so I brought a mini wireless camera that connects to my phone. It's small enough that we should hopefully find a way to peek inside."

"You're brilliant." He was grateful Sun was on top of things since he was a mess. He glanced at Diana. "We'll find a way to prove Bryn is or isn't inside."

Diana nodded, her expression hopeful.

"Let's go," he said to Sun. When Diana followed, he hesitated, glancing over his shoulder at her. "It might be better for you to wait here."

"She's my daughter."

His too, but he decided to let it go. "Diana, it's dangerous. The last warehouse blew up in our face. Wait here. We won't be long."

He could tell Diana didn't want to, but she reluctantly nodded. "Please hurry."

He nodded and crossed the street with Sun. The shiny padlock looked exactly like the one on the door of American Lumber. Giving it a wide berth, he and Sun slipped around to the side of the building, the one where a single window was located.

Maybe they wouldn't need the camera. He held out his hands, weaving his fingers together to make a sling. "I'll give you a boost. Check out the window."

Sun readily put her foot in his hands and rested a hand lightly against the side of the warehouse. He lifted her up as high as he could.

"See anything?"

"No, it's completely dark. But there is a narrow opening in the frame where the wood has warped, so I'll try the camera."

He held his breath, half expecting the building to blow up any second as Sun gently inserted the slim camera through the opening. "Well?"

"I've got it. Let me check my phone." Her weight shifted, straining his muscles as she pulled her phone from her pocket. "It's a large space, no people from what I can see, but it's full of boxes of some sort. I can't quite make out what's written on the label."

Boxes? "You're sure there's no people? Maybe a corner room where they might be holding Bryn?"

"Not from what I can see, but I'll take some pictures for you." After about ten minutes, when his arms felt like they might pop out of their sockets, she said, "I'm finished."

He lowered her to the ground and reached for her phone. Scrolling through, he could see that the building was full of boxes but otherwise empty.

No sign of their daughter.

CHAPTER EIGHT

September 9 – 11:36 p.m. – Baltimore, MD

Diana twisted her fingers together, counting off the seconds in her head as she waited for Jordan and Sun to return to the ancient Buick.

She wasn't sure if she should pray that they found Bryn inside the booby-trapped building or not. So many things could go wrong, but she desperately needed to see her daughter. To hold her little girl in her arms.

Dropping her chin to her chest, she struggled to maintain control. She couldn't bear the thought of losing her daughter. They had to find her, soon.

Before Mustaf landed on US soil.

Please, Lord, show us the way!

The sound of footsteps startled her, and she swung around in panic, relaxing when she recognized Jordan and Sun. She peered at their expressions. "Bryn?"

"No sign of her." Jordan's voice held a note of resignation. He'd been her rock through this ordeal, she couldn't stand the idea of him being dejected.

"No sign of anyone being held there, but there were

dozens of boxes stored inside," Sun said, resetting the tone to a more positive approach. "Maybe we can find out more about what Freedom Shoppes is up to once I can play with the camera images a bit."

"Will that help us find Bryn?" Diana moved closer to Jordan.

"Possibly," Sun responded. "But no guarantee."

She glanced at Jordan. "What do you think? We don't have time to spin our wheels, hoping for a break. We need a direction to go. A way to find her."

Jordan pulled himself together with a nod. "To do that, we need to investigate every single lead, no matter how small or seemingly insignificant. And that includes finding the third location, Justice Textiles, Corp."

"Actually, I found two other possibilities as well," Sun said. "As I was searching for more keywords, I came across United Secrets, Inc. and Liberty Bell, Corp. They both seem to be fronts for other businesses, so I'm trying to search for properties they might be linked to as well."

"Two more?" Diana suddenly felt light-headed, swaying a bit on her feet. Jordan stepped close and slid his arm around her waist. "But . . . there could be dozens of others we don't know about."

Sun didn't say anything but shot Jordan an apologetic look.

"We still have time," Jordan said. "Almost eight hours until Mustaf lands."

A flash of anger hit hard. "What good is that when we don't even know where he's going to be? And what if we don't find Bryn by the morning, then what?"

"We can't play the what-if game." Jordan tightened his hold around her waist. "I need you to trust me for a while longer, okay?"

She closed her eyes and rested her head on his shoulder for a moment. Truthfully, she did trust Jordan, and Sun. God most of all.

But the hollow feeling in her chest remained. The emptiness would not be refilled until they'd found Bryn.

SEPTEMBER 10 – 12:02 *a.m.* – *Annapolis, MD*

Having Diana in his arms felt right, as if the twelve years between them had melted away. Her agony resonated deep within, but he knew he had to pull himself together and fast.

She needed him to be strong and confident. He held her for several moments before she straightened and pulled away. "What's our next step?"

He glanced at Sun. "Let's find a hotel to set up a temporary office. We'll need to dig into these other companies, see if we can determine those locations."

Sun nodded. "Sounds reasonable. Where do you want to go?"

He thought about it. "I feel certain we need to be closer to DC. There's a motel in Brookmont that will take cash without an ID if the price is right. Sloan and I used it in the past with good results."

"Too far," Sun said, waving her hand. "Mitchellville is closer and more centrally located." She named a motel he'd never heard of but had to agree the location was better, closer to DC, which was what he wanted.

"Sounds good, we'll meet up there."

Sun melted into the shadows, leaving him to steer Diana toward his grandmother's Buick. The foghorn went off again, and she dug in her heels, balking at getting into the car. "Did you hear that? I don't think heading to

Mitchellville is a good idea. We need to stay here, along the coast."

"Diana, we're not going far. Please, get in the car."

She hesitated. "How far?"

"About twenty minutes, especially this time of night. No traffic jams to worry about."

She finally relented, sliding into the passenger seat. When he climbed in behind the wheel though, she continued to protest. "Twenty minutes seems a long way to go if one of those other businesses are located along the coast. All this driving back and forth is a waste of time."

"But DC is also on the coast." There was a lot of coast-line to consider if you thought about Maryland and Virginia, both close enough to DC to be a place they'd have stashed Bryn. He battled another wave of desperate frustra-tion. "Besides, I feel certain Mustaf will be brought to DC."

"Why hasn't your FBI contact told you more about that?"

"Because that information is only provided to those who need to know. And since my former employer doesn't know about Bryn, or the kidnappers' demand, I can't very well force him to provide me high security clearance type of information."

She frowned. "But I thought they asked you to infiltrate a possible terrorist cell? Couldn't you use that somehow as a reason to find out?"

He'd considered that approach but wasn't convinced it would work. "I'll go there if I need to. Right now, I'd rather concentrate on finding other possible locations where they might be holding Bryn. The foghorn is the only clue we have, we need to keep working from that angle."

"It feels like this is taking too long." Diana whispered. "We should have another clue by now."

He didn't argue because she was right. They needed something, anything to go on besides the sound of a foghorn.

He glanced at the rearview mirror, his gut tightening when he saw the pair of square-shaped headlights maintaining a three to four car-length distance behind him. He told himself there was no reason to panic, but he wasn't driving all that fast, staying in the right-hand lane, so why wasn't the vehicle behind him moving over to pass him?

Jordan pushed his foot down on the accelerator, picking up speed. If the car was being driven by someone who wasn't in a hurry, he'd leave them in the dust.

The square headlights kept pace.

Not good. He tightened his grip on the wheel, wondering how on earth he could have picked up a tail.

He pulled out his phone and handed it to Diana. "Call Sun, ask where she's at."

Diana did as he requested, placing the call on speaker so he could hear.

"Yes?" Sun asked.

"Are you behind me?" Jordan asked bluntly.

"No, I left before you did, so I'm probably ahead of you. Why?"

His chest tightened as he glanced once again at his rearview mirror. "I've picked up a tail."

Diana sucked in a harsh breath and swiveled in her seat to peer out the back window. "How is that possible?" Sun asked.

"I don't know. But I need to shake him loose."

"In your grandmother's car?" Sun's tone held a note of sarcasm, and he hated knowing she had a point. The old Buick wasn't built for speed. "Where are you?"

"Heading west on Highway 50 coming up on Interstate 301."

"I'm already there. I'm taking the on-ramp to head south. Follow me, I'll stay in touch." Sun disconnected from the line.

A stoplight up ahead turned red. Jordan slowed down, looked both ways, then gunned the engine and ran the light.

The square headlights did the same.

They were in trouble. Deep trouble. Jordan pushed the old Buick as fast as he dared as he estimated the distance to the on-ramp.

"Jordan? What if they catch us?" Diana asked, her fingers digging into the armrest.

"They won't. I need you to hang on." The markers along the side of the highway flashed past, and then he saw the blue sign for the interstate. Again, blowing through another red light, he abruptly wrenched the wheel and sped up and onto the interstate.

For a moment, there were no headlights behind him. His phone rang, and Diana pressed the talk button.

"Take the first exit off the interstate. I'm here, waiting for you. We'll sandwich this guy between us."

"Got it." Cars flew past him, the Buick was so not a race car, but that didn't matter. The exit loomed, and he did his best to stay on the road. Sun's black SUV was sitting off to the side of the road. He slowed his speed and continued past her.

The square headlights showed up a heartbeat later. He couldn't see anything behind the headlights following him and had to trust that Sun was doing her part. His hands were so tight on the steering wheel that the tips of his fingers went numb.

Putting himself in danger was part of his job. Something he did often and without complaint. But Diana was sitting beside him. The mother of his child.

The woman he'd once loved. The woman he'd thought had betrayed him.

Despite the fact that he still wasn't absolutely sure she hadn't betrayed him, he refused to let anything happen to her. Or to him, because if that was the case, Bryn was dead.

The square lights got closer, then suddenly hit him from behind with such force that his head jerked forward. The old Buick swerved under the impact, but since it was as big as a boat, he was thankfully able to keep it on the road.

Another bone-jarring hit. He sent up a silent prayer as he struggled to keep the Buick on the road, then the square lights vanished, the vehicle behind him, careening out of control, going over the shoulder of the road and coming to a stop.

He belatedly realized Sun must have been the one hitting square lights from behind with enough force for that vehicle to hit him. He hit the brakes, bringing the Buick to a halting stop. Pulling his weapon from its holster, he pushed open the driver's side door. "Stay here."

Without waiting for Diana to respond, he eased along the back of the Buick, his gaze fixed on the vehicle in the ditch. The square headlights were directly in his face, hampering his ability to see.

The sound of two sharp gunshots had him dropping to his knees, his heart hammering in his chest. Where was Sun?

He waited, despite every nerve in his body screaming at him to move. To do something.

Then more gunfire as a dark shadow came tumbling from the driver's side door. He reacted instinctively, firing at the driver who was shooting at him.

The shadow went down and didn't move.

Still, he waited. There could be others in the vehicle.

After another five minutes, he made a quick run for it, heading straight for the passenger side of the vehicle. Another shadow moved. He lifted his weapon, then lowered it.

Sun.

"The vehicle is clear," she whispered. "Driver's down, bleeding bad and unconscious."

He battled a wave of frustration. "That's not good, we need information from him."

"I know. I'm sorry, but he shot at both of us, so we had no choice but to return fire." Sun's expression reflected her dismay. "I know we didn't intend to kill him."

He blew out a breath. "Let's see what we can find on him or in the car."

The driver was of Arab decent, but there was nothing in his pockets or in the vehicle. There was a disposable phone, which Jordan picked up but didn't expect to get much information from.

"Let's get out of here." Sun put a hand on his arm. "You and Diana need to come with me. Your vehicle has been compromised."

"I know." Jordan hurried back to the Buick to get Diana. What he didn't know was how they'd been found and who was after them?

SEPTEMBER 10 – 12:37 *a.m. – Baltimore, MD*

Meira couldn't rest. Couldn't stop thinking of what Bryn had said.

My mother can help you start over, like she helped so many others.

Elam hadn't contacted her in days, and she very much

feared he might be dead. There was no limit to what these men would do to get what they wanted.

She bowed her head and silently prayed. Elam had embraced Christianity, but it was difficult for her to give up the way she'd been taught. And privately she thought his God and Allah were one and the same.

She prayed for wisdom and guidance. Was the child right? Were these men going to kill her despite their promises? Sliding her hand in the deep pocket of her cloak, she fingered the two plastic spoons she'd hidden there. Both had been sharpened as best she could by rubbing the edges against the rough concrete.

Yet they were flimsy. Plastic. Not close to being lethal enough to use in an escape attempt.

We must go. Soon. Tonight, the child's voice echoed in her mind.

Yet she couldn't do it. She couldn't risk the life of her unborn child in an attempt to escape that was surely doomed.

Elam, my love. Where are you? Why haven't you come for me? What is going on?

Bryn made a soft sobbing sound. Her heart ached for the girl.

Meira fingered the crudely sharpened plastic spoons again, then rose to her feet. Moving quietly, knowing the cameras were always there, watching over them, she bent over Bryn.

"Shh, it's okay. You have nothing to fear. Allah is here." She said the words loud enough for the microphones located near the cameras to pick up.

"I want my mommy," Bryn sobbed.

"Shh. It's okay." Meira took one of the plastic spoons

from her pocket and pressed it into Bryn's hand. "I'm here for you, *fatat saghira*." Little girl.

Bryn stopped crying the moment she realized the plastic spoon was a potential weapon.

"Sleep now, I'm here for you. Everything will be all right."

"Thank you," Bryn whispered.

Meira placed a finger over the child's lips, indicating she shouldn't say anything more. Bryn nodded as if understanding.

Meira moved away, turning various possibilities over and over in her mind.

If Elam didn't return soon, escape may well be their only option.

SEPTEMBER 10 – 12:43 a.m. – Mitchellville, MD

Diana sat on the edge of the motel room bed, twisting her fingers together to keep herself from falling apart.

Someone had come after them. Had tried to kill them.

It didn't make any sense. The demand was for Jordan to free Mustaf. Why try to harm him before he'd accomplished his task?

Jordan and Sun were both logged into their respective satellite computers, making her feel useless.

"I'd like to do something to help," she said.

Jordan glanced at her. "I know, but you need to let us work for a bit. Just hang tight, okay?"

She blew out a breath. As if she had a choice?

"The car was reported stolen a little over two hours ago," Sun said.

"From where?" Jordan asked.

"Washington, DC." Sun tapped the screen. "The suburb of Walker Mill."

Diana stood and crossed over to look at the computer. She frowned. "That's not far from here."

"No, it's not. And the two-hour timeframe from the time the vehicle was stolen and you guys picking up the tail is interesting too." Sun looked up at her. "It feels a bit, I don't know, amateurish."

"No ID, money, or other identifiers on the driver or within the vehicle doesn't match that theory," Jordan pointed out. "It's more along the lines of a professional."

"Maybe." Sun didn't sound convinced. "I wish we could figure out how they found you."

"I wish I knew who *they* were," Jordan countered. "I mean, I was assigned to infiltrate an Islamic terrorist cell by Yates, who is heading up the multiagency task force. Bryn's kidnappers want me to find and free Mustaf. Makes no sense that any of them would want to kill me."

"I agree," Diana chimed in. Out of nowhere, her phone vibrated. When she glanced down, there was an unknown number reflected on the screen. The only calls she'd gotten on this phone was from her WITSEC handler or the kidnappers, who always used a blocked number.

"Who's calling you?" Jordan's gaze drilled into hers.

"I don't know, it's a number I don't know." The phone continued to buzz.

"Is that your personal cell?" Jordan's expression turned grim.

"Yes, it's also the phone the kidnappers used, so I didn't dare get rid of it."

"I don't like it," Jordan muttered darkly. "Answer it."

She quickly pressed the button to answer. "Yes?"

"Is this Deborah Martin?" a male voice asked.

She glanced at Jordan, wondering if he remembered that the name she was now living under was Deborah Martin. "Who is this?"

"I need to speak to Deborah Martin about a beach rental."

She felt the blood drain from her face. "Beach rental" was the secret phrase provided to her by the US Marshals. But this wasn't Chris's number. "I might have a place, depends on who is interested."

"Deborah, this is US Marshal Frank Carlson. I'm sorry to inform you that US Marshal Christopher Wallace is dead."

Dead? She reached out to grip Jordan's shoulder to prevent herself from collapsing to the floor. First Bryn, then being followed and shot at, and now this. "When?"

"His body was discovered at the bottom of a ravine in the Smoky Mountains. We can't be certain yet if this was an accident or murder." There was a pause as he added, "I've been assigned as your new handler, and I need you and your daughter to come in ASAP. I'm afraid your identity has been compromised."

CHAPTER NINE

September 10 – 1:03 a.m. – Washington, DC

The ringing of his burner phone pulled him from sleep. Scowling, he grabbed the device and hissed, "This better be good."

A long silence before his man cleared his throat. "It's not. The professional failed to execute as ordered and was found dead along the side of the road from a couple of gunshot wounds, one to the chest, the other a head shot."

He tightened his grip on the device. "There better be no way to trace him to us."

"Of course not, and your plan B is still in play. We believe we'll get her location very soon."

He muttered a vile curse. "You must deliver by the deadline. There's a lot riding on this."

"Yes, sir." The guy clicked off.

He rose and stalked over to the window, looking over at the top of the White House easily seen off in the distance. It was a symbol of everything he detested yet longed for. It was so close yet remained far out of reach.

Because of the incompetence surrounding him. He

closed his fingers into a fist and tried to wrestle his red-hot fury under control.

After several deep breaths, he unclenched his hands and forced himself to relax.

This was just a minor setback. There was still time. He'd have what he wanted, no matter what the cost.

However, if the situation didn't improve—and soon—he'd have to find someone more capable than his current contact.

It shouldn't be this difficult to find them.

SEPTEMBER 10 – 1:07 a.m. – Mitchellville, MD

Jordan was close enough to hear the conversation between Diana and the US Marshal. She was clearly reeling from the death of her handler and was quizzing the guy for more information. In turn, the new handler kept repeating how she needed to come in for protection.

Jordan shook his head and made a slicing motion with his hand, indicating she needed to end the call.

Her eyes were wide with distress. She must have been on the same page as he was because she quickly interrupted Frank Carlson. "I'm sorry, I have to go. I'll be in touch, later."

"Wait—" he protested, but Diana didn't hesitate to disconnect the call. The phone immediately vibrated again, and she quickly shut it off.

"We should go," Sun said. "That was long enough for a trace."

Jordan sighed and rubbed the back of his neck. She was right. "Yeah, okay. Let's pack up. Oh, and Diana? Keep the number the Marshal used to call you, just in case we need to reach out to him, but lose the phone."

"What do you mean, 'lose the phone'? What if the kidnappers need to get in touch with me?"

"They know we're together and have used several email accounts to reach me." Jordan met her worried gaze. "Trust me, they'll find a way."

"Why would the US Marshals trace the call?" Diana protested. "They're supposed to protect those in the program, not track them down like criminals. Not to mention, participation in WITSEC is always voluntary."

"It's possible the US Marshals are working with someone in the government," Jordan explained as he packed up his satellite computer.

"Yes, of course they are, they work with the Department of Justice."

"I mean someone else, maybe even someone on the task force. You heard what he said, they're not sure if Wallace's fall into the ravine was an accident or murder. Was he the type of guy who liked to hike in the mountains?"

There was a slight hesitation before she said, "I don't know."

"We'll find out the truth from the ME's office eventually, but I'm leaning toward murder. For your sake, and Bryn's, we can't afford to assume everything is legit."

"I don't understand." Diana rubbed her hands over her arms as if chilled to the bone. "None of this is making any sense."

He couldn't argue. "Let's hit the road, find a new place to stay, and try to think things through. Leave your phone here."

"Where are we going? I thought this was the ideal place for us because it was centrally located."

"It was, but we'll find something." He hoped. He glanced at Sun. "Ideas?"

Sun had her satellite computer packed up too. She nodded. "I think we should try Edgewater. It's farther from DC, but still coastal."

He didn't like being farther from DC, but he trusted Sun's instincts. They were functioning better than his at the moment. "Okay, Edgewater. I hope they have a place we can go without showing ID."

"I'm sure we'll find a way," Sun said as they headed back out to the parking lot. "Offering money usually works."

And made them memorable too, but what choice did they have? First being followed, then the news of the Marshal's untimely demise.

He held out his hands for the car keys, and Sun dropped them in his palm with a flash of annoyance in her eyes. "I'm a better driver than you are."

"I need you to help me find a place to stay." He knew it was chauvinistic to insist on driving, but he couldn't help himself. The only driver he was comfortable with was Sloan, but he wasn't here.

"Idiot," Diana muttered as she slid into the back seat.

"Guilty as charged." He pulled out of the parking lot, keeping a keen eye on the vehicles behind him as he headed back to the interstate.

Ten minutes later, they were heading east on Highway 50 without any hint of a tail.

They were in the clear. For now.

His mind drifted back over the recent twists in the case. Diana was right about the fact that the puzzle pieces weren't fitting together. Diana and Bryn being in witness protection was to avoid her cousin Tariq, which wasn't linked to Bryn's kidnapping or to the ransom demand to free Mustaf.

Or was it?

Exhaustion pulled at him; it had been a long time since he'd gotten any sleep. He knew only too well that they needed at least a few hours of downtime.

Yet the clock was ticking. Less than eight hours until Mustaf's transport plane landed, hopefully, in DC.

"If Frank's right and my identity has been compromised, Bryn is in more danger than ever," Diana said. "I wouldn't put it past Tariq to place a high price on her head."

He met her gaze in the rearview mirror. "From what you said, Tariq wouldn't have any knowledge of you and Bryn. The Feds did a good job of faking your death."

"He shouldn't know about us, but with my identity being compromised, how hard would it be for him to find out? I know he has many connections. Word will filter out, eventually." Her voice was tinged with despair.

"We'll find Bryn." Jordan glanced at Sun. "We need to keep working on those locations."

"We will." Sun yawned. "But if we don't get some sleep, we're apt to do more harm than good."

"I can't sleep, not when Bryn is out there somewhere suffering at the hands of terrorists," Diana said sharply. "And I don't understand how you can."

"I want her back as much as you do." He kept his tone even with an effort. Snapping back wouldn't help. Not when the pressure was getting to both of them.

Besides, he knew where she was coming from, he really did. He felt the same sense of helplessness driving him forward too. But if they didn't get some sleep, they'd all crash and burn.

Which in their current precarious position could be deadly.

. . .

SEPTEMBER 10 – 2:09 *a.m. – Somewhere over the Atlantic Ocean*

Mustaf couldn't sleep, couldn't relax. Everything was all wrong, and he expected to be beaten with hands and feet at any moment.

But so far they'd left him alone.

He tensed. A whisper of fabric, the hushed footstep. This was it. This was what he'd feared all along.

They had no intention of delivering him to the United States of America alive.

"Can you hear me?" a low voice asked.

Mustaf feigned sleep.

"I know you're awake, your breathing is too fast." The voice was calm, measured.

"What do you want?" he finally whispered back.

"There is a plan in place for when we land. Be prepared."

A plan? Mustaf tried not to show his elation. He gave a brief nod, unable to do much more with his wrists and ankles chained together.

The man moved away, leaving him alone again.

Except he wasn't alone. His people hadn't forgotten him.

There was a plan to free him once he arrived in the US.

And yes, he would be more than ready.

SEPTEMBER 10 – 3:38 *a.m. – Edgewater, MD*

Diana jerked awake when her chin slipped off her hand. She blinked in an effort to clear her blurred vision.

The computer screen was the only light in the room. Sun had stretched out on one of the two beds, Jordan on the floor. He'd tried to convince her to rest in the second bed, but she'd stubbornly refused, angry at Jordan for his apparent disregard for their daughter.

No matter how hard she tried, she couldn't get the images of Bryn trying to look and sound brave while blindfolded and tied to a chair out of her mind.

She tried to focus on the screen, but it was no use. The words remained blurred by fatigue. There was a nagging headache residing in her temples. She pressed her fingertips there in an effort to relieve the pain.

She hated to admit that Jordan was right. That they needed some sleep if they were to be successful in rescuing Bryn.

Turning from the computer, she managed to step over Jordan's lean frame stretched out on the floor to reach the second bed. Easing onto the mattress, she pulled up the blanket and rested on the pillow.

The bed was likely far more comfortable than what Bryn was forced to use. She squeezed her eyes tightly against a fresh spurt of tears. She tried placing her daughter's life in God's hands, but it wasn't easy.

She believed in God, had faith in His abilities, but still resented the fact that Bryn had been kidnapped by these evil men. Terrorists. Why, God, why? Why should Bryn have to suffer?

There was no answer.

She must have fallen asleep because a strange clicking sound brought her awake. The room was still dark, but she could barely make out the shadow of a man looming over her.

She opened her mouth to scream just as a hand clamped over her mouth. "It's me, Jordan. Get up, we need to go."

Cold fingers of fear trailed down her spine. With his

hand over her mouth, she couldn't speak, so she gave a nod to indicate she understood.

He removed his hand and helped her up, pushing her behind his lean frame as he made his way toward the door. It took her a moment to realize the other bed was empty.

Where was Sun? Why did Jordan think they were in danger?

She didn't voice her questions. Jordan handed the satellite computer case to her and pulled his Glock from its holster. He pressed the snub-nosed revolver from his ankle holster into her hand. Her mouth went dry as he quickly positioned them behind the door.

The motel room only had one way to go out, the same way someone would enter.

As if on cue, the door handle turned with a loud click as someone accessed their room with a key card. In what seemed like slow motion, the door stealthily opened inch by inch.

Jordan didn't move, and she found herself holding her breath, afraid to breathe. A shadow moved into the room, but Jordan didn't immediately take action.

Then suddenly he attacked in a blur of movement, striking the intruder on the back of the head. She fully expected the guy to go down, but he didn't. He turned toward them, raising his hand where she could clearly see a gun.

No!

Without thinking, she threw the computer case. It hit the man's wrist, and the muffled sound of a gunshot went off, the bullet harmlessly hitting the floor. Moments later, the gun fell too.

Jordan jumped him, taking the guy to the floor and

pinning him there. He pressed his forearm across the man's windpipe. "Who are you? Who sent you?"

The man didn't speak but struggled to break free of Jordan's grip, kicking his legs wildly and attempting to wrap them around Jordan's torso. Jordan shifted so that he pinned one of the man's legs, keeping the upper hand.

"Who sent you?" Jordan repeated.

She gingerly picked up the computer case, staying out of the way. She went and stood over the man's head, holding the case up in a way that indicated she'd drop it on him if needed.

The intruder went lax, but still Jordan didn't move. Diana wondered how much pressure it would take to choke him to death.

Jordan locked gazes with the intruder. "If you don't talk to me, I have no reason to keep you alive."

Diana tried not to gasp, feeling certain Jordan was bluffing. The man she once loved, all those years ago, wasn't capable of cold-blooded murder.

Then again, she didn't really know the man Jordan was now, did she? She knew he'd been kind to her and determined to find Bryn, but she had no idea what his moral boundaries were.

"Have it your way," Jordan said as if they were having a normal conversation.

"W-wait," the guy gasped. "I . . . can help."

She could tell Jordan eased up on the pressure and felt dizzy with relief. His tone remained harsh. "Start talking."

"I . . . was hired by a guy in the task force," the man said slowly.

"Tell me something I don't know," Jordan countered. "Who? Why? What's the real threat here?"

The man's gaze flickered to her, and in that moment she

knew. Jordan had been right all along. Their daughter had been kidnapped because of her. Because of Tariq.

Her evil and horrifically brutal cousin knew about her daughter.

A sound from outside drew her attention. Another large shadow, and Jordan acted instinctively, lifting to shoot as the man on the floor once again struggled to get free.

Jordan lurched off-balance as the gun went off. She dropped the computer onto the man's head with as much force as she could muster. She heard a grunt, and the intruder went lax.

"Let's go!" Jordan levered up from his position on the floor. There was a second man dressed in black lying on his back in the doorway.

The intruder hadn't come alone.

"Grab the computer," Jordan said in a hoarse tone. He was searching the dead man's pockets, pulling out a set of keys. "Hurry."

She picked up the computer bag, horrified by the intruder's broken nose. Had she killed him? She hadn't meant to. A soft mewling sound came from her throat, and she reached down to check him for a pulse.

"No time, we have to go before he regains consciousness." Jordan grabbed her hand and tugged her away from the intruder.

"I . . . didn't kill him?"

"With a computer bag? Doubtful." Jordan used the keys in his hands to find the vehicle, then pulled her toward it.

"I . . . don't understand. Where is Sun?"

Jordan slid behind the wheel, waiting for her to get in beside him. Without answering, he pulled out of the motel parking lot and drove for at least a mile without using the headlights.

Her hands began to shake, so she interlaced her fingers, trying desperately not to fall apart.

"You left your phone in Mitchellville, right?" Jordan asked grimly.

"Yes." It hadn't been easy, but in the end, she'd believed Jordan was right. The kidnappers knew they were together and knew how to get in touch with Jordan if needed. "Why? What's going on? Where's Sun?"

There was a long pause before Jordan responded. "I don't know. When I woke up, she was gone, along with her sat computer."

"That doesn't make sense. Why would she leave us without telling us? She must be within walking distance as she didn't take the vehicle."

Jordan shook his head, his attention focused on the road before them. "I don't know, and a better question is how did they find us?"

"Do you think Sun is the leak?" She forced the question past her tight throat.

There was only the barest hint of hesitation before Jordan responded. "No. I trust Sun with my life. I'm sure she found some sort of lead and took off rather than wake us up."

Diana didn't respond because she wasn't so sure. Granted, it appeared Sun worked for Jordan's company, but that didn't make her trustworthy.

Jordan reached up and touched his left shoulder with a grimace. When he removed his hand, it was covered in something dark.

Blood?

"You're hurt?" She couldn't hide the flash of panic.

"Yeah, but it's okay. The bullet only grazed me."

CHAPTER TEN

September 10 – 5:05 a.m. – Washington, DC

His burner phone rang, and he sighed heavily when he recognized the number. "Now what?"

"Contact was made, but she refused to come in."

He hadn't really expected her to rush into the arms of the US Marshals Service. "I don't care, your job is to find her."

"I'm trying, but—"

He let out a string of curses, interrupting the idiot who couldn't seem to get a simple job done without listing excuses. "Enough. I don't want to hear it. Don't call me until you have something important to share or you have her. Understand?"

"Yes, sir."

He disconnected from the call and barely refrained from throwing the phone at the window. Time was running out. Things needed to happen and soon, or all his careful and precise planning would be for nothing.

Unacceptable.

He considered the possibility of hiring someone else.

He still had connections that could be tapped. Favors that were owed.

While he couldn't afford to raise suspicions about what he was doing, this issue needed to be contained and soon.

Using the untraceable phone, he took a deep breath and punched in a series of numbers. Drastic times called for drastic measures.

He would get what he wanted. What he needed. Whatever the cost.

Because the end absolutely justified the means.

SEPTEMBER 10 – 5:07 *a.m.* – *Annapolis, MD*

The bullet only grazed him? Diana did her best not to panic. "How bad is it?"

"I'm fine." Jordan's tone was curt. "We need to ditch this vehicle and find another place to stay."

The idea of getting rid of the vehicle was scary, but she reminded herself that Jordan was good at his job. He'd get them through this. She squinted through the windshield. "Why are we back in Annapolis?"

He glanced at her. "You have a better place in mind?"

Wherever Bryn was being held. A useless wish, so she shook her head with a sigh. "No. But all this running around seems counterproductive. Now we need to get rid of this vehicle, find another, then a place to stay. And we have no idea where Sun is, which worries me. We'll never find Bryn at this rate."

"I know." Jordan's tone softened. "We'll keep looking, but we also need a game plan for when Mustaf lands in"— he glanced at his watch—"less than three hours."

Her stomach knotted with tension. "You need to

contact the task force. There has to be a way to figure out where his plane is landing."

"Let's hope and pray he's not headed to Guantanamo Bay."

Jordan's statement sent a jolt of fear stabbing through her. "Cuba? How will we ever free him if he's being transported to Cuba?"

"Honestly, I don't think he is heading to Cuba. I think he'll land in DC. Either in the Naval District or at Andrews Air Force Base."

The news didn't help her sense of panic. "That's not much better. You're not a member of the armed forces, and gaining access to a tightly controlled military base will be just as impossible as flying to Cuba to grab Mustaf."

"I think I can get access with help from the government," Jordan pointed out.

She momentarily closed her eyes, the magnitude of their task hitting hard. It was all so impossible. Free Mustaf from a military base? Bring him to the kidnappers so they'll hand over Bryn in exchange?

No way. As much as she wanted to believe it, she knew it wouldn't happen that way.

Better to focus on finding Bryn. Finding and freeing their daughter had to be easier than getting to Mustaf.

She couldn't bear to imagine the alternative.

SEPTEMBER 10 – 5:18 *a.m.* – *Washington, DC*

Elam walked to the Metro, doing his best to ignore the pain that reverberated through him with every step. He'd spent the past few hours thinking through his situation and had come to a horrifying conclusion.

They were going to kill him.

Oh, not right away. They still needed him, still desired his expertise. His job was only half finished, but he now realized that the moment he'd fulfilled his duty, they would kill him without blinking an eye.

Meira would suffer at their hands too. As would their unborn child. The very thought made him feel sick to his stomach.

Knowing how vulnerable Meira and his baby were frightened him more than any beating they could threaten him with.

Until now, he'd thought they had a chance of surviving this. That these men would honor their promise.

Now he knew the truth. The Master had no honor.

Seeing the Metro sign up ahead, he approached and used his card to access the terminal. He headed downstairs, striving for anonymity. He didn't make eye contact, most people didn't notice him anyway, which made him good at his job, yet he didn't delude himself into thinking his so-called employer wasn't tracking his movements. Between the Metro card and the phone they'd provided him, they were all knowing.

And all powerful.

Elam had some emergency cash stashed away, but he wouldn't use it until he absolutely needed to. After the explosion and his beating, he knew the time was coming, soon.

But first, he had to find Meira. He couldn't live with himself if his wife and unborn child suffered because of him.

He'd die to protect them. And knew in his heart that was the most likely outcome. When the train pulled in, he entered and took a seat. After the train pulled away, he considered his options, accepting and embracing his new role.

There were several places Meira might be. He'd search them one by one until he found and rescued her.

Dear Lord, protect my family.

SEPTEMBER 10 – 5:32 *a.m.* – *Annapolis, MD*

The wound along the edge of his shoulder ached like a son of a gun, but Jordan ignored it. The couple of hours of sleep he'd managed to snag before he'd heard someone outside their room at the motel had helped take the edge off his exhaustion, but he still didn't understand where Sun had gone.

And why she'd sneaked out of the motel room, with the computer, without telling him.

He spied a drug store that had a sign indicating they were open twenty-four hours a day. He quickly pulled in. They needed dressings and another set of disposable phones. From there, he needed to find a place to ditch the dead guy's SUV and pick up a new ride.

Diana was right, all of this ridiculous running around was getting in the way of finding Bryn. Was that part of their plan? The guy who'd tried to kill him had confirmed there was a leak within the task force but hadn't given them anything more.

Who could he trust? Sun? Once he would have answered that with an unequivocal yes, but now?

Heaven help him, he wasn't sure.

"What do we need? I'll get it," Diana said, pushing her door open.

"No, stay here." He lightly caught her arm to prevent her from getting out. He couldn't explain his wariness, but he was all for trusting his instincts. "I promise I'll be back in a few minutes. And you can watch through the window for me."

She glared at him for a moment, then relented, closing her car door and settling back in her seat. His black T-shirt hid most of the blood, but he intended to find a restroom to finish cleaning up the wound.

The bright lights made him squint. The restrooms were in the back, and he headed there first. It didn't take long to clean up, and he was relieved the bullet hadn't caused much damage. When that was finished, he grabbed a couple of throwaway phones, dressings, and over-the-counter painkillers.

The woman behind the register eyed him warily as he checked out. He forced a smile, trying to put her at ease.

She did not look reassured.

He paid for everything in cash, then headed back out to the SUV, stopping short when he recognized Sun in the driver's seat of another SUV parked beside it.

Sun lowered the driver's side window. "Get in. We're leaving that SUV here."

Seeing Diana already settled in the passenger seat, he had little choice but to climb in behind Sun. "How did you find us?"

"Followed you from the motel." Sun backed out of the parking spot and took a right-hand turn out of the parking lot.

"There wasn't anyone behind us," he protested.

"I drove without lights." Sun met his gaze in the rearview mirror. "I'm sorry, I shouldn't have left without telling you. I couldn't sleep, so I decided to grab a rideshare to head over to where you left the SUV. The one in the parking area not far from the first warehouse explosion, remember?"

"Yeah," he admitted slowly. "But what made you think of that?"

She shrugged. "That's just the way my brain is wired. We needed another vehicle, so I went to get it. On the way back, I tried to find someplace that was open twenty-four seven to pick up something to eat. By the time I reached the motel, I noticed you and Diana driving away in an SUV."

He narrowed his gaze. "You really think I missed you tailing us because you were driving without lights?"

"Yes, I do." Sun made another turn, then headed toward the interstate. "I believe that was also how we were followed after the US Marshal contacted Diana."

He tried to think back at how he'd checked the rearview mirror. Maybe it was possible to tail someone in the middle of the night, driving without lights and keeping a safe distance back. Still, he was more observant than most.

"Are you hungry?" Diana asked from the passenger seat. "Sun brought bacon, egg, and cheese biscuits. They're cold but still edible."

He hesitated, hoping, praying Sun was right and they were finally out of danger. He winced when Sun hit the gas pedal, taking them to freeway speeds in a nanosecond, wishing he was the one behind the wheel. "Why not."

Diana handed him a sandwich. It was cold, but he ate it anyway. He frowned when he saw Sun take the lane that indicated they were heading back toward Baltimore. "Where are we going?"

"I found the location of another warehouse," Sun said in a calm voice. "I was going to check it out myself but figured you'd want to be there to check it out."

Another warehouse? He sat up straighter in his seat. "Which one?"

"United Secrets, Inc." Sun met his gaze in the mirror again. "It's in Baltimore, not that far from the place known as Freedom Shoppes."

He tried to take heart in the fact that Freedom Shoppes hadn't exploded the way American Lumber had, but it wasn't easy. "Three of the locations have been found in Baltimore. That can't be a coincidence."

"I concur." Sun kept her gaze on the road. "We need to stay there until we find all the warehouses with suspicious names."

"Yeah, that's a good idea." He took a deep breath and let it out slowly. It bothered him that they were heading away from the DC area. Deep down, he knew Washington, DC, was the key to this mess. The main target for the terrorists.

New York had a higher population, but DC was the epitome of what terrorists despised. Government and rules. The President of the United States.

There was no way they could get close to the White House. But there were plenty of other places to go. Other areas they could infiltrate to make a statement.

To make their presence known.

He closed his eyes, conflicted by his priorities. Who could blame him for putting his daughter first? Granted, he hadn't known about Bryn, but now that he did, he absolutely couldn't allow anything to happen to her.

But what about his duty to his country? To his city? The place most politicians called home? Most Americans had a love/hate relationship with politicians, yet mass disaster involving those who manage the country would result in unprecedented chaos.

As he and Sloan Dryer had discovered just a few months ago.

Sloan and Natalia were deep in another case, working undercover to get to one of the main members of the Russian Mafia, but he wanted to pull them off their current assignment and bring them in on this.

He and Sun needed all the help they could get.

Especially since he couldn't ignore the suffocating sense of doom hanging over him.

SEPTEMBER 10 – 6:01 a.m. – Baltimore, MD

"Wake up, little one." Meira's whispered words caused Bryn to blink up at her sluggishly. She had no idea if it was nighttime or morning because of the blindfold.

Wait a minute. She could see shapes in the dim light. The light?

The blindfold was off!

Bryn froze, wondering what was going on. Had she accidentally pulled it off and Meira hadn't noticed? Or had the woman tending to her taken it off herself?

"Time to eat." Meira pushed the usual bowl of pasty crud into her hands.

Bryn looked down, seeing for the first time the contents of what she'd been forced to eat. Then she looked up at Meira. The woman's kind dark eyes could be seen through the mesh of her burka. "Eat," she repeated.

Meira had removed the blindfold. Bryn swallowed hard, trying to understand if this was a good thing or a bad one.

"My blindfold. I . . . thought they were watching us," she whispered, lifting the bowl and taking a bite of the gloppy stuff. It tasted blah, as usual. But since she was hungry, she continued eating.

"Yes. We must be prepared." Up close, the woman was younger than Bryn had imagined, even with the heavy dark cloak and burka she wore. Meira patted the pocket of her jeans where Bryn had hidden the sharpened plastic spoon. "Prepared."

Bryn froze as the implication of her words sank deep. "You mean . . . we're going to try to escape?"

Meira tipped her head in a slight nod. "When the time is right."

"Good." Bryn set the bowl aside, but Meira stopped her.

"Eat for strength," she whispered.

Bryn reluctantly did as she was told, although her mind was whirling. As much as she'd longed for this moment, spidery threads of fear snaked their way into her mind.

What if they couldn't do it? A woman and a child going up against a big man? Maybe more than one big man? What if they couldn't escape? What if they did manage to get away but ended up captured by the icky men again? He would be so angry.

Bryn knew that if they were captured, the horrible slap would become something far worse.

The gloppy stuff lodged in her throat, making her gag.

"Easy," Meira murmured, putting a reassuring hand on her shoulder. "When the time is right."

She nodded and forced herself to swallow hard and keep eating. Meira was right. They had to be smart about this. They had to make sure they chose the right moment to make their move.

Bryn told herself that being out on the streets had to be better than being locked up in this cold dark room. The sound of the foghorn could be heard in the distance, and Bryn wondered how far they were from the water.

She'd helped her mother with the boat plenty of

times. Maybe she and Meira could steal one to help them escape. The icky men wouldn't think to search for them on a boat.

Would they?

Bryn finished her meal and handed the empty bowl to Meira. The woman took the bowl to the other side of the room. Bryn noticed the stupid bucket she was forced to use as a toilet was in the other corner.

As if sensing what she needed, Meira came back over to escort her to the bucket.

"Maybe we can use this to throw in stinky man's face," she whispered.

The woman's eyes crinkled as if she were smiling. "We will use whatever we need."

Bryn felt better knowing that she and Meira were in this together. When she was finished, she sat again on the edge of her pallet, holding the sharpened spoon in the palm of her hand.

And waited.

SEPTEMBER 10 – 6:17 a.m. – Baltimore, MD

Sun had made good time, he'd give her that much. Jordan watched as she navigated the streets down to the warehouse district.

"We should park and go on foot," he suggested.

"After I do a quick drive-by." Sun kept her gaze on the road. Traffic was already picking up, despite the early hour. All too soon, they'd hit the height of rush hour and be crawling at a sloth's pace.

He peered through the window, searching the warehouses for a hint of anything labeled United Secrets. But like the others, the signs were missing, old, or faded. Not one of them said anything near to what they were looking for.

"There, the building covered in peeling blue paint," Sun said.

Blue as in red, white, and blue? Not very original. Still, he stared at the warehouse jammed between two other buildings, much like American Lumber had been. Sun drove as slowly as she dared, and he stared until the building was out of sight.

There hadn't been a brand-new padlock on the door.

Because he'd missed it? Or because it wasn't there? And if it wasn't there, what did that mean? So far the other two warehouses they'd identified had one.

His heart raced. The lack of a padlock might mean they'd finally found Bryn.

"Okay, now that we've seen it, I'm going to find a place to park. We'll go in on foot to investigate." Sun turned left at the next intersection, then turned again, until she found a public parking lot.

Even at this early hour, it was nearly full. She drove in, paid the fee, and maneuvered into a spot. Then she turned in her seat to see him.

"It's daylight, so we need to be careful not to draw unwanted attention," she said. "Three of us can't go at the same time."

"I'm not staying here," Diana quickly interjected.

Sun glanced at him. He stifled a sigh. "You allowed us to go by ourselves last time, remember? We only want to take a look. If Bryn is inside, we'll come back to get you."

Diana's gaze clung to his. "Promise?"

He nodded. "Yes. I'm very aware that Bryn will be most comfortable with you."

She slowly nodded. "Okay, then."

He slid out of the car as Sun did the same. "Let's approach from opposite sides."

Sun nodded.

After leaving the parking area, they split up. Jordan felt very much out of place as he strolled past the various warehouses. Large trucks rolled by, the drivers often looking at him with what he felt was suspicion.

He paused at the corner, waiting for a moment before peeking around the corner.

A man wearing traditional Islamic garb came out from one of the buildings.

Jordan instantly stepped back, his heart hammering. He debated between making a grab for the guy or retracing his steps to put distance between them.

Distance won. He moved swiftly, searching for a place to hide. But there was nothing. The sound of the potential terrorist's footsteps grew louder behind him.

Any second now, the guy might see him and recognize him.

CHAPTER ELEVEN

September 10 – 6:19 a.m. – Baltimore, MD

Diana couldn't sit still, her mind whirling with possibilities. She pushed open the car door and stood, trying to get a glimpse of Jordan or Sun. She caught glimpses of people milling around, but not Jordan or Sun.

The overcast sky above only added to the gloom.

She paced back and forth in the parking lot, then wandered farther away from the vehicle in the direction Jordan had taken. So what if he'd told her to stay in the car? Bryn was her daughter, and she needed to know what was going on.

Even if the news wasn't good. The last two warehouses hadn't produced anything of value regarding Bryn's whereabouts.

The third could be the charm.

She found herself quickening her pace, anxious to get a glimpse of Jordan. When he abruptly rounded a corner, heading straight toward her, she abruptly stopped. The intense look in his dark eyes scared her.

Instinctively, she began to run toward him, her heart

lodged in her throat making it impossible to speak. Recognizing her, he picked up his pace. When he was within arm's reach, he hauled her into his arms and crushed her close.

"Wh-what . . ." she managed.

"Shh." He covered her mouth in a searing kiss. Taken by surprise, she found herself kissing him back, reveling in the passion they'd once shared while hanging on to his broad shoulders as if she might drown if she let him go.

The kiss went on for what seemed like endless minutes. Memories of happier times flooded her. Before her mother's family had shown their true murderous intent.

Before the terrible explosion and car crash that had nearly taken her life and Jordan's.

When they both needed to breathe, he lifted his head far enough to rest his forehead against hers. She gasped, feeling a bit like she'd run a marathon. Was it her heart or his that hammered so against her chest?

She opened her mouth to speak.

"Shh," he whispered again. "Not now."

She didn't understand what had gotten into him, then she heard the sound of footsteps. She froze, her chest squeezing with fear. Who was there behind them? One of Bryn's kidnappers? She clutched Jordan's shoulders in a deathlike grip.

"It's okay," Jordan murmured in her ear. "We're okay. He's leaving."

He who? She wanted to ask a myriad of questions, but then she heard for herself the sounds of footsteps growing more distant.

Until she couldn't hear anything at all.

Jordan lifted his head, then straightened enough to look down into her eyes. "Thanks for coming when you did."

"I . . . you're welcome." She flushed with embarrassment. Here she'd thought Jordan had kissed her because he'd wanted to, but now she understood that he'd been merely playing the role of a man greeting his lover to throw off whoever the person had been behind them.

"Diana." Jordan lifted his hand to cup her cheek. "I kissed you because I wanted to."

She wanted to believe him but forced herself to take a step back. "Yes, because you wanted to throw off whoever that person might be."

"No, that's not it," he countered, a flash of annoyance crossing his features. "I could have just held you in my arms to accomplish that. I kissed you because I wanted to. From the moment you walked back into my life."

"Does this mean you believe I didn't betray you?"

He shrugged. "If you say you didn't tell your family where we were hiding, then I believe you. Besides, it doesn't matter."

Yes, it did matter. She wanted, needed him to believe her. She stared at him for a long second, then changed the subject. "Any idea who was behind you?"

Jordan let out a sigh and shook his head. "No, but he was dressed in traditional Islamic garb and emerged from one of the warehouses. I couldn't afford to take a chance that he might be Bryn's kidnapper and recognize me."

A flash of hope hit hard. "You think Bryn's here in one of these warehouses?"

"I haven't gotten close enough to check, although Sun may already be there." He lightly caressed her cheek, then stepped back and caught her hand in his. "Let's go."

Jordan's warm hand helped keep her emotions in check as they headed back toward the faded blue building sandwiched between two others.

Up ahead, she saw Sun hovering near the doorway of the building. Jordan walked faster, and Diana kept pace.

"Find something?" he asked as they approached.

"No new padlock," Sun said. "But there is an oddly shaped doorbell on the front of the door."

"What kind of doorbell?" Diana frowned. "One that requires some sort of secret code to get inside?"

Sun hesitated. "I'm not sure. I don't have a good feeling about it." She gestured toward the door. "See for yourself, but don't touch it."

She glanced at the elaborate rather ornate frame surrounding what appeared to be a push button doorbell. "I don't understand, why is this suspicious?"

"We know American Lumbar had a padlock on it that may have contained a bomb since the structure exploded practically in our faces," Sun pointed out. "I have a feeling this is a decoy, something that invites a person to press the button, which may lead to another explosion."

Diana instinctively took a hasty step back, swallowing hard. "Is there a way to test it?"

"With a bomb-sniffing dog, maybe," Jordan said. He glanced at Sun. "Did you get a good look at the guy who came out from one of these doorways?"

"Not a good look at his face, but I can guarantee that he didn't come out of the blue building." Sun gestured with her hand. "He came from that one."

Diana stayed close to Jordan's side as he walked toward the building Sun indicated. This doorway didn't have a padlock or an ornate doorbell. When Jordan lifted his hand, she quickly stopped him. "Wait. I'm not sure this is a good idea."

He glanced at her in surprise. "Not even if Bryn is inside?"

She gnawed on her lip. "What if it's booby-trapped in a different way? If we trigger some mechanism, it could explode with Bryn inside. We can't take that risk."

"We can try our camera," Sun offered. "I still have the equipment in the car."

Jordan nodded slowly. "Okay, but it's growing lighter by the minute. I don't like being out here in the open."

"But . . . we can't wait until nighttime, it will be too late by then." Diana glanced between Sun and Jordan. "We have to know *now*."

"She's right," Sun said in a low voice. "Especially considering the deadline provided by Bryn's kidnappers."

Diana held her breath as Jordan considered their options. "Fine, but we can't all three be out here, that's too noticeable."

"Allow me," Sun said, her gaze on Jordan. "I will not be viewed as a threat the way you would."

Diana could tell he didn't like it but nodded in agreement. "I need to get in touch with my FBI contact anyway."

"Good." Sun gave a nod of satisfaction. "Let's return to the vehicle."

Diana had to force herself to step back from the doorway, a panel of wood that might be all that separated her and Bryn.

Hang on, baby, stay strong. We're coming for you!

SEPTEMBER 10 – 6:36 a.m. – Baltimore, MD

After Sun disappeared with the camera equipment to check the warehouse, Jordan used his disposable cell to call Special Agent Ray Pallone. It occurred to him that it had been twelve hours since he last tried to contact the guy, and even longer since they'd last spoken.

The phone rang several times before clicking off. There was no way to leave a message.

A sick feeling oozed in his gut. The inability to connect to the task force charged with infiltrating the terrorist cell was bad news. It meant his position was compromised or that Ray Pallone was dead.

Should he call Clarence Yates? The deputy director of the FBI trusted him, but he didn't want to raise the guy's suspicions. He was supposed to be undercover, not working on freeing his daughter from ISIS terrorists.

Even though he was beginning to believe they were one and the same.

He placed a call to Sloan, leaving a brief message. His partner returned his call in less than five minutes. "What?" Sloan sounded as if he may have been asleep.

"I need your help." Jordan didn't beat around the bush. "Time is running out, and my FBI contact is in the wind."

"Okay," Sloan responded slowly. "But just know we're very close to getting a face-to-face with Viktor Azimov. If we leave now, we'll lose whatever momentum we've gained over the past couple of weeks."

Jordan sighed and massaged his temple. The Feds wanted Azimov very badly, believing he was still connected to the Russian Mob, but the guy had gone underground after the Fourth of July terrorist attack had been derailed. Sloan and his wife, Natalia, have been working undercover in an attempt to find him. "How close?"

There was a slight hesitation. "We have a meeting at eleven with someone claiming to have direct access to Azimov. Our goal was to arrange a meeting directly with Azimov for tonight."

"Okay, fine." Jordan avoided Diana's pointed gaze.

"Keep your eleven o'clock meeting. If it's a no go for tonight, call me back at this number."

"Will do," Sloan agreed. "You think there's a problem with Pallone?"

"Yeah, I'm afraid so." He didn't want to elaborate with Diana sitting right beside him. "Later, Sloan."

"I'll be in touch," his partner confirmed.

Jordan slid the phone back into his pocket and reached for the satellite computer. After booting it up, he scoured the Washington, DC, news stories.

"What meeting is more important than our daughter?" Diana demanded.

Jordan tore his gaze from the screen. "Nothing is more important to me than our daughter. But even if Sloan dropped everything right now, what would we ask him to do? Sun is checking out the warehouse, and I'm trying to get in touch with someone who can help me get close to where Mustaf will be landing."

"Sloan can help do both of those things." Diana's tone was stubborn. "We need all the help we can get."

He didn't know what to say to that, so he returned to the computer. There was a news story that caught his attention. The color drained from his face.

"What is it?" Diana asked, craning her neck to see the screen.

"A dead body was found in Rock Creek Park." He met her gaze. "Identified as FBI Agent Ray Pallone."

SEPTEMBER 10 – 6:48 a.m. – Washington, DC

He tossed the newspaper aside. Idiots. He was working with nothing but a bunch of incompetent imbeciles.

Ray Pallone shouldn't have been found this soon. What

was wrong with his hired contact? What part of burying him deep in the park didn't he understand?

His work cell number rang. His boss. Great. Just what he needed after being up half the night dealing with idiots. He drew in a deep breath, doing his best to swallow the rage that threatened to burst forth, and answered. "Yes, sir?"

"I assume you've seen the news." Yates's tone was sharp.

"Yes, sir, just now." He tried to sound concerned. "Do we have any idea what Agent Pallone's cause of death was?" If he was lucky, they'd arranged for his death to appear natural, like from a heart attack.

"Gunshot wound to the back of his head, execution style," came Yates's dry response. "You know anything about that?"

He tightened his grip on the phone. "Why would I? I haven't seen him since our task force meeting yesterday at three in the afternoon."

His boss didn't respond. The prolonged silence was a trick, but an effective one. Good thing he'd been trained well.

"I need you and the rest of the task force in my office by eight thirty a.m." His boss didn't wait for a response but abruptly disconnected from the line.

He let out a series of curses, knowing that this was partially his fault. He should have hired better help. Someone intelligent who knew how to follow orders.

The dome of the White House seemed to mock him. He turned his back and glanced at his watch.

He had an important errand to run, one that might make him late for the meeting.

But damage control was his top priority at the moment. His boss and the rest of the task force would have to wait.

He had a loose end that needed to be cut off —permanently.

SEPTEMBER 10 – 7:03 *a.m.* – *Baltimore, MD*

Diana wanted Jordan to get more help but was interrupted when Sun approached the vehicle, a somber expression on her face.

"What did you find?" Diana demanded.

"No prisoners inside the building," Sun said. "It looked oddly like an office workspace, with office equipment inside. No signs of anyone being held there."

"But what if she's in one of those offices?" Diana wasn't ready to let go of the possibility that they'd reached yet another dead end. "I'm sure your little camera thingy couldn't see inside."

"That's true, but I watched for several minutes, looking for any sign of activity. There was none." Sun lifted a hand to prevent her from interrupting. "And let's face it, no guard on the outside of the building or near one of the office doorways? No way would they be holding Bryn there without someone keeping watch."

"Thanks for checking," Jordan said. "I'm glad we can mark that one off our list."

Diana wanted to protest, but she knew it was no use. Sun was probably right. Why would the kidnappers have Bryn in an office without someone standing guard?

"Ray Pallone is dead," Jordan added grimly. "It appears our contact with the task force has been severed."

"That's not good." Sun's normally impassive expression turned alarmed. "We need someone within the government to help us with this."

"I know." Jordan drummed his fingers on the steering

wheel. "I'll have to try going directly up to Clarence Yates. I don't see an alternative."

Diana knew Yates was the FBI director himself. In her opinion, the higher up the better for all of them. She glanced impatiently between Sun and Jordan. "Okay, great. How do we do that?"

"Sun, we need to head back to DC." Jordan actually slid out from behind the wheel. "I'll make phone calls while you drive."

Diana waited until Sun had gotten behind the wheel, with Jordan taking up residence in the back seat. She swiveled in her seat to face him. "Could Sloan get to Yates quicker?"

Jordan hesitated, then nodded. "Maybe."

She settled back in her seat as Jordan made another brief call to Sloan. Within five minutes, his phone rang. She listened, hoping Yates was already on the line, but was disappointed.

"Okay, thanks for trying, Sloan," Jordan said. "I'm sure Yates will call when he can."

She strove for patience. "He left a message?"

"Yes. Knowing Yates, he'll call back soon enough."

But it wasn't soon enough. Mustaf would land somewhere, hopefully in DC, in less than an hour.

They needed a plan. To get close to Mustaf and to find Bryn.

SEPTEMBER 10 – 7:35 *a.m.* – *Washington, DC*

He waited impatiently in the coffee shop, their designated meeting spot. His contact better show—especially since he'd made a concerted effort to gloss over the monstrous error in judgment the idiot had made.

He sipped his coffee, then glanced at his Rolex again. The idiot was late. Much longer and he'd be just as late attending the task force meeting. Traffic at this time of the morning was ridiculous.

Did Rashid know that Pallone was found dead this morning? Or was he so far undercover the news hadn't reached him yet? He hoped for the latter but knew enough to plan for the former.

Who would Rashid go to with Pallone out of the picture?

Only one possibility.

Yates.

He shifted in his seat, trying not to appear as impatient as he felt. He'd give his contact five more minutes before heading to the task force meeting. It could be that Yates would give them information that might help him find Rashid.

The door to the coffee shop opened, and his contact stepped over the threshold, his gaze nervously sweeping the interior, stumbling to a halt when their gazes collided.

He forced a smile and nodded, indicating his contact should join him. He had a cup of coffee ready for him, just the way he liked it—heavy on the cream and sugar.

His contact moved slowly through the shop, as if sensing he was about to meet his doom. "It wasn't my fault," the idiot said as he sat across from him. "I gave explicit instructions. I have no idea why they weren't followed."

He battled a wave of fury, lifting his cup and eyeing his contact over the rim. "Perhaps you should have taken care of the matter yourself."

"Yeah, I know." His contact played with the coffee cup for a moment before lifting the cup to his lips. "Trust me, I won't make that mistake again."

"I'm sure you won't. But we need some damage control. I don't want his cause of death to be leaked to the media."

"Already taken care of. The news will be told he died of natural causes."

Natural causes? Really? He was tempted to throw his coffee into the man's face. "With a bullet wound in the back of his skull? Seems irrational. What I meant was that this needs to look like Rashid did the deed." He needed Rashid out of the way, or at least out of Yates's good graces.

"Oh, yes. Of course." His contact took another nervous drink of his coffee. "I can do that."

Actually, that was impossible, but that didn't matter at the moment. "Call me when it's done." He casually stood and moved away from the table, leaving his contact behind.

He didn't glance back until he was outside and even then just long enough to see the idiot was still drinking his coffee.

He smirked as he used his phone to call for a rideshare.

Drinking his coffee would be the last thing he'd ever do.

CHAPTER TWELVE

September 10 – 7:55 a.m. – Washington, DC

Jordan stared out at the sea of cars crowding the highways leading toward DC. Even though they were skirting the downtown area itself, traffic was crawling.

At this rate, they'd never make it to Andrews Air Force Base in time.

Who was he kidding? Once they'd made it to the base, he had no credentials that would grant him access inside.

Come on, Yates, where are you?

"What are we going to do if the kidnappers find out we don't have Mustaf?" Diana asked, a wobble in her voice. "They could hurt Bryn, or worse."

"They gave us until eight o'clock tonight to bring him in," he reminded her. "They won't do anything yet."

"Twelve hours," Diana murmured. She shook her head helplessly. "We're no closer to getting Mustaf or finding Bryn. You're only guessing about him being brought into Andrews Air Force Base."

She was right, it was an educated guess on his part. "It

makes the most sense to have him land there. I need you to trust me on this."

Diana didn't respond, and he imagined her faith in him was wearing thin. He couldn't blame her. It was as if the kiss they'd shared never happened. She was as aloof as when they'd first met.

For years he'd thought she'd chosen her family over him. Only now he believed that was wrong. Diana hadn't turned her back on him. With a wry shake of his head, he turned his attention back to the computer. He'd been digging into Liberty Bell, the last property they'd found with the suspicious naming convention so far. But the weird doorbell on the building owned by United Secrets niggled at the back of his mind.

A bomb? Was this something that the terrorist group was using as a way to keep their operations secret? Anyone knowing about the booby trap would obviously be smart enough not to trigger it, but he wondered about those who were simply curious about what might be inside. He imagined a lot of people might be tempted to push the button to summon someone from inside. Salespeople, tourists, anyone.

Why blow up all the contents of the warehouse just because someone was nosy?

It didn't make sense.

"Look, isn't that a plane way off in the distance?" Diana had her face pressed against her passenger side window. "Do you think that's Mustaf?"

Jordan scooted over to get a better view. It was still far enough away that it wasn't going to be landing at eight o'clock. "Could be anyone, really."

"Maybe Mustaf's plane was delayed." Diana's voice echoed with hope.

He didn't want to be the one to burst her bubble. After all, anything was possible. The pilot may have been bucking a headwind the entire trip. "Could be, we'll know soon enough."

Sun caught his gaze in the rearview mirror, showing disapproval. He looked away. Easy for her to be nonchalant about all of this, but it was his daughter's life hanging in the balance.

Not hers.

Their car moved forward, hitting a whopping speed of twenty-five miles per hour, before Sun tapped the brakes again. The plane in the sky slowly grew larger. He could tell it wasn't a regular passenger plane; it was boxy in shape, like a cargo plane.

His pulse jumped. It could be Mustaf's plane.

The sign for Andrews Air Force Base loomed before them. They were getting close to the front gate. The plane hadn't landed yet but obviously would in the next fifteen minutes.

He called Sloan again. "I really need to talk to Yates."

Sloan sighed. "I'll try again, but I'm sure the guy has stuff going on."

"Nothing is more important than this," Jordan insisted. "Please get someone's attention."

"I'll do my best." Sloan disconnected from the line.

There were several cars in front of them also trying to get onto the base. Air force employees and a combination of civilians he assumed.

Sun inched their vehicle closer. He stared at the disposable cell, willing it to ring. When it chirped, he instantly answered, "Hello?"

"Now what?" Yates sounded irritable.

"Sir, I need you to get me access to Andrews Air Force Base ASAP."

There was a pause as Yates digested this. "How did you know Mustaf was being transported there?"

He let out a soundless sigh of relief that he'd guessed correctly. "More chatter, sir. It's important for me to be there when Mustaf arrives."

Another long moment of silence. "I don't think that's even possible, Rashid. And I need to tell you about Ray Pallone."

"I heard about his death, sir. I assume he was murdered."

"Yeah." Yates sounded grim. "I think there's a leak within the task force."

They inched closer, only two cars ahead of them now at the gate. "I hate to say this, but I think you're right about that. Is there further news on the US Marshal who was found in the Smoky Mountains?"

"Not yet. Still waiting on the preliminary autopsy. But that's two unexplained deaths of government operatives in less than twenty-four hours. I don't like it."

Only one car ahead of them now. Jordan understood Yates was frustrated, but he knew, deep in his bones, that this was all connected to him, to Bryn, and to the terrorists. "I don't like it either, and I suspect the terrorist cell is related to the murders of these two men. I have Sun Yin with me, and we're nearly at the gate at Andrews Air Force Base. I need you to find a way to clear the way for us to get inside. I wouldn't ask if it wasn't important."

Another moment of silence before Yates relented. "Okay, fine. I'll get you in."

Jordan momentarily closed his eyes in relief. "Thank you, sir."

The vehicle up ahead went through the gate. Sun drove forward, lowering her window. "We're here on direct orders from Clarence Yates, Deputy Director of the FBI."

The airman on duty frowned. "I don't know anything about that, ma'am."

"Sir? Will you please speak to Airman Troye?" Jordan asked. When Yates agreed, he held out the phone. "Deputy Director Yates is on the line. This is a matter of national security."

The airman hesitated, then reluctantly took the phone. "Sir?" He listened for a long moment, his initial dubious expression turning to respect. "Yes, sir." He handed the phone back to Jordan. "You'll need to keep your weapons locked in the car and pick up visitor passes inside."

"Thank you." Sun drove through the gate and found a place to park. As they climbed out of the car, the plane overhead grew larger and louder as it approached. Jordan felt his gut clench.

There was no doubt in his mind. Mustaf was on board the plane and would be landing on US soil very soon.

There wasn't much time, they'd need to hurry.

And they needed a plan to intercept Mustaf before he could be whisked away and taken to the closest detention center.

But how?

SEPTEMBER 10 – 8:20 *a.m.* – *Baltimore, MD*

Elam made his way through the streets of Baltimore to the location known as Bell. Liberty was the main location, but Liberty Bell was the second most important location, at least for him.

After hours of searching, he felt certain Meira was there.

He remained hidden behind a trash bin, watching from afar as a man lounged outside the door to the building. He didn't look particularly terrifying, but Elam knew every one of the men involved in this plan was lethal.

And their ultimate goal was just as horrific.

He ignored their plan with an effort, focusing on what he needed to do. Now that he'd arrived, he wasn't sure how to proceed. Especially in broad daylight. The sense of urgency that had brought him here was fading away.

No. He couldn't fail to free Meira. Their lives and that of their unborn child depended on getting away.

Ignoring the stench of garbage, he began to formulate a plan. A diversion might be necessary, and for that he'd need time to prepare.

Elam inched backward until he was able to leave his hiding spot without being seen. The diversion would only work for a brief period of time, the Master would suspect something right away.

He'd have just a few brief moments.

He'd have to make every one of them count.

SEPTEMBER 10 – 8:32 *a.m.* – *Andrews Air Force Base, DC*

Diana clipped her visitor pass to the collar of her disheveled blouse, wondering why on earth these military people were going along with this so easily.

Yates had power, clearly, but surely their trio looked more than a little suspicious. Her clothing had been slept in, and there was blood staining Jordan's shirt, a white dressing partially visible beneath the edge of his T-shirt sleeve. Sun looked the best of all of them, making Diana feel even more cranky that she looked serene and beautiful without an effort.

And what good was a visitor pass anyway? It wasn't like they were going to be allowed anywhere near Mustaf. Especially not with an airman standing right at their side.

This was nothing more than a waste of time. They should be searching for Bryn. Their sweet, innocent, eleven-year-old daughter was all that mattered.

"Now what?" Sun asked in a low voice as they were led down the hallway to the observation area. There was a wall of glass ahead through which a variety of planes and helicopters could be watched coming and going.

"Let's get as close as possible," Jordan said, heading toward the wall of glass.

Diana swallowed her protest, joining Jordan and Sun in the observation area. There were double doors that led out to the landing pad, but they were monitored by two uniformed airmen.

"This is stupid," Diana hissed in a low voice. "We're not going to get close to him."

"Maybe not." Jordan didn't look at her, his attention focused on the plane approaching the runway.

The plane grew larger, the engines loud enough to be heard inside the building. The plane didn't look like a normal passenger plane, but she supposed the air force wouldn't transport people in a 747.

The wheels of the plane touched the ground with a bump, then gradually decreased its speed. At least a dozen or more airmen dressed in camo from head to toe emerged from a hangar to meet the plane.

Diana wanted to scream in frustration. There was no way in the world they'd have a chance to free Mustaf. *None.*

This was nothing more than a wild-goose chase intended to keep them from finding Bryn.

A ploy both Jordan and Sun had fallen for, big time.

SEPTEMBER 10 – 8:42 a.m. – Baltimore, MD

Bryn leaned on the wall next to the doorway, already feeling exhausted, exactly the way she had the time she'd gone to Sophie's sleepover party and they'd stayed up all night giggling and laughing.

Her head ached, her stomach felt a little sick, and she feared she wouldn't have the strength to lift the stinky bucket of waste long enough to throw it at the icky man's head the way they'd planned.

She looked at Meira who stood on the opposite side of the doorway with seemingly infinite patience. Meira had the plastic spoon sharpened into a knife in her hand, while Bryn's was still in her pocket. They weren't sure when the icky man would come in, but normally he showed up by now.

Earlier, they'd decided the cameras were either not on or not being watched as they moved freely around the interior of the building testing their limits without anyone coming in to yell at them. She really, really hoped that meant they actually had a chance to make this work.

The idea of never seeing her mom again made her want to cry. She sniffled and swiped at her eyes. This had to work.

It just had to.

A deep voice from the other side of the door made Bryn

tense. Was this it? Was the icky man going to come through the doorway?

She looked at Meira. The woman gently shook her head. Bryn frowned, not understanding, until she heard nothing but silence.

Whoever was out there had moved away from the door, leaving them alone, again.

Now what? She looked at Meira for direction, but the woman had turned away.

Bryn swallowed a sob. What if they'd done all of this for nothing?

What if they didn't get a chance to escape their prison?

SEPTEMBER 10 – 8:46 a.m. – Andrews Air Force Base, DC

Mustaf remained lying on his side on the floor of the plane with his wrists bound behind his back. It had been the most horrific flight, far too much turbulence, as if the pilot had wanted him to throw up on purpose. Then, finally, the plane had landed on US soil and had slowed down, indicating his ordeal would soon be over.

Mustaf clenched and unclenched his fingers, trying to increase the circulation in limbs that had gone numb.

The man who'd whispered to him hours ago hadn't approached again. Mustaf had been kept blindfolded as well, so he had no idea who was on his side.

He wished the man would say something or do something that would help him understand what he should expect. Logically, he knew there had to be a plan to capture him right out from beneath the noses of the Americans, but how?

"Get up," a harsh voice commanded. Someone reached

down and roughly jerked his arm. Pain shot through him, but he refused to cry out in pain. In his mind, he tightened his fingers around the man's throat until he couldn't breathe.

Until he died by his hands.

But that wasn't meant to be. Not yet.

Mustaf did his best to get his feet underneath him as two men hauled him upright by his arms.

The plane was still rolling, but his two guards stood on either side of Mustaf, waiting for it to stop. He found himself holding his breath.

This was it.

Freedom was close enough to taste.

His people would come through for him.

SEPTEMBER 10 – 8:47 a.m. – Andrews Air Force Base, DC

The plane taxied forward, turning so that the side door to the cargo space was facing the dozen or so airmen waiting to escort Mustaf to a prisoner transport van.

So close, yet so far, Jordan thought sourly.

Still, he couldn't tear his gaze from the scene unfolding before him.

The plane stopped. The dozen men in camo didn't move. The cargo door slowly opened, revealing the interior.

A short thin man stood facing the open cargo door with his arms behind his back, a blindfold covering his eyes, his gray streaked hair disheveled, his skin wan. Two men wearing camo stood on either side of him.

Mustaf.

A thrill of anticipation threaded through his veins. The

man who was responsible for so many deaths across the globe was just twenty feet from him.

On the other side of the glass, of course.

The two men on either side of Mustaf urged him forward. He took one step, then another, leaning heavily on his muscular escorts.

A gunshot rang out, and Mustaf buckled. He would have fallen to his knees if the two airmen weren't holding him upright.

"He's been hit!" The shout was loud enough for them to hear.

What in the world? Jordan reached out to put his palm on the glass. No, it couldn't be. Mustaf couldn't have been shot the moment he was being taken off the plane.

Instant chaos reigned as several men spread out in an effort to identify the shooter while others went up to surround Mustaf. The transport van was moved out of the way to make room for emergency personnel.

Jordan took a step back from the glass, glancing at Diana and Sun and the airman assigned to them. "We need to leave. We have to notify the deputy director about this."

"Finally," Diana muttered. "I knew this was nothing more than a waste of time."

"This way," the airman assigned to them said.

"Are you sure?" Sun whispered. "This may be a part of the plan."

Jordan nodded slowly. Sun was right about that. This was indeed part of the plan. But not the time for him to try to get Mustaf. Quite the opposite.

"Where's the closest hospital?" Jordan asked the airman.

"There's a medical center here on base," the airman replied.

"They'll only stabilize him there until they can transport him to the closest trauma center." Jordan searched his memory. "I think there's one in Marlow Heights."

"If they're transporting him by chopper, they'll likely take him to Washington Hospital." Diana glanced between him and Sun. "Don't you think?"

"She's right." Sun nodded. "If he's a high-ranking terrorist here to be interrogated and to stand trial, they'll for sure want him at Washington."

"Yeah, okay." Jordan glanced around, before following the airman outside.

"Do you think this shooting was part of the plan all along?" Sun asked in a whisper.

"Highly likely," Jordan confirmed.

"But . . . what if they killed him?" Diana protested.

"I think he was shot in the lower abdomen." Jordan hadn't exactly seen the entry wound, most of the blood had come out from the exit wound. "If they'd wanted to kill him, they'd have aimed for his chest or his head."

The airman stood by as they entered their vehicle and headed for the gate. They were stopped as they attempted to leave. "What was your business here?" the airman demanded.

Jordan thought fast. "We were sent by the deputy director of the FBI to witness the transport of Ahmed Mustaf from the plane to the transport vehicle. Instead, we ended up witnessing an attempt to assassinate him."

The airman scowled. "How do I know you weren't responsible?"

"Because you forced us to lock up our weapons prior to being allowed inside, and one of your airmen was with us the entire time." Jordan leveled him a stare. "Meanwhile, every airman on base has their weapon, correct?"

The airman didn't respond. He irritably waved them through.

Jordan slid behind the wheel and quickly drove out of the air force base.

Mustaf had been shot, and he knew they'd be hearing from Bryn's kidnappers any moment.

CHAPTER THIRTEEN

September 10 – 9:19 a.m. – Washington, DC

"Cunningham, North, or Slater, do you have anything to add?"

He glanced at his colleagues, trying not to show his irritation. After listening to Yates drone on for the past fifty minutes, he was more than ready for this *urgent meeting* to be over.

"No, sir."

His boss's cell phone rang interrupting him. He straightened in his seat when Yates frowned and picked up the call. "What?"

The abrupt silence amongst the task force members was surreal as they all sensed this wasn't good news. His boss's face turned red, his eyes narrowing into slits.

"Keep me posted." The call was disconnected, and his boss's gaze landed directly on him. It took every ounce of willpower to keep his expression neutral.

"What happened?" He furrowed his brow with concern.

The way Yates's gaze bored into his was creepy. He'd done nothing to raise his boss's suspicions. *Nothing.* A minute later, Yates glanced around at the others in the room.

"Within minutes of Ahmed Mustaf landing at Andrews Air Force Base, he was shot by a sniper."

"How could that happen?" asked one of the task force members. "Who knew he was landing there? We kept that secret, knowing most would assume he'd be taken directly to Guantanamo Bay."

"Good question." Again, his boss's gaze landed on him, before moving on to the others seated around the table. "I'd like to know that myself."

"Do they have the shooter?" He showed nothing of his internal satisfaction.

"They don't have the shooter, yet." His boss let out a heavy sigh. "We need to keep this out of the media at all costs."

"Is Mustaf alive?" another member of the task force asked.

"So far, but he's being treated as we speak."

"Where?" He tried not to show an inordinate interest in Mustaf's location. "I would think he'd need to get to the closest trauma center."

Yates declined to answer, instead rising to his feet and sweeping his gaze once more around the room. "Stay in touch, we may need another meeting later today."

He was about to ask something more, but it was too late. His boss left the room, leaving the task force sitting there in stunned silence.

Yet he didn't allow his internal elation to show and didn't immediately leave the room either. He stayed and spoke with the others to blend in with the group.

Still, he loved it when a complicated plan came together.

SEPTEMBER 10 – 9:32 *a.m.* – *Washington, DC*

Diana turned to look at Jordan. "Who shot Mustaf? And why?"

Jordan glanced at her, then turned his attention to the road. They were heading into DC against her wishes. She wanted to hunker down somewhere to continue searching for Bryn.

"I have no idea who took the shot, but I suspect the reason was to get him into a hospital."

She narrowed her gaze. "You mean the shooter wasn't trying to kill him? That the goal was just to injure him enough to get him out of the air force base?"

"Makes sense," Sun said from the back seat. "Helping him escape from a hospital should be easier than getting him out of a military base or a federal prison."

Diana stared at Sun in shock. "But . . . I don't understand. They shot him to help him escape? And if that's the case, why have they kidnapped Bryn to force Jordan to free him? They seem to have a plan in place already."

"Yes, that's been bothering me too," Jordan admitted. Traffic grew heavier the closer they came to the city, which only fueled her frustration. "It seems as if there are two prongs to this plan, and it's not clear who is in charge of either of them."

Okay, that was not at all reassuring. She squeezed her eyes shut to prevent herself from bursting into tears. "Turn around," she begged. "Let's go back to working on finding Bryn. The rest of this doesn't matter."

There was a long silence before Jordan spoke. "Diana,

we will continue to look for Bryn. But we can't simply ignore a terrorist threat. Rescuing Bryn won't stop them, and we could all end up dead regardless. We need to work on both aspects of this case at the same time."

No. *No!* She wanted to rant and rave and scream at Jordan. Bryn was all that mattered. As soon as they had their daughter, they could get out of the area, away from any potential threat.

She had to swallow her protest though, knowing it would sound selfish. Jordan was right. They couldn't ignore the threat to their country.

But she didn't have to like it.

Drawing a ragged breath, she forced herself to calm down. There was only one thing she could do. Lift her heart and pray.

Please, Lord, keep Bryn safe in Your care!

SEPTEMBER 10 – 9:41 a.m. – Baltimore, MD

Holding his breath, Elam carefully packed the bag with what he needed in order to help free Meira. When he finished, he gently eased the straps over his shoulders so the bag hung in the center of his back.

Transport would be the biggest risk to him, but it was one he'd gladly take. He'd rather die than to have Meira and his unborn child suffer.

If this was God's plan, then so be it. He would do whatever was necessary, whatever God called him to do.

But he didn't want to die yet, not until he'd freed Meira from the men who held her against her will.

After pulling the last of his cash from its hiding place, he made his way across the room and out the door. Avoiding the subway was critical now, he didn't dare allow anyone to jostle him or the backpack.

He walked for several blocks before looking around for a taxi. It took several more blocks before a driver pulled over to offer him a ride. Elam slipped the backpack from his arms and gently set it on the floor behind the passenger seat before sliding in. When the taxi pulled into traffic, he breathed a little sigh of relief.

So far, so good.

I'm coming, Meira. I'll be there soon . . .

SEPTEMBER 10 – 9:50 a.m. – Baltimore, MD

The stupid icky smelly men seemed to have abandoned them.

Bryn watched Meira from the filthy mattress on the floor. They still had the bucket of waste near the doorway, but as the minutes had passed into hours, they had given up standing there waiting for someone to show.

She blinked, trying not to cry. Now that she'd convinced Meira to escape, they didn't have the means.

Why, God, why?

Her mom had taught her to pray, to lean on God's strength, but it was growing difficult. Hour after hour of doing nothing, hearing nothing, having only Meira around, was wearing on her.

Meira came over as if sensing her distress. Bryn sniffled and swiped a hand over her eyes. Meira was the only good thing about being here, at least she wasn't alone.

"You must get up and move often, to build up strength," Meira whispered.

Bryn nodded and pushed up to her feet. Since realizing

how weak she'd become, Meira had insisted on brief bouts of exercises. She'd started doing Tae Kwon Do forms to keep her blood moving and her muscles warm.

She dropped into the typical fighting stance and went through the moves, punching and kicking, following the pattern her instructor had taught her. Exhaustion pulled at her, but there was no point in complaining.

When the opportunity to escape arrived, she wanted to be ready.

Give me strength, Lord, she chanted beneath her breath. *Give me strength!*

SEPTEMBER 10 – 10:12 *a.m.* – *Washington, DC*

Jordan pulled into the George Washington University Hospital parking lot. He shut off the car and pulled out his phone.

Diana stared at him, clearly annoyed with his decision to come here to check on Ahmed Mustaf. He understood her concern, but he had Sun working on the warehouse location via the satellite computer, so they were pretty much multitasking the best they could.

He waited for someone within the FBI top office to answer his call. He really needed to speak directly with Clarence Yates and was tired of jumping through hoops every time he wanted to connect with the guy.

Since Ray Pallone was dead, he wasn't about to discuss anything with anyone other than Yates himself.

Too bad trying to reach the guy directly was about as difficult as calling POTUS. Maybe more so.

"Who may I ask is calling?" the woman asked on the other end of the line. No greeting, no acknowledgment of who she worked for, just the question.

He hesitated, then gave his name. "Jordan Rashid and I need to speak with Clarence Yates directly. No one else."

"I'm sorry, Mr. Yates is unavailable. I can give him a message."

"You don't understand, this is an extremely urgent matter. I need to speak to him as soon as possible. Please ask him to call me at this number, it's a matter of national security."

The woman answered in an almost jovial tone. "I will be happy to do that, thank you for calling."

He disconnected the call and blew out a breath before turning toward Diana. "I'm going in, but I need you and Sun to stay here." When she opened her mouth, he held up his hand. "Please don't argue. It will be a miracle if I can get anything out of these people with all the privacy laws. Alone I might stand a chance, but three of us going in together is asking for trouble."

"Fine." Diana crossed her arms over her chest. "But hurry. We need to find Bryn."

"I will." Jordan pushed open the driver's side door and stood. He formulated a plan in his mind on how to best approach this. He didn't have his FBI credentials anymore, but he did have Clarence Yates's business card. It wasn't much, and he knew his chances of getting through were less than ten percent, especially since he was dressed very casually in a black T-shirt and black jeans.

Feds always wore dark suits, white shirts, and muted ties. Men in Black.

He approached the front desk with an air of purpose. A woman he estimated to be in her midfifties, wearing what looked like a black security guard uniform, was seated behind the desk. He held up Clarence Yates's business card so she could see it. "I'm reporting in as directed by Clarence

Yates, Deputy Director of the FBI to help protect Ahmed Mustaf."

"You're early, he hasn't arrived yet." She frowned, then leaned forward to peer at the card. "Are you an FBI agent? Shouldn't you have a badge?"

"I'm a private security, hired by the FBI because I speak Farsi and Syrian. We need someone fluent in Arabic languages to speak directly to Ahmed Mustaf."

Her eyes rounded with reluctant admiration. "I see. Well, like I said, you're early. We're not expecting him for another fifteen to twenty minutes, according to the computer."

He gave her a brief nod. "Thank you. Can you give me his room number?"

"I don't have one." Now she turned suspicious. "Aren't the FBI agents meeting you here? They know all of that."

"Yes, of course, but we came from opposite sides of the city." Jordan replaced Yates's business card in his pocket. "Thanks for your help, I'm sure I'll hear directly from Mr. Yates soon."

He turned and strode away, glancing at his watch as he left, hoping and praying she wouldn't hit the panic button he was certain was hidden under the edge of the desk. Heading back outside to the car, he was glad he'd gotten part of what he needed.

Mustaf was definitely being transported here, likely via medical helicopter.

If Yates would ever call him back, he'd emphasize to the deputy director how important it was for Jordan to get in to see him.

Hopefully before Bryn's kidnappers contacted him again.

. . .

SEPTEMBER 10 – 10:24 a.m. – Washington, DC

As he walked past his boss's office, he heard Rashid's name. He slowed his steps, straining to listen.

"Thanks, April, I'll call him back as soon as possible." Yates sounded harried, and he wanted to smile at the way these events were unraveling the normally stoic guy.

When the admin came out of the office, he gave her a nod and kept walking to avoid calling attention to himself.

Interesting that Rashid had contacted Yates, just as he'd assumed. Rashid must have somehow heard about Mustaf, although he wasn't sure how. The security expert was really starting to piss him off.

Was there a way he could trace all incoming calls to Yates's phone? No, that was impossible. As much as he didn't care for Yates, there was no denying the guy was smart. He hadn't gotten to such a prestigious position at the Bureau by being stupid. Despite the people in key positions he paid to get him information, getting his boss's direct phone number hadn't happened.

At least not yet.

But soon it wouldn't matter one way or the other. His job would be done, and he'd be gone before anyone was the wiser.

SEPTEMBER 10 – 10:35 a.m. – Washington, DC

"Where are we going?" Diana asked Jordan.

"There's a motel near the hospital where we can wait for a bit until Yates calls me back."

Another hotel. She blew out a frustrated breath.

"I think I found something," Sun said.

Hope flared in Diana's heart, and she turned to face the woman. "The place they're holding Bryn?"

"Maybe. I discovered Liberty Bell is another shell corporation, but I've been able to dig down far enough to find that it, too, has a physical location in Baltimore."

"Baltimore." Diana shot Jordan a narrow look. "I told you we shouldn't have left."

Jordan glanced at her but didn't say anything. He pulled into the parking lot of a local hotel, then shut down the vehicle.

"She's right, Jordan," Sun said, lifting her gaze from the computer screen. "So many of these crazy warehouses hidden beneath shell corporations named United Secrets, Freedom Shoppes, and so on have been in Baltimore. And this one is located about five miles from the others."

Jordan scrubbed a hand over his chin. "We can head over there as soon as I've spoken to Mustaf. Let's not forget the kidnappers want him freed by eight o'clock tonight."

"We're going to have Bryn safe long before eight o'clock," Diana protested. "Or we would if we continued looking for her."

"Again, she has a point," Sun said. "I say we get to Baltimore ASAP."

"We could split up," Diana said. Then frowned. "But we'd need another car."

Jordan didn't look convinced. He stared down at his phone as if will alone would make it ring. Finally, he glanced at her. "Give me thirty minutes. If I haven't heard from Yates in thirty minutes, we'll go to Baltimore."

"Okay, but it will take us at least that long to get there, which means you're getting over an hour." Diana didn't bother to hide her frustration. "I want to go now, Jordan."

His phone rang, and he quickly answered it, placing it on speaker so she and Sun could hear. "Rashid."

"Now what?" The deep voice sounded annoyed. Jordan mouthed Yates so she knew that it was the deputy director of the FBI on the phone.

"I'm sorry to bother you, sir, but this is really important. We were at Andrews Air Force Base when Mustaf was shot."

"Yes, I'm aware of that. But I hired you to infiltrate the terrorist cell, not watch over Mustaf."

"I know, sir, but the terrorist cell is likely involved in the shooting." Jordan's tone reflected infinite patience, even though she could see the tension in his jaw. "I'm at Washington University Hospital now. I'd like your permission to speak with Mustaf."

Silence on the other end of the line, then, "I don't think that's necessary."

"Sir, you must know I wouldn't ask if it wasn't important."

"I understand you're just trying to help, but you won't be able to speak with him anytime soon, he's going straight into surgery. The bullet damaged one of his kidneys."

It was Jordan's turn to be silent for a moment. "Okay, but I need a number to contact you directly. With Ray Pallone dead, I don't want to speak to anyone else. Things are unraveling fast, and I believe a terrorist attack is imminent."

"Fine." Yates rattled off a number. "You're one of five people, including the president, who have that number, Rashid. Don't abuse the privilege."

"No, sir, I won't. Thank you." Jordan disconnected from the call and looked at her. "Okay, time to get to Baltimore."

Diana didn't say anything. Jordan started the car and pulled back out into traffic.

Still, while they drove, she silently vowed to stay in Baltimore until they'd found Bryn.

Even if that meant she'd remain in the city alone.

SEPTEMBER 10 – 10:44 a.m. – Baltimore, MD

Elam paid the driver in cash and climbed out of the taxi. He carefully pulled the backpack out and stood for a moment until the vehicle pulled away.

After easing the pack onto his shoulders, he began walking toward the northeast corner of Federal Hill Park. He did his best to blend with the crowd, hoping he looked like a college student searching for a place to study.

He knew he had to choose his location carefully. The park was close enough to the water that the sound should carry all the way over to Liberty Bell.

The area was busier than he would have liked. He didn't want to harm anyone, which was ridiculous since all those men wanted from him was to kill Americans.

After walking around to scope things out, he decided the parking structure was probably his best bet. There would be a lot of damage to the vehicles parked there, but less chance of hurting people.

He raised his eyes heavenward, praying for forgiveness for what he was about to do.

Entering the structure, he went to the northwest corner farthest from the elevator and slid the backpack off. Then he took his latest masterpiece and carefully affixed it to the top of a concrete separator, looking at it critically to be sure it wouldn't garner undue attention.

He'd created the device to look like a small seagull. There were always many gulls flying around the Baltimore area, and while his little bird wouldn't hold up to close scrutiny, from a distance, no one would glance at it twice.

When he finished, he pulled the backpack on again and retraced his steps, verifying the time. Once again, he hailed a cab to take him to the other side of the harbor.

He needed to be hidden somewhere close by the location known as Liberty Bell before creating his diversion.

CHAPTER FOURTEEN

September 10 — 11:03 a.m. — Washington, DC
He'd been shot!

Mustaf opened his eyes just enough to see his surroundings, trying to understand where he was. It took a few minutes of ignoring the overwhelming pain to figure out he was once again airborne in a helicopter. There were headphones of some sort placed over his head, and he caught glimpses of two people, a man and a woman working over him, but he couldn't understand the gibberish they spewed.

He shifted on the gurney, but the movement only caused another shaft of pain to spear through him. He couldn't believe he'd been shot at the air force base. In front of how many soldiers? It was ridiculous.

Yet if the US wanted him dead, they could have killed him at any time during the initial plane ride over from Lebanon.

If not the US Military, then who? Who had tried to kill him?

The movement of the helicopter made him feel sick to his stomach, so he closed his eyes and tried to breathe normally. As he calmed down, some of the words the medical staff said began to make sense.

"His abdominal bleeding is under control, and his vitals are stable. I don't think he needs a blood transfusion," a male voice said.

"I have two units of O Neg if needed, but I agree he seems to be holding his own," the female voice said.

He was appalled at how this woman was seeing him and touching him like this. Didn't she know her proper place? He felt himself go tense with distaste.

Never would he understand these heathens.

"Ahmed? Can you hear me? Lift up two fingers if you can hear me," the female voice urged.

He shied away from her touch and ignored her request. Better for him if they didn't realize how much he understood what they were saying.

Besides, speaking to the woman was beneath him.

"Karl, what's our ETA?" the male voice asked.

"Six minutes."

There was more poking and prodding, which he didn't like but forced himself to tolerate. The more he listened, the more he understood he was being flown to a hospital. The idea of receiving medical care helped him relax. They weren't just going to let him die. Instead, they'd provided basic care and were now transporting him to what he assumed was a better place to be treated.

He wasn't sure who'd shot him, or why, but at this point, he didn't think he was going to die.

But when this horrific nightmare was over, he would find those responsible and make them pay.

Every. Last. One.

.   .   .

SEPTEMBER 10 – 11:112 a.m. – Washington, DC

A trickle of sweat rolled down his spine.

There was a long line to get through customs at Dulles International Airport, and he stood with an impassive expression on his face, portraying confidence that his fake passport would hold up to scrutiny, allowing him through without a problem.

He'd chosen American dress: slacks, polo shirt, and a light windbreaker jacket. Nothing that would raise concerns. According to his carefully crafted background, he possessed dual citizenship in both Syria and the USA. There was absolutely no reason for anyone to believe differently.

Another bead of sweat slipped down his back. The line moved, and there were now only two people in front of him.

Then one.

When he stepped up to the window, he offered a wry smile. "Rough flight," he said as he slid his passport through the opening. He went on, "A baby cried the entire time, but eventually I helped the mother offer a distraction, and the infant quieted down."

The customs agent didn't respond to his attempt at casual conversation. Instead, the customs agent stared down at his passport for a long moment, then turned to type something into the computer. He felt his shoulders tense, knowing full well the name on his passport was being run through the database, searching for aliases related to anyone with known ties to terrorism.

It had been twelve years since he was here last.

He yawned and glanced at his watch. "I need coffee."

It seemed like forever before the customs agent turned back toward him. The agent stared up at his face, comparing it to the photo, then reached for the stamp and pressed it on an empty page of his passport.

"Coffee shop is in the luggage area," the agent said, sliding the passport back to him and turning his attention to the next person in line.

"Thanks." He strove for a casual tone, shouldering his duffel bag and slipping his passport back into his pocket. As he entered the luggage area, a surge of adrenaline hit hard.

He'd accomplished the first step in meeting his goal. There wasn't much time, he needed to hurry if he was going to be back on a plane out of here by late tonight.

Once he contacted his second-in-command, he'd understand what had happened with Ahmed Mustaf.

And hopefully learn who was messing with the timeline.

He needed everything to go according to plan.

There wasn't a minute to waste.

SEPTEMBER 10 – 11:22 *a.m. – Washington, DC*

What in the world? They'd barely dispersed from the conference room when Yates called yet another urgent meeting, demanding their presence immediately. He was beginning to think he'd given the guy too much credit. From what he could tell, the moron couldn't manage his way out of a paper bag.

He made sure to take a different seat this time, avoiding the chance of being directly across from Yates's piercing gaze. No matter how much he despised him, he didn't like the way Yates often glared at him.

There was a full minute of silence before their boss spoke.

"Aaron Cooper was found dead outside a coffee shop

earlier this morning." The blunt statement hung in the air for maximum impact.

He glanced at the others in the room. "You mean, our Aaron Cooper? Berkshire's assistant?"

"Yes." His strategy to avoid Yates didn't work because his boss's gaze bored into his even from an angle.

"What happened?" someone asked. "Did he have a medical emergency of some sort?"

"No." Again, his boss's gaze hit him, then moved on to look at every one of them seated around the table. "The ME is ruling Cooper's death a homicide."

What? No! That was impossible! He'd been careful to use cyanide, that usually looked just like a heart attack via autopsy. Getting toxicology results from autopsies took at least fourteen days, maybe more.

His contact hadn't been dead more than three and a half hours.

"What happened?" This time another voice broke the silence. "How was he killed?"

Their boss didn't answer for a long moment. "The better question here is why? Why was Aaron Cooper murdered in cold blood?"

His mouth went dry, and he wished he'd thought to bring a cup of coffee or a water bottle with him. He spoke fast. "We need to open an investigation into his recent activities. See if we can understand what happened."

"We?" Yates's voice was soft but held a note of steel. "We aren't doing any such thing. I have a different task force set up to deal with Cooper's murder."

It took all his willpower not to shift in his seat. Instead, he nodded thoughtfully. "I can see the wisdom in that approach."

"Can you?" Again, Yates's voice was dangerously soft.

"Of course." He put an earnest expression on his face. "I think you should include the NSA and others with high-level security ranks to investigate this. I'm sure there's video feed somewhere. This is terrible news, just awful."

"Yes, it is." Was it his imagination or was there a sarcastic note in his boss's tone? "Two deaths within the FBI offices so close together must be related."

"That's an interesting theory. One your special task force should run with." He felt himself relax. Yes, this was exactly what he'd hoped would happen. There were no video cameras, he'd made sure of that. His plan was to have Cooper's death linked to that of Ray Pallone.

With absolutely no evidence coming back to implicate him.

SEPTEMBER 10 – 11:27 *a.m.* – *Baltimore, MD*

"Jordan? We have another link that just popped into your email from the kidnappers."

He tightened his grip on the steering wheel and searched for a place to pull off. "Took longer than I thought," he admitted, spying a strip mall. Wrenching the steering wheel to the right, he cut off the car behind him in order to make the turn into the parking lot.

"Please, God. Please don't let them hurt Bryn," Diana whispered.

He silently echoed her prayer. Choosing a parking space off to the side, he threw the gearshift into park and turned in his seat. "Give me the computer."

Sun handed him the device. This time, the link was labeled *Rashidsfailuretofreemustaf.*

Failure. He swallowed hard and clicked the link.

This time, the room appeared to be empty. Yet he knew

it wasn't. His phone rang, and with an acute sense of dread, he placed the call on speaker. "This is Jordan Rashid."

"Your daughter's blood will stain your hands," the mechanical voice said.

Diana's dark eyes filled with horror, and she opened her mouth to respond, but he held up his hand to stop her and gave her a warning look. "I don't know why you're upset, Mustaf is right where I need him. He's been transported to Washington Hospital where he's already undergoing surgery."

"If he dies . . ." the mechanical voice began, but Jordan swiftly interrupted.

"I've already checked in with the hospital staff," he said. "I assure you Mustaf's injuries are not life threatening. If the gunshot had been meant to kill him, trust me, the sniper would not have missed his chest or his head. He would already be dead. This is all part of my master plan."

There was a pause as the caller digested this information.

"I can get him out of Washington Hospital easier than I'd be able to break him out of an air force base or a federal prison," Jordan continued. "I have every intention of meeting your eight p.m. deadline."

"Ask about Bryn," Diana mouthed in a whisper.

"I'd like to see my daughter." He kept his gaze on Diana. "I need to make sure Bryn is okay. If you've hurt her or already killed her, then maybe I'll have to make sure Mustaf suffers the same fate." It was an idle threat. He didn't kill people unless he was firing in self-defense. Besides, he wasn't going to worry about Mustaf even if they'd harmed Bryn. But he didn't think they'd done anything to their daughter.

Yet.

"We will contact you in thirty minutes and send a link so you may see your daughter." Instantly, the line went dead and the webcam disappeared from the email link.

He let out a heavy sigh. "I think they bought it."

"I hope so." Diana didn't sound convinced. "What if they've already hurt her?"

"We can't think like that." He handed the computer back to Sun and took Diana's hand. Her fingers were ice cold, and despite the heat of the sun warming the interior of the car, she was shivering. "Our daughter is strong, you taught her well, Diana. She's a survivor. We're going to find her." He glanced back at Sun. "How far is the warehouse known as Liberty Bell?"

"Another fifteen minutes, maybe less." Sun offered a grim smile. "Maybe we'll beat mechanical voice there."

"What do you mean beat them there?" Diana looked perplexed. "The kidnappers are already with Bryn."

"I don't think so," Sun mused slowly. "Have you noticed that every time we ask to talk to Bryn they make us wait a specific timeframe? Last time it was within the hour, this time thirty minutes. If she was right there close by, they wouldn't need to delay, they could simply carry the phone into the next room, switch cameras, and be ready to roll."

Jordan slowly nodded, thinking about the empty room on the link. Was it just a decoy room? Not the place where Bryn was being held? "You're right. I should have put that together sooner. Even when they sent that very first video, they made us wait to talk to her." He glanced at Sun. "Which means they have two locations."

"Yes," Sun agreed. "At least two, if not more."

"But you think Bryn is being held at Liberty Bell, right?" Diana asked.

"I think it's a very real possibility," Sun hedged. "We won't know for sure until we check the place out."

"Let's hurry, Jordan, please?" Diana's dark eyes pleaded with him. "If she's truly being held there, and these guys are going there so we can talk to her, we need to find her before they arrive."

"It might be better to keep eyes on the place to see if we even have the correct location," Jordan countered. "If they show up prior to the thirty-minute window, we'd know for sure Bryn was there."

"Normally, I would agree with a wait and watch approach," Sun said. "But getting Bryn out of the place might be easier without additional men being there and tipping the odds in their favor."

Sun had a point. Fanatics were a dime a dozen, so there could already be several men watching over Bryn. Adding more would only create a larger obstacle for them to break through in order to free Bryn.

"Okay, we'll go to the warehouse ASAP." He put the car in gear and pulled out of the strip mall parking lot.

"Thank you," Diana murmured.

He glanced at her. "Thank me when we have Bryn safe and sound."

Diana shook her head, lightly touching his arm. "I have confidence in your abilities, Jordan."

He didn't answer. Having Diana's vote of confidence was nice, but she wasn't considering the possibility that Liberty Bell might not be where Bryn was being held. It could very well be the terrorist's main headquarters.

Which would be great if he had an entire team backing him up, but he didn't.

Sun was lethal in her own way, an expert in martial arts, not to mention an excellent shot with any gun you put her in hand, but Diana wasn't used to this kind of thing. It was too late to call Sloan or Yates for additional help.

At this point, they were on their own.

SEPTEMBER 10 – 11:36 a.m. – Baltimore, MD

Elam watched the man in front of Liberty Bell for what seemed like forever. Even from here, he could tell the guard was bored. The sun was out, a cool breeze wafting in from the ocean, but the man standing guard fidgeted and paced, glancing frequently at his watch.

Elam took a deep breath in and let it out slowly. What was he waiting for? There was no way to know how many guards were inside the warehouse. At this point, he needed to take care of the one he could see.

Then he'd worry about the others.

No more stalling. He picked up the detonator and stared down at it. How many people would be hurt by this act he was about to commit?

Too many.

But he couldn't let that matter. This diversion was necessary to get Meira out of there. Together, they would find a way to escape these men.

And survive.

He closed his eyes and sent up a whispered prayer. "Please forgive me, Lord."

Before he could change his mind, he pressed the trigger. Seconds later, an explosion rocked the earth.

SEPTEMBER 10 – 11:36 a.m. – Baltimore, MD

"What was that?" Diana asked harshly, bracing herself with a hand on the dashboard. "Another explosion? Bryn?"

Dear Lord above, had these mad men killed their daughter?

"Hang on, we're going to find out." Jordan's voice was terse, and he was maneuvering through traffic like a Formula 1 racer, cutting people off without caring about the series of horns that followed him.

"Try to remain calm, Diana," Sun said from the back seat. "I'm pulling up the news now."

Calm? Diana wanted to scream in frustration. As if the Korean woman would be calm if her daughter was kidnapped.

And maybe dead.

No! She couldn't imagine her life without Bryn. This couldn't be happening. It just couldn't.

"Sun, give me directions for the Liberty Bell warehouse," Jordan said.

"Take a left here, then six blocks down take a right," Sun directed. "That gets us close, but we'll need to park and walk from there."

"I see smoke"—Diana pushed the words through her tight throat—"coming from near the water."

"I know." Jordan sent her a grim glance. "Try not to worry."

Impossible. He was asking the impossible. She'd trusted Jordan to get to Bryn, but they were too late.

The kidnappers didn't buy their ruse of helping to arrange for Mustaf to be shot for the sole purpose of getting him out of the hospital.

What if Bryn had paid the ultimate price?

SEPTEMBER 10 – 11:42 a.m. – Baltimore, MD

Jordan felt sick but did his best to stay focused on

getting them to the warehouse. He noticed that several of the cars were headed in the opposite direction, which didn't bode well.

Please, God, please keep Bryn safe in Your care.

"Pull over," Sun said, distracting him. "The warehouse should be on the next block.

"There isn't smoke coming from these buildings," Jordan said as he wedged the car into the parking spot. "It looks like it's farther away."

"A-are you sure you have the right address?" Diana asked, her eyes bright with unshed tears.

"I'm positive." Sun looked out the window again. The sounds of fire engines and police vehicles echoed around them. "I don't think the Liberty Bell warehouse is the location of the explosion."

Jordan was more than willing to keep praying for a miracle. "Sun, you and I will go to the warehouse. Diana, wait for us here."

"No, I'm coming too."

He wasn't sure why he bothered since she never listened to him. Still, there was no time to argue. He and Sun led the way down the street to the corner. Diana kept pace, staying directly behind him.

Without a word, Sun went first, slipping around the corner and walking up a block, then she turned again and headed directly toward a large reddish-brown building. Jordan swept his gaze over the area but didn't see anyone lurking nearby.

When they reached the warehouse, there was no sign on the outside and no lock on the door like the previous times.

In fact, the door was hanging ajar.

His pulse quickened, and he joined Sun. Together they

flanked the door, each with their weapons drawn. He wrinkled his nose at the horrible stench of urine and bodily waste. It was as if the place had been used as an outhouse of sorts.

Giving Sun a nod, he went first. He swept his gaze over the interior of the building. He took note of the mattress on the floor in the corner and a small chair and table. There was a bucket lying on its side and excrement all over the floor.

He heard the foghorn in the distance and knew in that moment Bryn had been here. His daughter had slept on the dirty mattress, had been tied to the chair. Likely forced to use the bucket as a toilet.

But not anymore. The warehouse known as Liberty Bell was empty.

CHAPTER FIFTEEN

September 10 – 11:55 a.m. – Baltimore, MD

Bryn ducked her head and squinted against the harsh daylight, gagging at the awful stench of human waste that clung to her.

Don't throw up. Don't throw up!

After being indoors for days, the bright sunlight beating down on them made her eyes hurt. She stumbled and would have fallen if not for Meira. Her caretaker kept a strong arm around Bryn's waist, anchoring her close as they followed the man who'd come to rescue them.

Secretly, she'd been disappointed their rescuer wasn't the man they claimed was her father or her mother. But just being away from the icky smelly men was enough to carry her forward. Especially since getting away from the man at the warehouse had been a minor miracle in itself.

Bryn had thrown the gross contents of the bucket in the man's face while Meira stabbed him in the neck with the spoon honed into a knife. When the man had screamed, swiping at his eyes and blood spurting from the knife wound, she and Meira had darted outside toward freedom only to be met by an Arab man whom Meira knew.

"Elam!" Meira had thrown herself into the man's arms. Bryn realized the man must be the husband she'd mentioned. He'd held her close for only a second.

"We need to go, now. Hurry!" Elam had led the way, leaving her and Meira to follow. He seemed to know where he was going, taking turns as if he'd been there before.

And maybe he had. Bryn tried to understand what had happened. It couldn't be a coincidence that this guy had shown up outside their warehouse just as she and Meira had made a run for it.

The moment they'd heard the explosion, they'd known their guard would come inside. That there had only been one man on guard outside was a miracle.

Elam took them down yet another street. There were a couple of rough-looking men hanging out at the corner of a building, eyeing them suspiciously.

"Meira, we need money," Bryn whispered, instinctively moving closer to the woman. "To get on a subway or get a taxi to get far away from here."

Meira didn't answer right away. They'd gone another block, taking yet another alley before she said, "Elam will take care of us."

Bryn battled a wave of frustration. "We're not helpless, Meira. We escaped, remember?"

Meira nodded slowly. "Yes, but Elam knows best."

Bryn's hopes sank to the pit of her stomach. She knew that Muslim women often deferred to their husbands, even when those same men treated their wives terribly. After all, wasn't that what she and her mother had been working on over the past few years? They were one step in a process that was designed to help Muslim women escape the clutches of their terribly abusive spouses.

She tried to take heart in the fact that Meira was pregnant. Men often wanted a son to carry on their legacy, girls apparently didn't mean anything to them, but a son was like a king. Maybe Elam would treat Meira okay until she gave birth.

But where did that leave her? Bryn wanted her mom.

She wanted desperately to go home.

But first, they needed to get far enough away from the icky men so they wouldn't be found and dragged back.

The mere thought made her stomach clench with terror. Instinctively, she ducked her head and avoided eye contact with anyone nearby. She picked up her pace, determined not to be left behind.

Please, God, help us find safety!

SEPTEMBER 10 – 12:03 p.m. – Baltimore, MD

"Gone? What do you mean, gone?" Diana couldn't believe the warehouse was empty. To be this close yet not have her daughter was a significant blow.

"The warehouse is empty," Jordan repeated. "Let's get back to the car."

"No, wait. I don't understand." Diana knew her emotions were getting the best of her, but she couldn't help it. "I need to know what happened. The allotted thirty minutes the kidnappers gave us as a timeframe to talk to Bryn hasn't passed yet. Do you think we missed them? Did the kidnappers move her?"

"I think she escaped." There was a note of pride in Jordan's tone, which only made her want to smack him. "I think the explosion caused the guard to go inside, where Bryn threw the bucket of waste on him and escaped. The place is a mess."

Diana abruptly stopped in her tracks. "If that's the case, we need to spread out and search for her. She has no money, no ID. Where will she go? What will she do?"

"Diana, please. We can talk when we get to the car." Jordan swept his glance over the area. "I don't want to be here when the kidnappers find out she's gone."

"But if she's hiding somewhere nearby . . ."

"Bryn is smarter than that. She'll have gotten as far away from this place as possible." Jordan tugged on her arm. "We need to go."

She reluctantly nodded. As much as she didn't want to leave, she knew Jordan was right. If Bryn had thrown the bucket of waste on her kidnapper and found a way to escape, she wouldn't stay close. She'd run and fight, run and fight.

The way Diana had taught her.

The shriek of sirens could still be heard heading toward the scene of the explosion, but she ignored them.

Bryn could be out here, somewhere. Without any money and no way to get to a phone to call for help.

Would she find a police station? Maybe. The thought gave her hope that her daughter would be safe in police custody.

Jordan opened the car door for her. Preoccupied with her thoughts, she slid into the passenger seat. Sun resumed her seat in the back as Jordan took the driver's seat.

"Okay, new plan," Diana said. "We need to find the closest police station because that is where Bryn will likely go. We need to let the police know she's alone and on the run from men who intend to harm her."

"She may not be alone," Sun said.

Diana twisted in her seat to face her. "What do you mean?"

"Sun's right, Diana. Think about it for a moment. Do you really think Muslim males would lower themselves to caring for an eleven-year-old girl? Feed her and help her to the bathroom?"

Diana thought about her late uncle Omar and his son Tariq. "No."

"Exactly. She's not alone, she has help." Jordan reached over to rest his hand on her knee. "In fact, if you ask me, the timing of that explosion was a bit of a coincidence."

"Yes," Sun agreed. "Just like the explosion when we were at that first warehouse, American Lumber. Remember? Something triggered the explosion, but there were not many people nearby. We were far enough away that we weren't seriously hurt. I believe the explosion was a diversion used to help free Bryn and whoever was inside with her."

Her chest tightened with tension. "But . . . she'll still go to the police, right? Bryn knows enough to get help from the authorities."

"Maybe." Jordan didn't sound convinced. He started the car and pulled away from the curb, melting into the traffic streaming away from the harbor.

"According to the media," Sun said, "the explosion occurred in a parking structure located at Federal Hill Park."

"Interesting. A bomb placed in a structure would cause a lot of property damage but may avoid human casualties." Jordan glanced at her. "A diversion for sure. Otherwise the bomb would have been planted near a location where people hung out, like within the park itself, for maximum impact."

Again, she hated to admit Jordan was right. Knowing her cousin's extremist beliefs, if he'd planned something like this, he would have absolutely found a way to impact a large number of innocent victims.

Bryn wasn't alone, she'd had help to escape. Diana tried to relax in her seat, to be thankful for the news, but it wasn't easy.

Before, they had clues to follow, information that led them to different warehouses as potential locations where they might find Bryn.

Now, they had nothing.

SEPTEMBER 10 – 12:15 p.m. – Washington, DC

"I need a status report." After finally getting out of Dulles airport, he was on his way to a local hotel. He'd called his first-in-command, but the man hadn't answered.

Nor had the second.

The fact that he was on his third-in-command was not a good sign.

"Well?" he snapped impatiently. "You still have the girl, right?"

"Yes, we have her in a secure location, but there have been a few unanticipated . . . complications."

He tightened his grip on the phone. What did he pay them for anyway? "What kind of complications? With Mustaf? Or something else?"

"Someone else is pulling the strings on Mustaf," his third-in-command said slowly. "The good news is that it appears we both want the same objective and that is for Mustaf to be freed from captivity."

It wasn't a good thing to have interference, especially since there was no way of knowing for sure what the objective was. "Who?"

"We're not sure. But we think Rashid is working with them."

"You think?" he echoed in a dangerously soft voice. "Or you know?"

There was a long silence before his third-in-command admitted, "We strongly believe Rashid is working with them."

Strongly believe wasn't good enough. He reined in his temper with an effort, not wanting the rideshare driver to have a reason to remember him. "I want to know who is behind the interference and why. Do you understand?"

"Yes, I understand. I will get on that immediately," his third-in-command quickly agreed.

He disconnected from the call before he could say something he'd regret and stared out at the annoying traffic.

He detested being here in the United States, especially being stuck in Washington, DC. There wasn't much time. His men, whom he paid well, needed to deliver. Soon.

The nagging questions remained. Who had escalated the timeline to free Ahmed Mustaf, and why?

To what end?

Everything he had planned would fall apart if he didn't get the answers he needed.

And failure was not an option.

SEPTEMBER 10 – 12:19 p.m. – Washington, DC

The news of a parking structure explosion in Baltimore rippled through the FBI offices faster than the speed of light. He happened to be seated in the conference room with two colleagues and mentally braced himself for the impending wrath of their boss.

The door to the conference room was flung open, slamming hard against the wall. "Can anyone in this office explain to me what in the world is going on?" Yates thundered.

He didn't have to pretend to be confused as he had no clue what had happened in Baltimore. "I haven't heard anything, what do we know so far? What was the cause of the explosion?"

"A bomb." Sarcasm dripped from Yates's tone.

He squelched the urge to snap back. "I thought it may have been a natural gas leak or a car failure. A bomb is bad news." He paused, then asked, "Have any of the known terrorist groups taken credit for it yet? Seems like something they'd do, especially considering the timing."

"No. Do you know something I don't?" his boss countered.

"Just trying to cover all the bases." He glanced at his colleagues. "You guys have any ideas on this?"

The two men shook their heads.

"This is the second bomb that's been detonated in Baltimore in two days. I want answers, and I want them now!" Yates's face was so red he feared the guy would blow a carotid.

Which wouldn't be a bad thing. In fact, he nearly smiled thinking about Yates falling flat on his face from a sudden heart attack.

"I'm hearing there aren't many casualties," one of his colleagues said. "That's good news."

"Nothing about this is good news, do you understand me? Nothing! Get me answers or get out of my sight." Yates stormed out, slamming the door shut behind him.

There was a long tense silence in the conference room after their boss left. "Now what?" he asked. "We need something to go on to make him happy."

"I've got a source within the Baltimore PD. I'll see what I can get from him." One of his colleagues rose to his feet and moved away, holding his phone to his ear.

"I'll check the chatter from overseas, see if there's any specific group trying to take credit for this." His other colleague also left the room.

He sat for a moment, trying to understand why things seemed to be falling apart. First, Aaron Cooper's death being ruled a homicide so quickly thanks to some astute detective wannabe cop who'd snagged the coffee cup as evidence and found the contents laced with cyanide, now this. He didn't have any intel on this recent detonation. Which meant his people weren't involved.

Unless they'd gone rogue? Decided on their own to deviate from the plan?

No, he didn't think so. Fanatics like the people he dealt with were all about planning for the maximum impact. One measly bomb going off in the warehouse district of Baltimore didn't come close to meeting their objective.

There was something else going on here. Something else interfering with his plans.

He desperately needed to know who exactly had set off the bomb. And why?

SEPTEMBER 10 – 12:38 p.m. – *Baltimore, MD*

"Where are we going?" Bryn tugged on Meira's hand, needing to slow down as she was growing weary. Her strength and excitement at being free of the icky men had slowly vanished, leaving a sick sense of panic and worry behind.

She wanted her mom and had no idea how to find her.

"Elam will take care of us," Meira repeated for what seemed like the tenth time. Bryn was irritated by the woman's passive attitude.

"We helped get away, Meira," she said sharply. "That means we get to be included in the decision of where we should go next."

Elam paused and turned to look at her. She tensed, but he didn't rake his gaze over her with the evil eyes that the icky men had used every time they came near. "Do you know your way around the city of Baltimore?"

Baltimore? Was that where they were? Bryn thought back to her school lessons and tried to picture where they were. Somewhere near the water yet not too far from Washington, DC. She swallowed hard. "No."

"Then be silent." His tone was mild, but his words cut to the bone.

"I will not be quiet." Bryn glanced frantically around, trying to figure out if she needed to escape once again. But where would she go? What would she do? She had no money, nothing with her but the clothes she was wearing, which reeked of sweat, pee, and poop. "I have a right to know where you're taking me."

"Hush, child," Meira murmured. She still wore the burka, but no one stared at them because of it. Bryn almost wished they would. "We are safe. Elam will not allow any harm to come to you."

Elam didn't respond, which wasn't the least bit reassuring. She stumbled again, about to ask for a break, when she saw a sign for the subway.

A mix of emotions hit hard. She dug in her heels, holding them back. "Wait, are we taking the subway? Where?" As much as Bryn wanted to be far away from the place where the icky men had kept her, she couldn't be sure getting on a subway with Elam and Meira—to go who knows where—was the right thing to do.

"Don't delay, little one. We need to be far away before the others come looking for us," Meira said softly.

Bryn tensed and instinctively glanced apprehensively over her shoulder. They hadn't known how many men were guarding them, and it turned out to be just one. Maybe there weren't as many of the others as they'd assumed.

But being found by even one of the icky men wasn't high on her list of things she wanted to do.

Drawing in a deep breath, she pushed onward, forcing herself to keep pace with Meira and Elam. The heat from the sun was giving her a headache, and her mouth felt incredibly dry. Going down the escalator to the dark and cool subway station was a welcome reprieve.

"Can we get something to eat and drink?" She collapsed on a bench as Elam went to purchase their tickets.

Meira sat next to her without answering. When Elam returned, they spoke briefly in Arabic. Elam nodded and went over to purchase bottles of water.

"We will get food later," Meira said. "Elam doesn't want to waste all of his money."

Bryn didn't think eating was a waste of money, but drinking the ice-cold water helped make her feel better. She pressed the bottle against her temple and closed her eyes.

Being inactive for these past few days had made her a wuss. She couldn't believe how weak she was. She needed to be strong to find her mother.

She finished her water and tossed the bottle in the recycle bin. Then she sat back down to rest. When the train arrived, Meira tugged on her arm. Bryn blinked and stood. From the corner of her eye, she caught sight of a cop with a beautiful German shepherd K-9 on a leash.

The police! Her pulse soared. Of course! Why hadn't she thought of that sooner? The police would help her find her mom! She took a step toward the cop, but he was already walking away, the dog sniffing at people's bags as they went by.

"Come," Meira said, grabbing her arm to prevent her from straying farther away. "The train is here."

"But, the police." Bryn was torn, should she leave Meira and Elam and go to the cops? Or should she stay with them?

"Were you serious about helping us escape?" Meira asked. "There are those that will kill and torture us for what we have done today."

Bryn turned toward her. She remembered how she'd convinced Meira that her mom knew how to help women escape. But that was normally from their abusive families, not a husband and wife together escaping icky men.

Meira put a hand on her abdomen. "Please?"

Bryn glanced back toward the cop. He was so far ahead now she'd never catch up. Was what Meira wanted so different from the others? No. The woman wanted nothing more than to raise her baby in a safe environment.

Bryn turned and joined Meira and Elam as they boarded the subway. "Yes, I'll help you escape. But we need money, and a phone. I need to call my mom . . ." Her voice trailed off.

"Thank you." Meira smiled wearily. "Elam can get us money and a phone."

The subway doors closed, and the train began to move. Bryn stared blindly at the people standing and sitting around them.

Had she made the right decision to stay with them? She honestly didn't know.

CHAPTER SIXTEEN

September 10 – 12:52 p.m. – Baltimore, MD

"The kidnappers missed their deadline," Sun said from the back seat.

Jordan glanced back at her and nodded. "Because Bryn escaped. Although I'm sure we'll hear from them soon enough. They'll do their best to find a way to pretend they still have her."

"Yes," Sun agreed. "And we'll need to play along."

"Why?" Diana turned to look at him. "What do we care?"

Jordan reached up to rub the back of his neck. He was driving through Baltimore without a firm destination in mind. He was loath to leave the city knowing Bryn was likely still here. He saw a sign for a motel and decided it was as good of a place as any to form a plan to find Bryn.

"Jordan?" Diana prodded when he didn't answer.

"We need to think this through," he said slowly. "I was asked by Clarence Yates, the Director of the FBI, to infiltrate a known terrorist cell here in DC. That mission had barely begun when I learned of Bryn's kidnapping." He risked a glance at Diana. "I've been worried my case is what caused Bryn to be taken, but things didn't play out the way they were supposed to. I'm honestly not sure if the cell I was to infiltrate is the same one who had Bryn or if there are two different factions at play."

"Two?" Diana frowned. "Okay, so there might be two groups involved. Why does playing along about Bryn help us?"

"I'd rather not tip our hand, at least not yet." He focused his attention on the road, following the signs to the motel. "We need some time to figure out our next steps."

"We can't forget about Mustaf," Sun reminded him. "He's key to the plan. At the very least, we need to assure the kidnappers there's a plan in place to free him."

"Yeah." Jordan fell silent, his thoughts whirling. "But everything that has happened to free Mustaf hasn't been from anything I've done. What does that mean? Who is doing the work for me, and why? It just doesn't make any sense."

"I know." Diana stared out the window for several long moments before she said, "Unless Tariq is involved."

"Yes, I've thought he might be. But we don't know how or where to find him." He pulled into the motel parking lot. "I doubt he's using his real name."

Diana let out a harsh laugh. "No, he can't use his name here in the States. After the way you took out Omar twelve years ago and he retaliated by trying to blow us up, he's on the list of known terrorists."

The memories of the night he'd thought Diana had betrayed him were not happy ones. Jordan stared at the motel, then pushed open his car door. But that had been a long time ago. "Let's get a room and come up with a strategy to find Bryn."

"Wait." Diana reached out to grasp his arm, preventing him from getting out of the car. "My phone."

It wasn't difficult to follow her train of thought. "You think Bryn will try to call you on your phone, but we got rid of it when we were followed."

Her grip tightened. "We need to get a replacement, right away. Bryn could be trying to call me right now! I'm forced to change numbers every six months, so Bryn has the most recent one memorized."

"Okay." He glanced back at Sun. "How much cash do you have?"

"Enough." Sun worked the sat computer. "There's a big box store six miles from here. We can get a replacement phone and arrange for the same number to be used."

"And the possibility of being tracked with the phone?" He met Sun's gaze in the rearview mirror.

"It's a risk." She shrugged. "But we only need it long enough to connect with Bryn."

"Sounds good." It was good to have something concrete to do to find their daughter.

Baltimore was a big city with far too many places to hide.

He had to trust that Bryn was smart enough to find a way to get in touch with her mother.

SEPTEMBER 10 – 1:16 p.m. – Washington, DC

Meira stayed close to Elam's side, resting her hand protectively on her abdomen.

He couldn't believe they'd gotten this far. His diversion had worked, and Meira, with the girl's help, had managed to assist in their escape.

Despite his actions today, it was humbling to realize God still looked after them.

"What is it, Elam?"

He shook his head, then spoke in their native tongue. "You need to convince the girl we need to stay away from the police. I set that bomb back there to help distract the guard in front of Liberty Bell, and it worked. I can't risk being caught."

She nodded. "I will, Elam. And I know finding me with the girl was a surprise, I'm sorry about that. I want you to know they didn't hurt me, or Bryn."

Relieved at the news, he said, "That's good, Meira. Seeing you with her was a surprise, although I should have realized they wanted you for a reason."

"That is how these men operate, yes? By keeping secrets." She paused, then added, "The child can help us, husband. I will make sure she won't take us to the police."

Elam's mouth tightened. Accepting help from a child was difficult. What could the girl possibly know? At the moment, he viewed her as a burden. Another mouth to feed. It wasn't as if he was given much money each day, and now that meager influx of cash would stop. They only had what was in his pocket to live on. "We should let her go," he finally said. "There is no need to keep her with us."

Meira glanced at Bryn, and he knew the child was watching them curiously and listening to their discussion. Of course, the child didn't understand Arabic, but still.

Meira switched to English, probably for the girl's benefit. "Bryn's mother has helped other Muslim women escape bad situations. We need to get far away from here if we want to survive. She can help us escape, for good." She waited, and when he didn't respond, she added, "For our unborn child, Elam. Do this for our baby."

He glanced over at Bryn, then down at the backpack he still carried. The close call with the K-9 cop had shaken him. He still had a couple of explosive devices, and the scent could have easily brought the dog over to them. He debated leaving it behind on the subway but thought it was possible he might need them.

It was the only weapon he had if they were caught.

At that moment, his cell phone vibrated. He tensed and glanced at Meira. He lifted the phone but didn't answer it.

"You have a phone?" The girl's voice was loud enough to attract attention. He instantly replaced the phone in the backpack.

"No."

"I saw it," Bryn protested. "Don't you understand? We can use that to call my mom!"

"Not now, later."

The girl opened her mouth to protest, but Meira put a hand on her arm. "Hush, child, we will call soon."

Elam felt the phone stop vibrating, then almost immediately start up again. His hands began to shake with fear. Every one of the men he'd been working for would be searching for him.

He glanced again at Meira. She was right. They needed to disappear, and soon.

To protect their unborn child.

SEPTEMBER 10 – 1:31 p.m. – Washington, DC

"Can you hear me? Open your eyes if you can hear me?"

Mustaf tried to do as requested, but the lights were so bright they hurt his head. His mouth tasted foul, his lips dry and cracked.

They must have tortured him. He hoped he didn't say anything about the upcoming plan while he was being worked over by these infidels.

"Ahmed, please open your eyes. I need you to take a big breath for me. I know it will hurt, but you need to breathe on your own."

The words were confusing, but the pain was very real. His abdomen felt as if he'd been stabbed with a thousand knives. He pried his eyes open and looked up at the face hovering above him. It took a moment to note the blue scrubs and the stethoscope hanging around her neck.

A nurse. He was in the hospital. Memories flooded back.

He'd been shot, then flown to a hospital via helicopter. Not tortured, unless you count the gunshot wound as torture, which at the moment he did.

"Water," he croaked.

"Good, I'm glad you're awake. I have an ice chip for you, no water until your belly starts working again."

His belly wasn't working? Was she speaking in riddles to confuse him? She used a plastic spoon to give him an ice chip, and it melted in his mouth providing a small relief.

"More," he said.

"Not too much or you'll throw up," she warned, but spooned another ice chip into his mouth. "Trust me, you do not want to throw up, not after the surgeon spent the last two hours repairing the damage from the gunshot wound."

He closed his eyes, savoring the ice chip. Now he understood. He'd undergone surgery. Had his abdomen repaired from the gunshot wound.

"Would you like something for the pain?"

The pain was horrific, but he forced himself to shake his

head no. He couldn't afford to have a mind fuzzy with pain medicines.

He needed to remain alert. If a rescue attempt was in process, he intended to be ready.

No matter what the cost.

SEPTEMBER 10 – 1:48 p.m. – Baltimore, MD

Diana clutched her new phone like a lifeline. It wasn't charged up and ready to go yet, but as soon as they were settled in the motel room, she intended to check her voice mail.

Maybe Bryn had already reached out to her!

Jordan pulled back into the motel parking lot and looked back at Sun. "Would you mind securing the room?"

"Of course." Sun closed the computer and slid out of the back seat.

"We're going to find her soon, Jordan. I can feel it," Diana said, breaking the silence.

"I know we will." Jordan's smile didn't quite reach his eyes. "I wish I knew what the plan was behind freeing Mustaf. I don't like the timing of all this."

Diana tensed, thinking again of her cousin Tariq. "When we have Bryn safe, we can focus on your terrorism concerns."

"Time is running out." Jordan sighed. "You know what time the plane hit the first tower?"

"Eight thirty-six a.m." She didn't have to think about it, the timeline was drilled into her mind.

"It's close to two p.m. now," Jordan said. "If they're planning something, I have to believe it will happen at the exact same time on the exact same date as nine eleven."

She swallowed hard, the news sobering. For hours now,

all she could think about was getting Bryn back safely. But Jordan was right.

They needed to figure out the rest of this mess.

Before it was too late.

SEPTEMBER 10 – 2:04 p.m. – Washington, DC

"What do you mean, she's gone?" He was settled in his modest hotel room that overlooked the Potomac River. He tightened his grip on the phone, hoping his first-in-command had made a mistake.

"There was an explosion that created some chaos, and somehow the girl and the woman caring for her escaped. We are actively searching for them now."

He cursed his first-in-command. "What is wrong with you? You allowed a measly woman and child to escape? How could you fail me like this?"

"We will find them. They can't have gotten far."

It was all he could do not to scream more obscenities. Remaining calm was difficult, but necessary. His first-in-command obviously had to die. But that wasn't his primary concern.

Without the girl, he didn't have the leverage he needed with Rashid.

And Diana.

He'd been looking forward to killing them all. To avenge his father's death. With the added bonus of freeing Ahmed Mustaf.

"Find them. I will see you soon." He disconnected from the call.

These imbeciles were useless.

As distasteful as it was, he'd need to get his hands dirty and take care of this himself.

. . .

SEPTEMBER 10 – 2:16 p.m. – Arbutus, MD

Bryn's stomach was rumbling from the various food scents surrounding her. Elam was skinny and didn't look as if he ate much, but she was worried about Meira and her baby.

"Can't we get something to eat?" She directed her question at Meira, even though she knew Elam was the one with the cash.

"Soon, little one," Meira said in a soothing tone.

Bryn glanced around, wondering if it was time to ditch Meira and Elam. She wanted to help Meira, she really did. But things weren't moving fast enough for her. She wanted to use the phone to call her mother. She wanted to wash up and get clean clothes. She wanted to eat real food, not the glop they made her eat over the past few days.

She needed to use the bathroom with a real toilet, not a bucket.

As the thoughts washed over her, she felt a sense of shame. She'd escaped from the icky men because of Meira and Elam's help. Without them, she knew she wouldn't have made it.

Didn't she owe it to them to provide help in return?

God wouldn't want her to be so selfish.

Bryn kept up with Meira and Elam as they headed away from the subway. The sun was bright, but now she tipped her face toward the sky to bask in the glow. It seemed as if she'd been kept in the dark for weeks instead of days.

After they went another couple of blocks, they turned toward a large store. Elam glanced at Meira, and she heard them talk in rapid Arabic. She couldn't follow the conversation but understood when Elam pulled a few dollars out of his pocket.

He didn't have much money, and they were trying to figure out what they could afford with the scant money they had.

Her breath came out in a whoosh. Bryn should have figured it out earlier. Elam obviously cared for Meira, he wouldn't refuse her food without a good reason.

"Please, Elam," she interrupted them. "If you'll let me call my mother, I'm sure she'll come and get us. She can buy food for us, and more water. Just let me use your phone."

Elam hesitated, uncomfortable with the idea. After a quick glance around, he directed her toward the side of the building where they were partially hidden from view.

"Be quick," he said, handing her the phone.

Bryn almost wept with joy as she punched in the numbers she'd memorized a few months ago. Her mother had to answer. She just had to!

SEPTEMBER 10 – 2:17 p.m. – Baltimore, MD

When the phone in Diana's hand rang, she was so startled she nearly dropped it. Staring at the screen, the number was one she didn't recognize, but it started with a DC area code.

"Hello?"

"Mommy?"

Bryn! "Oh, baby, yes, it's me. Where are you? Are you okay?" Diana reached out to grab Jordan's arm, her eyes filling with tears. "We'll come pick you up right away."

"I'm okay, it's so good to hear your voice." Bryn sounded as if she was going to break down and cry, so Diana quickly wiped her own tears away.

"Everything is going to be just fine, baby. Can you tell me where you are? What city you're in?"

"Baltimore." Bryn paused, then said, "We're at a Walmart Supercenter." Diana heard a man's voice and tightened her grip on the phone. "In a suburb called Arbutus."

"Who is with you, Bryn? Does a man have you captive?"

"Huh? Oh, no," Bryn hastened to reassure her. "I'm fine. I'm not alone, I had help getting away from the icky men, and to be honest, Mom, they need your help too."

"They?" She glanced at Jordan who was right next to her and listening in. "How many?"

"A man and his wife."

"Okay, baby. That's fine, we can help." Anything to get Bryn back safely. "We can be at the Walmart Supercenter within fifteen minutes. Can you stay on the phone with me while we drive?"

Again a male voice mumbled in the background. Diana couldn't understand the words, but her stomach clenched in warning.

"No, I'm afraid not. I have to get off the phone now. But you'll come soon, right? I'm hungry."

"Oh, baby, yes. I promise we'll be there soon. I love you, Bryn." Tears welled in the back of her throat.

"I love you, too, Mommy. Please hurry." Bryn didn't wait for a response but disconnected from the line.

"We have to go right now." Diana leaped to her feet, still clutching the phone. "Sounds as if she hasn't eaten in a long time."

"We'll get her." Jordan glanced at Sun. "You'll need to stay here, okay?"

"Got it." Sun smiled. "I'm really glad you've found her.

"Me too." Diana was almost dizzy with relief. But she still couldn't relax, not until she was holding Bryn in her arms.

Jordan took the wheel, which was fine with her. She stared out at the streets, glancing back down at her phone as if willing Bryn to call back.

"Did she say anything about who helped her escape?" Jordan asked.

"No, other than she was with a man and his wife." She glanced at him. "You think they were her caretakers?"

Jordan shook his head. "Not the man, but the woman? Maybe."

Diana didn't care who they were, even tiny green people from Mars would be welcomed with open arms. "I'm so glad she wasn't alone the whole time."

"Me too." Jordan reached over to touch her knee. "You did a great job raising her, Diana. I'm not sure what she'll think of me, but I hope you allow me to be a part of her life."

It was something she'd worried about early on, but now? How could she possibly refuse? "Of course, Jordan. Just . . . give her time, okay? I told her you were dead because that was part of our cover in witness protection. I also told her the men who killed you were dangerous, which is why we had to always be careful, learn self-defense, and change our phone numbers frequently."

"I know." He gently squeezed her knee. "At some point we'll have to rehash the past, but not now. Let's focus on getting Bryn and whoever this couple is who helped her escape."

"Yes. Thank you." Diana peered out the window. "Is that the Supercenter?"

"Yes." It took Jordan longer than she had patience for to get from where they were located to the Walmart. As he entered the large parking lot, she anxiously raked her gaze over the area.

Where were they?

Jordan drove up and down a couple of aisles before she spotted them. "There, Jordan, see? Next to the building."

He narrowed his gaze and quickly headed in that direction.

Without waiting for the car to come to a complete stop, she opened her car door and jumped out. "Bryn!"

Her daughter rushed forward, throwing herself into her arms. Diana clutched her close, pressing a kiss to the top of her head.

Safe. *Dear Lord, thank you for keeping Bryn safe!*

"Hello, Elam," Jordan said in a calm voice.

Diana glanced toward the tall thin Arab man who was staring at Jordan as if he'd seen a ghost.

And maybe he had. It took a moment for her to understand the implication.

Elam must have been the contact Jordan had been given to infiltrate the terrorist cell operating out of Washington, DC.

CHAPTER SEVENTEEN

September 10 – 2:37 p.m. – Arbutus, MD

"You know Elam? And Meira?" Bryn eyed him curiously. "How?"

"We'll discuss this later," Jordan said, keeping his gaze on Elam. "Let's get back to the motel, okay?"

"Can't we eat first? And get new clothes" Bryn protested. "I'm hungry and so is Meira. We didn't get any food since this morning, and she's pregnant."

"Pregnant?" Diana's eyes widened in surprise.

Jordan hesitated, then nodded. "Let's make a quick trip inside for clothes, then we'll stop and pick something up from a fast-food restaurant along the way."

The clothes didn't take long. Minutes later Jordan, Diana, and Bryn were back outside. Elam and Meira were still huddled near the building.

"Let's go, I need you all to get into the car," Jordan said.

"Even me?" Elam asked in a low voice.

Jordan nodded slowly. "Yes, I think you and I have a lot to discuss." He was stunned to see his contact linked to the terrorist cell here with Bryn. And the man's wife.

"It's okay, Meira." Elam spoke in Arabic, reassuring the woman standing beside him. "We can trust him."

"Yes, you can," Jordan agreed, using their native language as well.

Meira and Elam climbed into the back seat. Diana reluctantly let go of Bryn so their daughter could join them, clutching the bag of clothes to her chest. The SUV was better than a sedan, but five people were the most that could be comfortably seated.

Jordan slid in behind the wheel, glancing at Diana sitting beside him. "Ready?"

"Elam, wait," Bryn said. "You forgot your backpack."

"Leave it," Elam said firmly.

Jordan met his gaze in the rearview mirror. "Are you sure?"

Elam inclined his head. "There is an explosive device inside. Best that it remains here."

Jordan didn't ask twice. It bothered him to realize that Elam had carried a bomb with him the entire time he'd been with Bryn. Sure, he assumed the guy knew what he was doing, but still, it was crazy dangerous to walk around with explosive material in a backpack.

"Did you set off the recent explosion in Baltimore?" Jordan asked as he pulled away from the store. "The one in the parking structure?"

Elam met his gaze without wavering. "Does it matter?"

Jordan understood the man's leeriness. "Not really, although I suspect you used it as a diversion to rescue Bryn."

Another long pause. "Yes," Elam said simply. "Although my sole purpose was to free Meira. I must be honest, I knew nothing about the child until I found the two of them together."

For a brief moment Jordan looked heavenward, knowing God had played a role in this. His heart swelled with gratitude and a humble relief. "I'm glad you were able to help them, Elam. Thank you."

There was a slight hesitation before the man nodded his head. "You are welcome."

Jordan had many, many more questions to ask Elam, but he didn't intend to do that with Bryn listening in. His daughter had been traumatized enough, no need to burden her with the terrorist attack that was in the works.

But he felt better now knowing that Elam had defected from the group.

With Elam's help, they might be able to prevent the terrorist act from moving forward.

If it wasn't already too late.

SEPTEMBER 10 – 3:01 p.m. – Washington, DC

"Okay, we're going to take you to your regular room now."

Mustaf peered up at the nurse, hiding his resentment and forcing himself to respond politely. "Thank you."

"You must be someone really important," she said while disconnecting wires from his chest. "There are soldiers standing guard outside, waiting for you." She flashed a smile. "We didn't let them into the operating rooms or the recovery area, but they told me they would be with you from now on." She smiled and lowered her voice. "I've never seen so many handsome men."

Soldiers? The unwelcome news hit hard. Until now, he'd been convinced that his people would find a way to free him from this place.

No easy task while being guarded by soldiers.

The nurse pushed his bed through the area, making his stomach lurch. He caught glimpses of health care workers and other patients on gurneys much like his as he was wheeled through the recovery area and into the hallway.

Two men stepped up beside him, one on either side of his gurney. They were clearly military men, with their ramrod straight posture and short haircuts. Neither one of them spoke but simply fell into step as the nurse pushed him forward. Mustaf couldn't see much of their uniforms but figured they had to be from the air force base where he'd been shot.

And he wanted to puke when the stupid woman gushed over them.

"Such handsome escorts, thank you so much for your service to our country."

"Ma'am," one said with a brief nod.

He closed his eyes in an effort to ignore them. Two soldiers walking alongside him ready for anything, but were there more? Located at various positions within the hospital, the entrances and exits? If so, how many in total?

He had no way of knowing. The gurney bounced against the wall, sending a shaft of pain spearing through him. He wanted to rant and rave at the stupid female who was being so careless but sensed the soldiers would not take kindly to an outburst.

He needed to remain calm. Lull them into a sense of complacency.

Waiting and hoping that his people would find a way to sneak in and save him.

SEPTEMBER 10 – 3:09 p.m. – Baltimore, MD

Diana had insisted her daughter shower and change her

clothes, but when it came time to eat, Bryn could only manage half her cheeseburger and a handful of fries before she pushed the remnants of her meal away. "I'm stuffed. That was good, Mom, thanks." She eyed Jordan shyly. "And thanks to you too . . . um, Dad."

Jordan's smile was gentle. "You're more than welcome, Bryn."

Diana had quickly told Bryn that Jordan really was her father, which Bryn seemed happy about. She reached out and rested her hand on Bryn's arm, unable to keep from touching her daughter. Bryn was alive and relatively unharmed. Oh, she knew very well her sweet little girl would be forever changed over this horrible experience. Bryn was acting normal enough know, but Diana knew she needed to be prepared for Bryn to suffer nightmares and flashbacks at the very least.

Her daughter would need professional help when this was over. But, for now, she was safe. And that was all Diana could ask for.

God had answered her prayers.

"I hope you don't mind that I told Meira you would help her and Elam escape," Bryn went on, oblivious to her inner turmoil. "She's worried about her baby. And you've helped so many others, I didn't think adding two more would matter."

Diana glanced at Jordan who was listening intently to this new turn in their conversation. The curious and determined expression in his eyes warned that she'd better fill him in on what Bryn meant, very soon.

She swallowed hard and nodded to indicate she understood what he was silently asking. She'd always feared this day would come. She'd done what she'd felt was necessary to honor her mother's memory, and she wasn't going to apologize for her actions. Besides, that was all in the past. It didn't matter, not anymore. "Of course, I don't mind, baby." She smiled and hugged Bryn close. "Happy to help those who protected you."

"How do you plan to do that?" Jordan asked with a frown.

"I'll explain later." She glanced at Elam and Meira. "I think we need to understand what we're up against first."

Elam glanced at Meira, then at Jordan. "It's better if we speak in private."

"Why? Because women don't understand enough about what's going on in the world?" Diana tried to take the edge from her tone. "Trust me, Elam, I come from a family with men who didn't hesitate to do whatever was necessary to get what they wanted. We're in this together."

Elam didn't seem to agree, but he didn't push the issue either. "I only know my role in the master plan, nothing more."

"And your role was to bring me to the men in charge?" Jordan asked.

Elam shook his head. "No, I believed you were one of them, like those in charge. I didn't know you were working for the US government."

Intrigued, Diana leaned forward. "You thought Jordan was one of the bad guys?"

"Yes. I was told there was a new recruit ready to die for the cause." Elam glanced at Jordan. "I believed you to be one of them. Your accent and your Arabic is flawless. Very impressive."

"Thanks, I think," Jordan drawled.

A hint of a smile tugged at Elam's mouth. The first Diana had witnessed since picking them up outside the Walmart Supercenter.

"What were the warehouses used for?" Diana asked.

"Various things," Elam responded. "The one I blew up contained bomb components; another is a location to make false IDs and passports. There were a few others, one specifically to store guns, but I was not involved in the level of detail you are asking for."

"Who's in charge?" Jordan pressed. "I mean, you must know something that will help us find them."

Elam was silent for a long time. "I do not know the name, but the main headquarters is known as Liberty."

"Liberty?" Jordan repeated, his gaze clashing momentarily with hers. "The warehouse where we believe Bryn and Meira were being held was known as Liberty Bell."

"Yes, but Liberty is the main location." Elam glanced at Meira, then reluctantly added, "It is located in Washington, DC."

Diana inwardly groaned. Of course, it was. Why on earth did all roads have to lead back to DC?

The terrorist plot couldn't be centered around the White House, there was no way in the world anyone would get close to planting a bomb there. The place was crawling with Secret Service, and anyone going in and out had to be carefully vetted.

No backpacks or other carry-ons were allowed in either.

"Do you know the target?" Diana asked. "Knowing that is half the battle."

Elam shook his head. "I make bombs, that is all."

Bombs. Plural. The magnitude hit hard. How many possible targets could there be? Five? Ten? A dozen?

She swallowed hard.

Too many.

. . .

SEPTEMBER 10 – 3:17 p.m. – Washington, DC

He slit the man's throat, grimacing at the copious amount of blood.

He despised getting his hands dirty. He paid men to do this for him. But they were useless, every single one.

Except perhaps his third-in-command. Yes, he believed the young man known as Amar was eager to make his mark within his command structure. Dropping the dead man to the ground, he moved back and turned toward his second-in-command. The guy stood stoic, as if unmoved by seeing his cohort's demise.

Then his second-in-command bowed down before him, offering the vulnerable back of his neck. "I understand the punishment for failure."

The sacrifice gave him pause. Maybe all was not lost. Maybe this man and Amar could turn this mess around.

Sadly, things couldn't get much worse.

"You will find Rashid, his woman, and the girl and return them to me."

"Yes."

He hesitated, wondering if he was getting soft. Normally he wouldn't tolerate any of this.

But the clock was ticking, and they were running out of time.

He needed answers, soon. And he needed to know everything was going to fall into place as planned.

"Amar, you are with me." He turned and walked away, with Amar following close behind.

His second-in-command remained kneeling with his head bowed low, knowing that he must deliver on his promise.

Or die.

. . .

SEPTEMBER 10 – 3:28 *p.m.* – *Baltimore, MD*

Jordan asked Sun to get a second motel room connected to theirs for Elam and Meira. He knew that Elam would require privacy for his wife. He plugged in the satellite computer that had no battery left, then drew Elam aside. Despite Diana's desire to be included, he wanted a few words alone with the man who had briefly been his contact within the terrorist cell.

"Tell me about the bombs," he said in a low voice.

Elam avoided his gaze and shrugged. "There is nothing to tell. I make as many as they order. When I'm finished, they take them to the appropriate locations."

"And you have no idea what the locations might be?" Jordan pressed. He knew that it was common for the plan to be parceled out in isolated pieces without any communication between members, but he wanted, needed more.

"No." There was no hesitation in Elam's tone.

Jordan battled a wave of frustration. "Come on, Elam, you must know something. Was each bomb the same size and type?" He thought for a moment about the padlock that was on the door of the warehouse. "Did you make a bomb in the shape of a lock for the warehouse known as American Lumber?"

"Yes, that was my work." Elam almost looked proud of what he'd created. "I'm sorry about detonating that device, but you and the woman were too close. I waited for you to be far enough away but needed to detonate the device to maintain our mission."

"I doubt the man who died felt it was necessary," Jordan said testily. "You realize more innocent people may have suffered or died in the parking structure explosion too."

Elam lowered his gaze to the floor. "Yes, I am aware. It was necessary to do as I was told until I could free Meira."

Jordan blew out a breath. "Yeah, okay. I get it. You did all of this for Meira."

"For my wife and our unborn child." Elam glanced up with a hint of defiance. "As I'm sure you would do the same for your woman and your daughter."

Jordan couldn't help glancing over to where Diana and Bryn were huddled together on the bed. Diana would bristle at being thought of as his woman, but he couldn't fault Elam's logic. "Yes."

"In answer to your question, no, the bombs I have made are not all the same size and shape," Elam said. "They are each different."

"Different how?"

Elam spread his hands wide. "They tell me what they want, and I make each device according to their request. There are often repeats, but in different sizes."

A thrill of anticipation hit hard. "Give me an example."

"I have made several birds, baby rabbits, pinecones, and rocks," Elam said.

"Birds, baby rabbits, pinecones, and rocks?" This wasn't at all what he'd expected. "How much damage can one of those small bombs do?"

"Plenty," Elam admitted. "I used a seagull for the parking structure. Have you seen the end result of the explosion on the television?"

Jordan hadn't, so he quickly crossed over and turned on the television. It wasn't difficult to find a news station covering the story. There would be drones and/or helicopters flying above the area taking photographs.

A female reporter stood in front of the camera, fire trucks, ambulances, and police cars cluttering the background. He couldn't tell how much damage there was to the structure from the current angle and was about to switch stations when the camera switched views and showed the gaping hole along the northwest section of the building.

A sick sense of dread settled in his gut. "That was done by one of your small devices?"

"Yes." Elam stared at the television screen with sad eyes. "I hope God will find a way to forgive my sins."

"God does forgive us, but we also need to do our part," he pointed out. "Elam, your part of this atonement is to help me figure out where your devices were taken. Can you make a list of what you've made?"

"Yes, but I cannot write very well in English."

"I'll write, you talk." Jordan pulled paper and a pen from the motel desk drawer. "How many birds, pinecones, and rocks?"

"Three birds, three baby rabbits, four pinecones, and four rocks," Elam recited. "And I have made a few"—he waved a hand, searching for the right word—"decorative types of things, like with flowers and such. They showed me a picture, and I made what I saw in the picture."

Jordan set the pen aside and glanced at Sun. "The decorative bomb with flowers might be a clue we can follow up on. Sun, use the sat computer that's fully charged to help Elam review all the tourist attractions in DC to see if he can identify any of the decorative things with flowers he made. Can you do that with him?"

Sun nodded.

Jordan stared at his brief list. Sixteen items so far, with likely a few more. All with the ability to leave gaping holes in structures or kill dozens of people.

They needed to find each and every one of Elam's devices, before it was too late.

. . .

SEPTEMBER 10 – 3:58 p.m. – Washington, DC

Mustaf heard the soft swish as the door to his hospital room opened and the muted squeak of footsteps on shiny linoleum approaching his bed. He kept his eyes closed and his breathing even.

Friend or foe?

He hated feeling helpless and at the mercy of others. Even if this was a foe, he was too weak to fight, doing his best to handle the throbbing pain in his abdomen.

"Can you hear me?" The low voice spoke in Syrian, his native language.

Still, he didn't move. Didn't acknowledge the stranger standing near his bed in any way. If this man was here to silence him for good, there was nothing he could do to stop it.

But . . . where were the soldiers who were allegedly standing guard outside his room? Had they been paid off by his enemies to leave their station?

"I know you can hear me, Ahmed Mustaf," the voice continued. "I am here to tell you to be ready to move in roughly four hours."

Be ready to move? Mustaf opened his eyes to see a man with a face mask covering his nose and mouth looming over him. "I will be ready," he said in a guttural tone.

"Good." The man turned and left.

Mustaf glanced at the clock on the wall. It was nearly four in the afternoon. It would seem he would be freed by eight o'clock as promised.

Nothing would get in the way of their mission.

Nothing!

CHAPTER EIGHTEEN

September 10 – 4:23 p.m. – Baltimore, MD

Diana slipped away from Bryn, who'd fallen asleep. Leaving her daughter's side wasn't easy, but she needed to do her part in helping Jordan understand what the terrorists planned to target.

"We need to talk."

Jordan glanced up at her, then nodded. They went to the far corner of the room, away from the spot were Sun and Elam were scrolling through websites.

"What did Bryn mean when she said you helped others escape?" Jordan asked in a low voice.

She licked her dry lips. "You already know that after my uncle found and murdered my mother, and his son Tariq tried to kill us, I was taken into witness protection. But after a few years, I learned about other women who were suffering at the hands of their husbands, fathers, uncles, grandfathers . . ." Her voice trailed off. "I did some research and found there was a Muslim Shelter in Raleigh, which was only two and a half hours from where we lived."

"You decided to volunteer?" Jordan asked when she paused.

"Yes, they welcomed me with open arms because I could speak Arabic." She hesitated, then told him the rest. "Soon, though, they asked for additional help."

"Like?"

She met his dark gaze. "There is an underground railroad of sorts, a way to transport women who fear for their lives from one area to the next. Because I lived close to the ocean, I became a drop-off point. The boats would come in at night, and I would take the woman and hide her until she could be transported safely to the shelter."

Jordan blew out a breath and rubbed the back of his neck. "You took a huge risk, Diana. Part of being in witness protection is to sever all ties to your former life. I doubt participating in an underground railroad for Muslim women is exactly keeping away from your roots."

"I know, but it was a risk I was willing to take." She glanced at Bryn, her heart squeezing in her chest. "Don't you see? If my mother had been able to find something like this, she'd be alive today. My attempt to save my mother backfired, so this was something I had to do. And I wouldn't knowingly put Bryn in danger. I was just one cog in a big wheel. It wasn't as if women came through on a weekly basis."

"I know you wouldn't put Bryn in danger." He surprised her by taking her hand in his. "But it was still a risk, one that could have had dire consequences."

"Yes." There was no denying he was right.

"How often would you take one of these women from the boat to the shelter?"

"Roughly once every two to three months. Things moved very slow, for obvious reasons, and the route was circuitous to avoid discovery." She tightened her grip on his hand. "There's more, Jordan. One of the women I helped maybe three months ago? Her name was Fadia Haram Shekau."

He sucked in a harsh breath. "One of Tariq's wives?"

"One of his five wives, yes." After holding the secret for so long, telling Jordan felt as if a weight had been lifted from her shoulders. "I didn't know it at the time, it's not like I get any personal information on these women before they arrive. In fact, just the opposite. They simply step off the boat, and I assist them into my car and take them home. But I recognized her, even after all those years, and she recognized me too. I saw the jagged scar on her face, and she told me that Tariq had cut her for disobeying . . ." She couldn't finish.

Jordan pulled her into his arms, cradling her close. She buried her face against his chest, reveling in his embrace. He sweetly kissed her temple, and she lifted her head to look up at him, silently asking for more.

Keeping his gaze on hers, he lowered his mouth. She eagerly met him more than halfway. This kiss was just as passionate as the first, which seemed like forever ago but was really just earlier that morning.

"Diana," he whispered when they both needed to breathe. "When this is over . . ."

"Yes," she whispered back. "I would like to spend some time with you, Jordan. And of course you'll want to get to know Bryn too."

"I'd love to spend time with both of you," he confessed.

"I know." Then her smile faded. "Do you think it's possible Tariq knows I helped Fadia? Is that how my cover within witness protection was blown?"

His gaze turned serious. "Maybe, if Fadia told him."

"No, I can't believe that." Her denial was swift. She paused, then added, "I keep coming back to the federal government. Chris Wallace was killed, maybe tortured to reveal my location. If he was betrayed by someone inside, they could have found me."

"But Fadia may have also told Tariq about you," Jordan persisted.

"Fadia was scared he would kill her. Tariq . . . is a violent man."

"That doesn't surprise me, but I don't see how Tariq could know about your role in Fadia's escape. Not without inside help."

Inside help. She went still. To her shame, she'd never considered this angle. "You mean if someone at the shelter or maybe even someone along the railroad told him?"

Jordan nodded slowly. "Unfortunately, money is a powerful motivator. Offer enough money and there will always be those who jump at the chance, no matter what horrible thing they're asked to do."

The thought was a sucker punch to the gut. She leaned heavily against Jordan for a long moment, then forced herself to straighten. "If that's true, then we'll need to disappear again. I can't allow him to hurt Bryn."

"We don't know for sure Tariq is involved yet," Jordan said. "As you pointed out, it could be someone within the FBI who broke your cover. I'd like to talk to Tony Balcome about that."

"Maybe, but again, why come forward now?" She shivered, despite the stuffiness inside the motel room. "Tariq . . . is a possibility I can't ignore, Jordan."

"Let's try to focus on one crisis at a time, okay?"

She drew a deep breath and let it out slowly. "Okay."

But as they worked on searching for information on the

computer, she couldn't help but think about the threat of her cousin Tariq finding them.

After the way her uncle had been killed by Jordan, she knew Tariq would show her and Bryn no mercy.

SEPTEMBER 10 – 4:58 *p.m.* – *Washington, DC*

Amar was anxious to please. "I believe Elam planted a bomb in Baltimore, causing the parking structure to explode. It was a diversion to create confusion that allowed him to breech the Liberty Bell location."

He nodded. "Elam will need to be found and silenced, permanently."

Amar inclined his head. "Yes, but remember there are three additional devices he has not provided to us."

That was not good news. "How many do we currently have?"

"Sixteen are in place and ready to go." Amar checked his phone. "I've been trying to reach Elam, but without success."

A kernel of unease slipped down his spine. "Do you think he will try to disappear? Or stick around in an attempt to disrupt our plans?"

"Disappear," Amar said without hesitation. "He doesn't know any details related to our plan, his job was only to create what we asked of him. And we did that by holding his wife hostage." Amar shrugged. "If he has rescued his wife, then he has no reason to stay."

He hoped Amar was right. "I would still like him found and punished. A message must be sent to the others."

"I have already put the man who allowed them to escape on Elam's trail."

"Good." It wasn't perfect, and having three fewer devices than originally planned wasn't a major concern.

As long as their plan went off without a problem.

SEPTEMBER 10 – 5:02 p.m. – Washington, DC

"Hey, I didn't realize you were still here."

He looked up to meet his colleague's gaze. His only purpose for sticking around the FBI office was to get information, a tactic that had clearly worked in his favor. He did his best to looked concerned. "I'm troubled by recent events and have been trying to come up with an angle to investigate."

His colleague held up his phone. "I just heard from my contact within the Baltimore PD. They found a backpack with an explosive device outside the Walmart Supercenter in Arbutus, a suburb of Baltimore. Inside was an explosive device shaped like a seagull."

He went still. Explosive device? "Are you sure?"

His colleague nodded. "My guy told me it looked real from a distance, but up close it was definitely made of explosives. They backed off and got the bomb squad there pronto. They're hoping to pick up some usable prints from the backpack. If they do, there's a good chance someone's name will pop in the system."

"I'd like to know what your friend finds out about that. A name would be very useful." He didn't have to feign interest—he knew this was big. If the bomb in the backpack was similar to the one used at the parking garage, then he had to believe the man who'd left it behind was working in parallel to them.

Toward the same goal? Maybe.

If only he could get his hands on Jordan Rashid. He

thought about the woman's phone that had been out of service since the failed attack in Annapolis and decided it couldn't hurt to give it another try. Even if the phone was off, it would give him their last known location.

Booting up his computer, he brought up the phone number and entered it into the database.

With a jolt, he stared at the location that bloomed on the screen.

Baltimore.

SEPTEMBER 10 – 5:11 *p.m.* – *Baltimore, MD*

Bryn still had trouble believing she was safe at last. The clothes her dad had purchased for her were nothing fancy, but Bryn was still grateful to get rid of her old stinky things. Her once favorite Minion T-shirt would never be worn again. She couldn't believe how much better she felt after a shower and a change of clothes.

Not to mention having her mom and her dad, the man she'd been told was dead, nearby.

God must have been looking out for her. And for Meira, although the woman spoke of Allah, which Bryn figured was just the Arabic version of God.

She had so many questions to ask her dad, but he was over talking to the beautiful Korean woman named Sun and Meira's husband, Elam.

Elam was a surprise. She'd heard him say something about asking God for forgiveness. He had specifically said God, not Allah.

It was all so confusing. They had to be one and the same, right?

"Bryn, can we talk for a moment?"

She glanced shyly at the man who was her father.

Secretly, she thought him very handsome and felt certain her mother must still care about him. "Sure."

He sat down beside her on the edge of the bed. "I'm very glad you're okay, and I don't want to bring up painful memories, but I need to ask if you remember anything about these men that might help us figure out who they are."

"No." She stared down at her hands. "They smelled awful and were mean. One of them hit me really hard." She put a hand to her cheek. The blow had hurt, but it was the sudden attack that had scared her most of all. Along with the fear of suffering another.

"I know, and I'm very sorry that happened." Her father lightly wrapped his arm around her shoulders. "Did they use any names? Or mention any places? Even the smallest detail could prove useful."

She thought back to those horrible hours she'd been locked in the room with Meira. She'd been so upset, her mind whirling with terror, she couldn't remember hearing any names. "I'm sorry, but I don't remember anything except how scared I was." She felt bad for letting her dad down. "Have you asked Meira? She might know more."

"Yes, actually, your mom is talking to Meira, and it's okay that you can't remember anything, Bryn. I know how frightened you must have been. But escaping the way you did was very brave. And you were so smart to call your mom."

"You think so?" Bryn gazed into her father's dark eyes, so much like hers. And her mother's. She leaned against him, needing the physical connection. She was afraid to be left alone again. "I'm so glad you found me."

"I'm very grateful for that too." Her dad kissed the top of her head, and she closed her eyes, soaking up his strength.

She didn't know what had happened between her mom and her dad in the year before she was born.

But she knew what she wanted when the danger was over.

Her mom and dad together with her, as a family.

SEPTEMBER 10 – 5:17 *p.m.* – *Washington, DC*

"Jordan?"

He turned toward Sun. He'd been disappointed that Elam hadn't been able to find the flower pattern he'd created in any of the landmarks.

It made him wonder if the guy was hiding something.

"What is it?" He crossed over to where she was seated with the satellite computer. "Did you find something?"

"Did you know Mustaf has a brother?" She gestured to the screen. "Daboor Kadir Mustaf."

A chill snaked down his spine. "So Daboor is likely the one bribing someone here in the US to free his brother."

"I believe so, yes." She stared up at him. "But here's what I don't understand. How would Daboor know about you and Diana and Bryn? How could he have orchestrated Bryn's kidnapping from North Carolina bringing her to Baltimore?"

He frowned. "That's a really good question." He glanced over to make sure Diana was still in Meira's room. "Diana has been working as part of an underground railroad to help Arab women escape their abusive situations. One of them was a woman named Fadia. She was one of Tariq's wives."

Sun's eyes widened. "That's an interesting twist."

"Tell me about it." He couldn't blame Diana for wanting to help women like her mother. "But that link to

Tariq as Diana's cousin doesn't mesh with a man by the name of Daboor."

"No, it does, don't you see?" Sun's gaze held a bit of excitement. "All along we've been wondering why there seem to be two parallel tracks to free Mustaf. Your daughter was kidnapped with the demand being to free him, yet before you could do anything, he was already in the process of being set free by someone else." She stabbed a slender finger to the man on the screen. "By his brother, Daboor."

Jordan nodded slowly. "Okay, I can buy that theory, except there are still holes. Like why these attempts to free him wouldn't be better coordinated?"

"That's been bothering me too. Except now that I know about Tariq, I think it makes more sense. If we operate under the assumption that Diana's cousin is the one who arranged for Bryn's kidnapping, the demand to free Mustaf was extraneous to the true purpose."

"The true purpose being . . ."

Sun looked at him as if he were dense. "To kill you, Diana, and Bryn."

SEPTEMBER 10 – 5:19 p.m. – Baltimore, MD

"Meira, please. I need you to tell me what you remember." Diana didn't quite know what to make of the woman. She owed Meira a huge debt of gratitude for taking good care of Bryn while her daughter was vulnerable and alone at the hands of the kidnappers. And she knew the woman was pregnant and worried about her and Elam's unborn baby.

But she wasn't cooperating the way Diana had expected.

"I have told you everything I know." Meira's soft voice

was firm. "I am but a mere woman, they would not speak freely in front of me and the child. More often than not, we were left alone, with men standing guard outside."

"I was raised in such a household too," Diana said. "And I know that women are often unseen. Men forget we are there and assume we are not paying attention." She'd been so thankful her mother had fought for Diana to attend college, which was where she'd met Jordan.

Before their lives had changed so drastically.

Meira finally lifted her gaze. "I only heard a mention of Syria, nothing more. No names."

"No one mentioned Tariq?" She held her breath, hoping Meira wouldn't recognize her cousin's name.

Meira shook her head. "No. As I said, only Syria was mentioned. I was given the impression that someone in Syria was giving the orders."

"Okay, thank you." Diana offered a wan smile. "And I want to thank you again for how you looked after Bryn. When you are a mother"—she swallowed hard—"you will learn that you will do anything for your child. *Anything*."

"I understand. Your daughter was very brave." Meira placed her hand over her abdomen. "My hope is that my child will be born in freedom and not in oppression."

"I can help, there is a woman who runs a shelter back in North Carolina where I live. She provides new identification for women in your position." They'd never before accepted a woman accompanied by a man, but Diana was determined they would make an exception in this case. "Once this is over, we'll get you and Elam to safety."

Meira nodded. "That would be good."

Diana knew there wasn't anything more to be gained by grilling Meira. She stood and made her way to the doorway.

"Diana?" She looked over her shoulder at Meira. "Thank you."

"As I thank you." She slipped through the door and closed it behind her. Movement caught the corner of her eye, and she frowned when she noticed a dark SUV rolling slowly down the street.

Using her key, she quickly entered the room. "Jordan! I think we've been found." She swallowed hard and added, "I had my cell phone on at first, but then shut it down. Maybe I was too late!"

"Get Bryn and hide in the bathroom with Meira," Jordan said, pulling his weapon from his holster. "Elam and Sun, you're with me."

Diana put her arm around Bryn, urging her daughter toward the small bathroom. Sun already had her gun in her hand. "But Elam isn't armed!"

"I have a knife and a plan, just go!" He looked as if he wanted to say more but headed toward the door.

Diana swallowed hard and urged Bryn into the bathroom, Meira coming up behind her. It was tight with three people, but she didn't care. "Into the bathtub," she whispered. "Both of you."

"But it's still wet," Bryn protested.

Diana pulled a towel off the rack. "Use this, but get in. Hurry. I want you and Meira to lie down in the bottom and don't move no matter what you hear, understand?"

"But, Mom." Bryn's voice wobbled with tears.

"We're going to be fine, just please do as I say." Diana practically shoved Bryn down into the bathtub, then helped Meira inside. This mess was her fault. Why hadn't she turned the phone off right away? Stupid, she'd been so stupid.

She quickly glanced around for something to use as a weapon.

The top of the toilet tank? It was all she could come up with.

She held it in her hands and waited, straining to listen.

Praying Jordan, Sun, and Elam would be okay.

CHAPTER NINETEEN

September 10 – 5:32 p.m. – Baltimore, MD

"Elam, use the knife to slice the tires." Jordan glanced at Sun. "You and I will take the two in the car."

"But she is a tiny woman," Elam whispered in protest. "They'll kill her."

"Trust me, she can hold her own." He didn't hesitate, even knowing he was putting his family's lives on the line by trusting Sun. "Go, hurry."

Elam went to the left, the direction that would place him behind the vehicle, while he and Sun headed toward the right, staying low behind other cars that were parked in front of the motel. The vehicle was rolling slowly through the motel parking lot. It was still light out, so he couldn't help but wonder if this was a test run rather than the real deal.

Grimly, he realized if Diana's keen eye hadn't noticed the vehicle, they would have been taken by surprise.

And possibly killed.

He should have told her to leave the cell phone at the stupid Walmart. Recognizing Elam and seeing his daughter alive and well for the first time ever had been a distraction.

He couldn't afford another.

Jordan paused alongside a truck, trying to come up with a plan. He was tired of playing defense and relished the thought of taking control of the situation.

"We move on three," he told Sun.

"I'll take the driver." A ghost of a smile creased her features.

He wasn't about to argue. "One, two, three!"

Jordan rushed out from behind the truck. Sun was hot on his heels, and she did one of her amazing gymnastic moves, leaping forward, planting her hands on the hood of the moving car, and vaulting over it.

The driver was so startled he stopped the vehicle. Jordan tried to open the passenger side door, but of course it was locked.

The passenger lifted his gun, but two seconds too late. Jordan slammed his gun into the window, shattering it, and grabbed the weapon from the surprised passenger's hand, while at the same time, Sun did the same maneuver on her side.

Elam must have slit the rear tires because at some level he noted the vehicle sank down a couple of inches. After both men were unarmed, Jordan stepped back from the vehicle.

"Get out of the car, slowly."

The two men glanced at each other, then the driver punched the gas. The vehicle lurched forward, but without speed thanks to the rear tires being flatter than pancakes. As if sensing escape was impossible, the driver hit the brakes, then thumped his fist on the steering wheel in frustration.

"Get out!" Jordan shouted. They were drawing stares

from people nearby, and he lifted his voice so it would carry. "FBI! Get out of the car with your hands up!"

Technically, he wasn't FBI anymore, but since he reported to Clarence Yates, he figured that it wouldn't hurt to fudge a bit.

The two men emerged from the vehicle. They were dressed in black from head to toe, much like the other guy who'd come after them in Annapolis. Jordan gestured with the nose of his gun. "Inside the motel room, now."

The two men reluctantly headed in that direction, but then they abruptly sprang apart, darting off in opposite directions.

He lifted his gun but hesitated, glancing over at Sun. She had one of the guys in her sights, too, but hadn't pulled the trigger.

It went against the grain to let them go, but he didn't want to leave the vicinity of the motel. Diana, Bryn, and Meira were vulnerable.

"Let them go," he said on a sigh.

"We need to get away from here," Sun pointed out, gazing at the man who'd disappeared around a corner. "There could be more."

"I know." Jordan glanced at Elam who came up to stand beside him. "But we need a larger vehicle for all of us to fit."

"I can secure us a van," Sun offered. "Give me fifteen minutes and be ready to leave when I return."

"Thanks." Jordan held out his hand for the knife. Elam placed it gently in his palm. "Do you know how to fire a gun?"

Elam shrugged. "I have but prefer not to."

Yeah, frankly he'd prefer not to shoot anyone either, but they needed to be able to defend themselves. "Would you shoot to protect Meira?"

"Yes," Elam said without hesitation.

"I thought so." Jordan led the way back to the motel room. "We'll secure another weapon after we get out of here."

Elam didn't argue. "I will be glad to get out of Baltimore," the younger man said quietly.

He would to. This time, they'd leave Diana's cell phone behind, but the technology to track a cell phone wasn't easy to obtain. He didn't see the terrorist cell having that ability.

So who was behind this latest attempt?

Jordan had no idea but suspected that someone within the multiagency task force Yates had put together was involved.

He glanced back at the vehicle with its flat rear tires and made a note of the plate number. No doubt he'd find the car had been stolen, but maybe, just maybe, there would be a link back to the government.

Diana wouldn't like it, but they needed to head back to DC.

SEPTEMBER 10 – 6:12 p.m. – Washington, DC

"What do you mean you didn't get them?" Of all the incompetent idiots, the two he'd hired to bring in Rashid, the woman, and the brat took the cake. They'd come highly recommended but were clearly useless.

"They got the jump on us."

"They?" He stared out the window at nothing. "He still has help?"

"Yes, and the woman looks fragile, but I can assure you she is not." The man's voice held a note of bitterness. "Somehow they disabled our car too. It was fortunate we managed to escape, not that we would have told them anything," he hastened to add.

"I'm sure." He resisted the urge to let out a string of curses. "And how did you escape, exactly?"

"We, uh, took off running. They didn't shoot at us and didn't follow either."

He narrowed his gaze, thinking that through. Rashid could have easily killed the two idiots, so why hadn't he? And why not give chase? Take the two morons out, permanently? It's what he would have done if the situation was reversed.

Then it dawned on him. Rashid had let them go in an effort to protect the woman and her brat?

They were likely already on the move, far away from the motel in Baltimore. He wanted to rant and rave in frustration but managed to keep his tone even. "You will finish your assignment or I will finish the two of you. Understand?"

"Yes, we're on it."

Doubtful, but what could he do? Disconnecting from the line, he returned to his laptop computer, quickly pulling up the last known location of the woman's phone.

It remained in the exact same location as an hour ago, the motel in Baltimore.

Slamming the laptop shut, he whirled away, panic tightening his chest. Those idiots had cost him his best chance at finding them.

He broke out in a cold sweat. He couldn't allow Rashid to interfere with his plan. There had to be a way to find him.

There just had to be!

. . .

SEPTEMBER 10 – 6:29 p.m. – Washington, DC

Mustaf awoke to the sound of his nurse entering the room. The soles of her shoes squeaked as she approached the bed. "How are you doing, Ahmed? Are you feeling okay?"

The casual way she called him by his given name set his teeth on edge, but he did his best to remain polite. "Yes, I am fine."

"You haven't taken much for pain," she said, her tone lightly scolding. "Are you sure you don't want me to give you something?"

"I'm fine," he repeated, even though he wanted nothing more than to be free of this reverberating pain. But the clock was ticking, and he needed to keep his mind sharp, not foggy with drugs.

"Okay, but your facial expression tells me you're hurting very badly."

It took considerable effort to smooth his expression. "I am a foreigner in a strange land, I refuse to take any of your narcotics."

"You know we're here to help you," she said. "With the soldiers outside your doorway, you're safe here. No one can harm you."

Little did she know. His enemies could infiltrate this hospital much the way his people already had.

He would not be safe until he was out of this place, and far away from the Americans.

SEPTEMBER 10 – 6:37 p.m. – Washington, DC

Yates was startled by the sound of his personal cell phone ringing. Hesitantly, he answered, "Yes?"

"It's Rashid. Someone within your task force is out to kill us."

"There was an attempt on you and Sun?" Yates let out a sigh. "I have my suspicion about someone being on the take, but no proof. There have been too many coincidences over the past thirty-six hours."

"Ya think?" Rashid's voice dripped with sarcasm. "You must suspect someone. I need a name."

"One name? Unfortunately, I have several." Yates didn't like sharing this kind of intel with Rashid. Oh, he trusted the guy, it wasn't that, but he hadn't even confided his suspicions to POTUS.

"Names," Rashid repeated. "There have been too many attempts against us already, and the next one could be the last." There was a pause before he added, "You should know I have Diana Phillips and our daughter Bryn with me now. They were in danger, and well, it's a long story, I can fill you in later. Right now, I need information. I refuse to let anything happen to them."

"Okay, fine." Yates blew out a breath. "Ben Cunningham and Rick Slater are two members of the task force that I have some concerns with. They are both FBI, but there's a third guy, Geoff North, who is on loan from NSA. I don't know much about Geoff, he's a bit of a wild card. So if you want names, those three are at the top of my list."

"Ben Cunningham, Rick Slater, and Geoff North," Rashid repeated. "No one else?"

Yates wasn't used to be questioned. "Don't you think I want answers as much as you do?" he snapped. "I'm dealing with several murders as it is, first Ray Pallone, then Aaron Cooper. If I knew anything more, I'd take care of it myself!"

"Who is Aaron Cooper?" Rashid asked, ignoring his outburst.

Yates scowled. "An administrative assistant here at the FBI. There were witnesses that saw him drinking coffee that was later found to be laced with cyanide."

"Not easy to get your hands on cyanide," Rashid muttered.

"Exactly. The tox screen is still pending, but the ME has already ruled Cooper's death a homicide."

"No camera footage from the coffee shop?"

"No, and that is no coincidence either," Yates said. "Interviews haven't helped yet either."

"I have another question, about FBI Agent Tony Balcome."

Yates frowned. "Why do you want to know about him?"

"I . . . think he's a potential leak within the department."

"Impossible, because he's dead."

"Dead?" Rashid sounded shocked.

"Crashed his car into a concrete barrier going at a high rate of speed two months ago. To be honest, they're suspecting suicide, although the investigation is still ongoing." Yates straightened. "You think Balcome was murdered?"

"Maybe." Rashid hesitated, then asked, "Anything else significant going on that I need to know about?"

"I don't report to you," Yates said dryly.

"No, sir. I report to you, but I can't help if my hands are tied by a lack of information."

Yates hated when Rashid was right. "I'm concerned about Ahmed Mustaf somehow escaping from Washington Hospital."

"I'm sure you have him guarded."

"Yes, by two airmen from Andrews Air Force Base. They're taking Mustaf's being shot rather personally."

Rashid grunted. "I can see why. Is the current theory that his brother, Daboor, is the one behind all of these attempts to free him?"

Yates straightened in his seat. "Yes, why? Do you have a line on that?"

"Not yet, but it's one of the angles we're working on." Rashid paused, then added, "Okay, thank you. I appreciate the information you've shared."

"Don't let me down," Yates said on a wave of exhaustion. "You and Dryer helped us out a few months ago, we wouldn't mind another win for the good guys."

"Security Specialists, Incorporated will do its best to deliver, thanks." Rashid disconnected from the call.

Yates set his phone aside and scrubbed his palms over his face. To have another mole within the task force was disheartening. Balcome may have leaked information in the past, considering Rashid was now protecting Diana and their child. He knew full well the agent had arranged for Diana to be placed into WITSEC, not that he fully understood how they were linked to what was going on.

Balcome might have talked, but not recently. There had to be someone else.

Cunningham, Slater, and North.

Which one had committed treason?

SEPTEMBER 10 – 7:03 *p.m.* – *Washington, DC*

Diana shifted in her spot in the back seat with Bryn, already weary of driving. Traffic was bumper to bumper, worse than usual as they approached DC. She glanced over, reassured to note Bryn was sleeping.

"What is the plan moving forward?" she asked, meeting Jordan's gaze in the rearview mirror.

"Sun is getting us a place to stay, a townhouse with two bedrooms, so that we can avoid hotels."

"And then what?"

"We need to figure out where Elam's explosive devices have been left."

"And if we miss some?"

Jordan's expression turned grim. "Then innocent people will die."

Diana turned to stare out the window. The thought of a terrorist act made her feel sick, yet at the same time, she wanted to turn and run away. She didn't want Bryn to be anywhere near DC when those bombs were detonated. And even if she and Bryn stayed behind, she had to worry about Jordan. What if he happened to be within the blast zone?

She couldn't imagine losing him for a second time. Not now.

"Wouldn't it be better to find the man in charge of detonating the bombs?" She'd been turning this problem over and over in her mind during the long drive back to DC. "If we take him out, then none of the devices will go off."

"Yes, but at this point, Elam doesn't know anything about him."

"Do you think he's being honest with us?" She kept her voice low, hoping Bryn was really asleep. She didn't want her daughter to hear her doubts about her rescuer. Since Sun had been unable to secure a van, they'd ended up in two vehicles. Sun had graciously taken Elam and Meira in her vehicle, leaving the three of them alone.

Now she wondered about them. She owed Elam and Meira a debt of gratitude, but Elam had to know something.

"I do." Jordan's response came without hesitation. "He did his part in slashing the tires back at the hotel. He could have just as easily doubled back and gotten Meira out of there."

"But that's only because I promised to help them get new identities," she protested. "Not because he is determined to stop this terrorist attack."

"Do you know how I met Elam in the first place?" Jordan asked.

She shook her head.

"There's a church in DC that works with Muslims, teaching them about Christianity. When I first met Elam, he seemed sincerely interested in understanding Christianity and how it compared and contrasted with the teachings of the Quran."

"Okay, so how did you know he was your contact, then?"

"I thought he was faking his Christianity, but after meeting up with him again, I realize he truly believes."

She buried a flash of impatience. "That doesn't make him a saint."

"I've heard him talk about God and about asking for forgiveness for the bombs he detonated. I get the sense we can trust him."

Diana wasn't convinced. Meira was different. She trusted the pregnant woman who'd cared for Bryn, who'd kept her daughter safe during captivity.

But she still felt that Elam knew more than he was letting on.

And for this to be over, they needed all the help they could get.

. . .

SEPTEMBER 10 – 7:14 p.m. – Washington, DC

"Are you ready to head down for your MRI scan?"

With confusion, Mustaf pried open his eyes to look at the man leaning over him. He hadn't seen this man before, even though he was dressed in hospital scrubs like all the others. And no one from the medical team had said anything about having an MRI scan. He opened his mouth to ask what was going on, but the man lifted a finger to his lips.

"Don't worry, this won't take too long." As he spoke, he disconnected the wires from the three patches on his chest, then proceeded to remove the patches themselves.

"How long?" He forced the question past his dry throat.

"Less than an hour." The man gave a slight shake of his head, silently indicating Mustaf shouldn't continue talking.

Mustaf forced himself to relax, although his heart was beating rapidly in his chest. Maybe this was part of the plan to rescue him, but he didn't understand how they'd escape the two soldiers standing guard in the hallway.

"Do you have any other metal on you?" the man in scrubs asked. "Any piercings that I need to know about?"

"No." Slowly he began to see the mastery of the plan. He vaguely recalled that MRI scans were giant magnets, which meant no metal was allowed inside the room.

That included guns or other weapons.

"Okay, we're ready to roll." The man pulled his bed away from the wall and pushed him through the open doorway. As before, the two soldiers came to walk beside him, one on each side of the gurney.

"Why is Mustaf having an MRI?" one of the soldiers asked.

"How should I know? I'm just following orders. His doctor ordered an MRI, so that's where we're going."

The soldiers fell silent. The man pushing his bed greeted several staff they passed in the hallway along the way.

Almost as if he really did work here.

"Sorry, you guys will need to stay behind the red line," the man in scrubs said in a cheerful voice.

"We go where he goes," the soldier said sternly.

"No can do. We can't allow anything metal beyond the red line. If you're bored, pull up a YouTube video on the power of an MRI magnet. You'll watch a cop who crossed the line lose his weapon right out of his holster, the gun flying across the room and hitting the magnet. It's pretty impressive."

It took every ounce of willpower not to smile as the man in scrubs pushed him past the red line, leaving the soldiers behind.

The minute the doors closed behind him, the guy stopped the bed. "Get up, we need to take you by foot."

Walk? After having surgery? Mustaf wanted to argue, but there wasn't a moment to waste. He did as instructed, getting out of bed and standing on his own two bare feet.

The man in scrubs handed him clothing, including running shoes. "Get dressed, hurry. We need you far away from here before the hour is up."

Every movement was agony, but not as much as being in jail for the rest of his life. Gritting his teeth, he pulled on the scrubs and the shoes.

He'd do whatever was necessary to obtain the freedom he deserved.

CHAPTER TWENTY

September 10 – 7:41 p.m. – Washington, DC

Jordan paced the length of the small house Sun Yin had directed him to. Where was she? Sun, Elam, and Meira should have been here by now.

They'd ended up with two cars. He'd left with Diana and Bryn first, but Sun and the others had been just a few minutes behind them.

Not fifteen minutes. Had something happened? Had Elam overpowered Sun and taken off with Meira?

No, he felt certain Sun could handle Elam, and Meira wouldn't try much being pregnant. Sun was a master at martial arts, she could disarm Elam as easily as she could squash a bug.

Yet he couldn't get Diana's doubts about Elam out of his mind. As much as he didn't want to believe the man was involved in the terrorist plot to kill so many Americans, he couldn't deny the fact that Diana was right.

Elam had mentioned the terrorist headquarters was known as Liberty. And that it was located in DC.

What else did he know?

When he heard the key in the front door, he shot over, taking position up against the wall just in case. But it was Sun's dark head that entered first, followed by Meira, and lastly Elam.

Jordan rubbed the back of his neck, wondering if he was beginning to lose it. He'd forgotten to make Diana shut down her phone, and now this paranoia. Lack of sleep and constantly being on edge were getting to him.

The weight of finding those involved in the terrorist plot rested heavily on his shoulders.

"Something wrong?" Sun asked, her dark eyes not missing a thing.

"Elam? With me." He jerked his thumb toward the kitchen. Diana and Bryn had taken one of the bedrooms, leaving the other for Elam and Meira.

Sun could have the sofa, since he wasn't planning to sleep much anyway.

"You are angry with me?" Elam asked.

Jordan dropped into a kitchen chair with a sigh. "I need to know the location of Liberty, the main headquarters of the terrorist cell."

Sun came in and sat across from him. "I was asking Elam about the location as we came in. We took a minor detour past the place. It appears deserted, but I'm certain there is more than one way in and out of the building."

He scowled, not liking the fact that they were already a step ahead of him. "Why didn't you say something to me?"

Sun's gaze didn't waver. "Jordan, you've been through a lot these past few hours. Your family is very important, but they are also a distraction. There is no harm in accepting help. When you offered me a position with Security Specialists, Incorporated, I was under the impression we would work as a team."

He sighed. "Okay, fine. Everything you said is true. I've been distracted, and I do view you as an important part of the team."

"Liberty is only ten minutes from here," Elam said. "I will be happy to take you there again." He hesitated, then added, "If they see me, they will kill me. If that should happen, I would ask you to make sure Meira and our baby are safe."

Jordan was secretly relieved his trust wasn't misplaced. "I promise, but they won't get to you, Elam. We just need to know how to get inside."

Elam slowly shook his head. "I cannot help you with that. I was brought in through the main doorway, and the situation was such that I was not able to look around."

"What was the situation?" Jordan asked.

"I was summoned there to be punished by the Master. When they were finished, they took me out the same way, leaving me on the street. I have no knowledge of another way inside."

He felt bad that Elam had suffered at the hands of these men yet felt even worse that Elam was unable to provide anything more to go on. Jordan shifted his gaze to Sun. "You have any thoughts?"

"No, but I haven't had time to examine the place or the surrounding structures more closely." She gestured to one of the two sat computers. Only one was fully charged and ready to go. "I was planning to search for other properties that are owned by the same corporation near or adjacent to Liberty. An added bonus would be to get blueprints of the buildings as well."

"Blueprints would be very helpful." Jordan glanced at his watch and grimaced. "But there's not enough time for that. We need to find a way inside their main headquarters, tonight."

"After dark would be best," Sun agreed. She opened the fully charged computer as Jordan plugged in the backup. Sun glanced at him as she waited for the device to connect to the closest satellite. "Give me a couple of hours, I'll do my best to get what we need."

"Okay." It wasn't as if he had a better plan. Except to drive around to each tourist attraction to see if Elam could find one of his custom-made bombs.

And that would only work if they'd already been planted. If he were the one in charge, he'd have a dozen men each with a device to be planted shortly before the agreed upon detonation time.

At exactly eight forty-six a.m. tomorrow morning.

SEPTEMBER 10 – 8:02 p.m. – Washington, DC

His second-in-command would not fail anyone ever again.

He rose to his feet and swiped the blood from the knife. He wanted to throw the blade across the room.

This wasn't supposed to be happening in this way. They were supposed to be working together and focused on one goal, that being proving once again who was superior.

Certainly not the Americans.

"Amar, I need you to take care of him." He kicked the dead man with the toe of his shoe. "And bring me a replacement."

"Of course." Amar bowed and quickly dragged the dead man from the room.

Tariq glanced around the interior of the warehouse that

served as their headquarters. If he could, he'd move the timeline up. But that was impossible.

As it was, the death count wouldn't be near what they'd seen with 9/11. The most famous attack his father had been connected with.

Then again, planning any level of attack these days was ten times more difficult. The government had tightened the borders to the point that getting in and out without being caught was a monumental task.

No, he wouldn't let himself be distracted by the incompetence surrounding him. The attack would go on as planned.

He would personally see to it.

SEPTEMBER 10 – 8:17 p.m. – Washington, DC

Mustaf sagged against the door of the car, not caring where he was being taken. He closed his eyes and struggled to control the waves of pain crashing over him.

He'd never felt so awful in his entire life. It was as if he was being slowly tortured beyond what the human mind could tolerate.

A flash of anger hit hard. Surely his escape hadn't had to happen this way, with him reeling from pain from surgery to repair the gunshot wound in his abdomen.

"Are you okay?" the driver asked. It was a different man than the one who'd taken him to the MRI scanner. He fleetingly wondered how the hospital worker had gotten away.

The soldiers wouldn't take kindly to losing him as their prisoner.

The idea of the soldiers being upset made him smile.

"Where are we going?" he forced himself to ask to take

command of the situation. He was Ahmed Kadir Mustaf and would be treated with the respect he deserved.

"Your brother sends his regards," the driver said. "I'm taking you to a secret location where no one will find you."

"Good." His eyes drifted closed. Then shot open again. "Is my brother here, in the US?"

"No, but his allies are. Rest now, we will arrive shortly. I can give you something for the pain when you are settled."

Mustaf gladly accepted the opportunity to rest. His previous irritation at how things had progressed melted away.

Daboor had freed him as promised.

This was, indeed, a good day.

SEPTEMBER 10 – 8:24 p.m. – Washington, DC

"I can't find a single blueprint." Sun gave the computer an annoyed shove. "I'm sorry, but we'll have to stake the place out to get the intel we need."

Nothing about these last two days had been easy, why had he thought it would change now? He nodded slowly. "When should Elam and I head out?"

"You?" Sun arched a brow. "Why not me?"

Elam had left to spend time with Meira, so it was only the two of them in the kitchen. He looked at Sun. "Because I need you to stay here to guard Diana and Bryn. They are the most important thing right now. I can't function without knowing they're safe."

Sun leaned forward. "All the more reason I should be the one to go with Elam. Your place is here with your family."

"No." This was his problem, not Sun's.

"As a woman, I'm bound to be underestimated by these

agreement. He rose to his feet and shortened the distance between them to draw her into his arms.

Diana clung to him, and he sensed Sun slipping from the room, leaving them alone.

He buried his face in her hair. "When this is over, we'll go away together, just the three of us. Someplace sunny and warm."

"I'd like that," Diana whispered. "And I know Bryn will too."

He didn't want to let her go, not now, not ever, but that wasn't possible. He forced himself to drop his arms and take a step back.

There was a lot of work looming ahead of him.

And less than twelve hours to get it done.

SEPTEMBER 10 – 9:06 p.m. – Washington, DC

He tensed when his phone rang. He'd been waiting for news on Mustaf for what seemed like forever and wasn't in the mood for more bad news. "Yes?"

"I have Mustaf at the safe house."

The relief was staggering. Finally, things were going his way. "Good. I'm glad to hear it."

"He's in rough shape from the surgery."

Yeah, too bad. He couldn't care less what shape Mustaf was in as long as the guy was alive and kicking. He couldn't deliver a dead guy, now could he? "His brother will be sending arrangements soon. Tell him he'll need to remain strong in order to get out of the United States without being caught."

There was a moment's hesitation. "Yes, of course he will be ready to go when you give the signal."

men," she pointed out with a canny smile. "And you
how much I like using that ridiculous macho attitude
advantage."

The image of petite Sun taking out several big
terrorists made him smile. If he hadn't seen her in actio
himself, he wouldn't believe she was capable of usin
hands and feet as lethal weapons. "Yes, I know. But I s
Arabic better than you."

She wrinkled her nose. "I understand enough to get

"But it's not your area of expertise." Jordan knew
grasp of Arabic and many of the dialects was the re
Yates had asked him to infiltrate the terrorist group in
first place.

"I can speak Arabic too." He turned to see D
standing in the doorway, her expression troubled. "I sh
be there if Tariq is involved."

"Absolutely not." Jordan's knee-jerk reaction came
harsher than he'd intended. "He would kill you with
blinking."

"And you think he'll behave differently toward yo
Diana asked. She ventured farther into the room. "I
found you again, Jordan. I don't want to lose you a seco
time."

Her admission caused his heart to swell with gratitu
but he quickly pushed the emotion aside. He would not p
Diana and Bryn in danger. Not under any circumstance.

"Diana, I don't want to lose you and Bryn either. B
this is my job. I was hired to infiltrate the terrorist cell
promise to be careful." When she looked as if she mig
argue, he added, "It will be easier for me to concentrate o
the task at hand knowing you and Bryn are safe here wi
Sun. Please don't fight me on this."

She stared at him for a long moment before nodding i

"I'll be in touch." He disconnected from the call and then quickly dialed his contact. "I need to speak to Daboor."

"You can speak to me."

His mouth thinned, he hated the arrogance of these people. "Fine. Tell him his brother is out of custody and is being held in a safe house. But things need to move fast if you want him to get safely out of DC."

"Good. You need to make arrangements for private transportation."

"I'll make it happen." Getting Mustaf out of DC wouldn't be a piece of cake. Any moment now, the news of his escape would send all sorts of alarms going off and every freaking governmental agency would be on the lookout for him.

Now, all he needed was for the next phase of his plan to go just as smoothly.

Once the money hit his offshore account, his time in DC was finished. He'd be out of here as soon as possible.

Leaving a disaster in his wake.

SEPTEMBER 10 – 9:16 p.m. – Washington, DC

Jordan inwardly groaned when his phone rang. Yates never called with good news. "What happened?"

"Mustaf escaped from Washington Hospital."

He'd half expected something like this. He straightened in his seat. "How?"

"Someone entered an order for an MRI procedure in his medical record. He was transported down to the radiology department, accompanied by the guards from Andrews Air Force Base. The airmen couldn't go into the MRI suite with him because of the metal on their uniforms, and of course their weapons weren't allowed anywhere close to the magnet either. After thirty minutes, they grew suspicious and demanded to be let inside, but it was too late. Mustaf was gone."

"We need to start following the bribery trail," Jordan said with a sense of urgency. "Someone was paid to enter that order, and someone else was paid to get him to the MRI suite."

"Already being done, but we've hit a dead end. The airmen gave a good description of the guy who transported Mustaf out of the hospital room, but the ID he was wearing was stolen. They're combing through video now to see if they can figure out what vehicle he might be in." Yates sounded frustrated, and Jordan could understand why.

Losing a terrorist who killed dozens of Americans never looked good as the leading news story.

"You have any ideas?" Yates asked.

"There are only so many ways out of the city." Jordan thought fast. If he was trying to move a terrorist who recently had surgery, what would he do?

"I've put all the airports in the DC area on alert for the next twelve hours," Yates said.

Plane? Jordan didn't think that was likely. "I think you should set up roadblocks for vehicles leaving the interstate, including ambulance services. What better way to get Mustaf out of the city to some remote airport? I feel certain they won't try to fly out of DC, expand your alert to all airports within a two-hundred-mile radius on alert."

"Ambulance?" Yates repeated thoughtfully. "You really think so?"

"They can go fast with red lights and sirens, without anyone stopping them. And once he leaves DC, there will be toll cameras to consider. Putting the photo of the guy who took Mustaf out of his room may help pin him down."

"Brilliant, Rashid. We'll get right on it." Yates hung up without saying another word.

"Mustaf escaped." Diana's expression was full of concern.

"Sounds that way." He glanced over to make sure Bryn wasn't within earshot. "Which makes the whole kidnapping scheme unessential."

"Unless the goal wasn't for you to free Mustaf but to get you in a place where you could be held hostage too."

"Yeah." But the pieces of the puzzle still didn't fit properly.

"I think we have to accept that the group behind Bryn's kidnapping is led by Tariq," Diana said thoughtfully. "But maybe using you to free Mustaf was only part of the plan. Maybe the other part of the plan was to keep you from infiltrating the terrorist cell."

That part made sense. "Because they learned of my mission to infiltrate the cell from someone within the joint terrorist task force."

"Yes." Diana regarded him steadily. "I know you and Elam are going to Liberty soon, but maybe me and Sun can try to find the leak."

It went against the grain to bring Diana into his world. Sun, sure, she was tough, but Diana? He didn't want her anywhere near these ruthless people.

But she was smart and knew Arabic.

"Okay." He sat back at the kitchen table and wrote out the three names Yates had provided. "These are the top suspects, but in all honesty, the mole could be someone whom Yates trusts implicitly."

Diana crossed the room and peered over his shoulder. "Benjamin Cunningham, Geoff North, and Rick Slater."

"These two"—he drew an arrow connecting

Cunningham and Slater—"are both FBI. Geoff North is from the NSA."

She blew out a breath. "Finding information on these guys isn't going to be easy. Not when they've been thoroughly cleared by the FBI to receive classified information."

"No, it won't be easy." He figured Sun and Diana would spin their wheels while he and Elam scoped out the terrorist cell headquarters. He added a phone number. "This is the personal cell number for Clarence Yates, Director of the FBI."

Diana stared at the number for a moment, then met his gaze. "You mean, if anything happens to you."

That was exactly what he'd meant, but he didn't say it. "Nothing's going to happen." He turned toward Elam who was hovering in the doorway. "Ready to go?"

The man nodded.

He drew Diana to her feet and gave her a quick kiss. "I'll be back as soon as possible."

Elam fell into step beside him as they headed for the door. He glanced back at Diana, struck by the need to see Bryn one last time.

Ignoring the deep sense of foreboding, he led the way outside, making a silent promise to see his family again, very soon.

CHAPTER TWENTY-ONE

September 10 – 9:55 p.m. – Washington, DC

Mustaf was roused from sleep by someone shaking his shoulder. Fighting a fresh wave of pain, he grabbed the man's wrist in a tight grip.

"Stop." The word came out harsh and rough through his dry throat.

The man easily broke free of his grasp, making Mustaf feel even more weak and pathetic. Two words that were normally not associated with him. He glared at the man who'd come to rescue him. "Watch yourself," he warned.

The man smirked. "For someone so dependent on others, you should be more grateful."

Mustaf didn't bother to dignify that with a response.

"Get up. The ambulance is here."

Gritting his teeth, Mustaf forced himself up and into a sitting position. The room spun dizzily around him, but he managed to stay upright. As much as he didn't want to force his weary and battered body to move, much less walk across the room and outside into a vehicle, he found himself glad they were moving onto the next leg of the journey.

Staying in one place for too long was a good way to get caught.

And he intended to never get captured and imprisoned again.

"Do you need help?" The question held a note of sarcasm.

He wished he had the strength to strike the man for his imprudence, but it took everything he had to maintain what little dignity he had left. Without answering, he rose to his feet and took a couple of shaky steps.

The man turned and led the way down the hall and to the front door. Through the window, he could see the rectangle-shaped ambulance sitting in the driveway, the red and white lights whirling.

Two men had brought a gurney out of the back of the ambulance and were wheeling it up to the house. Mustaf stood where he was, glaring at his rescuer.

There had been no reason to make him get up and walk if they were taking him out of here on a gurney. He muttered a Syrian curse, not caring if his rescuer heard or not. When the two men brought the gurney inside, he gladly headed toward it.

"He's all yours," his rescuer said.

The two men were dressed as paramedics. Whether they had any actual training or not was debatable. Still, Mustaf wasn't in a position to argue. It appeared his rescuer was handing him off to this pair.

Fine with him.

Lying on the gurney, he suffered through the bumps and jostles as they wheeled him outside and lifted him up and into the ambulance.

"Where are we going?" he finally asked.

"Virginia."

He closed his eyes, envisioning the map of the DC and surrounding area in his mind. Virginia was as good of a place as any.

But he wouldn't be able to relax until he was back in his homeland of Syria.

SEPTEMBER 10 – 10:14 p.m. – Washington, DC

The trip to Liberty didn't take long, even as they took a circular route to avoid being followed, but they wasted time searching for a good place to leave the car and making their way back to the building on foot.

When Elam had told him which structure was the terrorist headquarters, Jordan had been surprised. It wasn't really a warehouse the way he'd thought.

The way the others had been.

It was a two-story brick building, but it didn't look like a house. More like a place that might house several small business suites inside.

He found a spot across the street that provided a decent view of the door. "There must be two ways into the building, one from the back and one from the front."

"I only know the front." Elam's gaze was full of fear. "They will kill us if they find us."

Jordan knew the man had every right to be afraid. "We won't be found."

Elam edged farther behind him. He remembered what the guy had said about the beating he'd sustained. These men didn't kill quickly, preferring to torture their subjects.

"Stay here," he whispered. "Send me a text if anyone shows. I'm going to check things out around back."

Elam gave a brief nod, indicating he understood.

Jordan stared for a moment at the front of the building.

The hour wasn't that late, yet there wasn't a single light on inside. The place looked deserted, but he knew it might be that the windows had been blacked out so that no lights or movement could be seen.

He needed to know one way or the other.

Staying in the shadows was second nature. After all, his years of working in the field had taught him well. He took his time, knowing that to rush was to risk exposure.

Making a wide berth around the block, Jordan eventually found a spot in which he could view the back door. It looked just as deserted as the front had been.

He glanced at his phone. No text from Elam.

After watching the place for a few minutes, Jordan decided he needed to get closer. If the windows had been blacked out, the occupants inside could be having a full-blown party and they'd never know it.

If the windows weren't blocked out, then maybe it was time to find a way to get inside.

Staying low, he stealthily crept up to the building. Up close, he strained to listen but heard nothing.

Had they soundproofed the place as well? Maybe.

Steeling his resolve, he slid over to the closest window. Drawing a deep breath, he peered through, bracing himself for the doors to bust open and for dozens of terrorists to come flooding out to grab him.

It didn't happen. The window wasn't blacked out either. In fact, the room he was looking into was empty.

Which didn't mean the entire building was empty, but it still seemed odd. He sent a quick text to Elam.

It was time to break in.

SEPTEMBER 10 – 10:48 p.m. – Washington, DC

"Mommy!"

Hearing Bryn's cry had Diana rushing into the bedroom. "I'm here, baby. You're okay. Everything is okay."

Bryn looked around wildly for a moment before throwing herself into her mother's arms. "I had a nightmare," she whispered.

Diana's heart squeezed tight. She stroked Bryn's hair. "I'm sorry. Would you like to talk about it?"

Bryn shook her head but didn't loosen her grip. "I wanna go home," she whispered.

Diana swallowed hard. "I know, me too. Hopefully, we'll be able to do that very soon."

Bryn took several deep breaths and lifted her head. "Where's Dad?"

It was humbling how easily Bryn accepted Jordan as her father. Maybe it was easier for her under these dire circumstances. Of course, the fact that she didn't have a father figure in her life was an added bonus.

Diana had always known, especially lately with Bryn's less than subtle hints, that her daughter had wanted a father. Even a stepfather would do.

But to have her biological father a part of her life? Added bonus.

"He's checking some leads." Diana didn't think Bryn needed to know about how Elam and her father had gone to the terrorist cell headquarters. The poor kid was having nightmares already, knowing the level of danger Jordan was facing would only make them worse.

Bryn frowned. "He'll be back soon though, right?"

"I'm not sure exactly when he'll be back, but we have Sun here with us, so don't worry, okay?" She smoothed Bryn's hair from her face. "Try to get some sleep."

"I don't want any more nightmares."

"I know you don't. Maybe praying will help."

"That's a good idea," Bryn admitted, stretching out on the bed. "I prayed a lot when those men had me in that awful room."

The admission made Diana's heart swell with love. "I'm glad to hear that, baby. I know I took comfort in knowing God was watching over you."

"I used to think God sent Meira to stay with me so I wouldn't be all alone."

"I'm sure God had something to do with Meira being there with you during that difficult time," Diana agreed. She definitely owed Meira a debt of gratitude. "Rest now. I'll sit with you for a while."

Bryn yawned and nodded, her eyes drifting shut. Diana thought it likely Bryn hadn't slept well while being held against her will and hoped that her daughter would feel more like her usual self come morning.

Sun appeared in the doorway, her expression grave. Alarmed, Diana eased away from Bryn and went over to join her.

"What is it?" Diana whispered, glancing nervously toward Bryn's room. She'd only partially closed the door, wanting to be able to hear if the little girl suffered another nightmare.

"I've seen the same SUV pass by the house twice," Sun said. "I think we need to get out while we can."

Get out? Leave the safe house? "Are you sure? How do you know the two SUVs are the same? Did you see their license plates?"

"I know they are the same because the plates are covered with mud." Sun glanced over her shoulder at Bryn. "You grab Bryn, I'll get Meira."

Diana didn't waste any time. She shook the girl awake and put a finger to her lips. "Shh. We need to leave."

Bryn's eyes filled with horror and fear, but she didn't say a word. Instead, she shoved her feet into her running shoes and drew on the dark blue hoodie Jordan had purchased for her.

Diana put her arm around Bryn and guided her out of the bedroom and toward the back door. Where she stopped abruptly. A tall Arab-looking man stood there, inside their safe house, holding a gun. Instinctively, she shoved Bryn behind her.

"Hello, cousin."

Diana's blood congealed with fear. The man's eyes bored into hers with eerie familiarity. She wanted to respond, but her throat was frozen.

Tariq had found them.

SEPTEMBER 10 – 10:53 *p.m.* – *Washington, DC*

"We need to get back," Jordan said. "I don't like the way we found the terrorist headquarters empty and seemingly abandoned."

There had been nothing left inside, other than maybe dust. Seeing the interior for himself gave him a nagging itch along the back of his neck.

Something was wrong. Very wrong.

Elam looked grateful as they hurried to the car. There was no need for stealth now, but he still made a couple of turns on the way back to the safe house. He thought about calling Yates and asking for a crime scene team to go to the building, just in case there may be a spare fingerprint that had been left behind.

But first he wanted—needed—to get to Diana and Bryn.

As he approached the street where their safe house was located, a black SUV parked on the road a few yards down from the place Sun had obtained for their use stood out like a sore thumb. At the last minute, he wrenched the steering wheel to the side, making a tight right corner at the intersection in an effort to avoid driving straight toward it. In that brief moment, he'd noticed the license plate was darkened out somehow.

His heart slammed against his rib cage.

The women were in trouble.

SEPTEMBER 10 – 10:58 p.m. – Washington, DC

"I told you, Jordan's not here." Diana had been doing her best to stall Tariq. "I'm not sure what you hope to accomplish."

Only she did know. Tariq wanted her dead. And Bryn and Jordan dead too.

But he didn't know about Sun.

She hoped.

"Please, let my daughter go. She's innocent. It's me you want, isn't it?" Once Diana had found her voice, she'd purposefully spoken loud enough so her words would carry.

"None are innocent," Tariq said with a sneer. "I will kill all."

Fear churned her stomach, but she tried not to show it. "It's over, Tariq. Mustaf has already escaped. That's what you'd wanted all along, wasn't it?"

"You know nothing of what I want. Now back up, slowly." Tariq ignored her questions, and she couldn't seem to tear her gaze from the business end of his gun. If she made him too angry, there was nothing to stop him from simply shooting her and Bryn.

She'd sent up a silent prayer the minute she'd recognized Tariq. But she didn't have any idea what God's plan was, leaving her determined to do whatever possible to stay alive long enough for Sun to make her move.

Or for Jordan and Elam to return.

Or both. *Please, God, please?*

There was the barest hint of movement behind Tariq. She did her best to keep her gaze focused on Tariq and the gun. She took one step back and then another, reluctantly giving him space to enter the room. Bryn gripped the back of her shirt tightly, and Diana thought she could hear her daughter softly sobbing.

But there was nothing she could do to reassure Bryn they'd be okay.

"Jordan works for the FBI, shooting a Federal Agent is a big deal. They won't rest until you're found. Are you really sure this is a smart move to make?"

"Shut up!" Tariq's abrupt shout startled her so badly she stepped back and tripped over Bryn, the two of them falling to the floor.

At the same time, something struck Tariq hard in the back of his head. His body jerked, then he dropped the gun and fell to the ground.

Sun ran forward, scooped up the weapon. She gestured to the back door that Tariq had used to come inside. "Let's go. Now!"

Scrambling to her feet, she helped Bryn up. "What about Meira?" Diana couldn't help glancing down at Tariq. He lay perfectly still, his eyes closed as if he'd been killed on the spot.

But how? What had Sun hit him with?

"She's behind you, hurry! The black SUV is still sitting

out front, there's no telling how long before the others will come inside to check on him."

Others? That was enough to spur Diana into action. Hauling Bryn close, she urged her daughter to follow Sun outside. She sensed Meira hovering close behind, oddly enough carrying one of the satellite computers, and risked a quick glance over her shoulder to be sure. Meira's posture was tense, indicating she might be upset, and Diana knew how she felt. She didn't necessarily want to leave without Jordan either.

But staying wasn't an option.

Sun moved with a silent grace Diana admired, holding her weapon ready as they made their way out into the very small backyard that was shared with the home adjacent to theirs. Diana saw a tree in one corner and wished she'd taken a better inventory of the backyard when they'd first arrived.

She'd gotten soft over the recent years of being in witness protection. In the beginning, she'd had trouble sleeping and had constantly looked over her shoulder everywhere she went. Had expected to see Tariq around every corner.

The reality of seeing Tariq with a gun had been worse than her imagination. Especially since he'd changed his features. But not his eyes.

She'd always remember his eyes.

Sun lifted a hand. Diana instantly stopped, once again edging Bryn behind her. She listened intently but couldn't hear whatever had caught Sun's attention.

"Jordan?" Sun's whisper was so soft Diana wondered if she'd imagined it.

"Sun? What happened? Where are Diana and Bryn?"

"Here." She stepped forward and noticed there was a dark shadow beneath the tree. "We're fine."

"But we need to move," Sun interjected. "One man is down, but there are more outside."

"I know, I saw them too. This way." Jordan and Elam stepped out from beneath the tree.

"Elam," Meira whispered in relief.

There wasn't time for a tearful reunion. Diana and Bryn followed Sun and Jordan to the vehicle they'd parked on another block. Meira and Elam were close behind them.

It would be a tight fit for all of them in the car, but no one voiced a single complaint. When they were finally on the road, Diana reached over to tap Jordan's shoulder.

"It was Tariq who found us, although I have no idea how he found the location of the safe house."

"Tariq?" Jordan's voice rose in alarm. "Are you sure it was him?"

"Positive. I recognized his eyes, and he greeted me by calling me *cousin*." She glanced at Sun who was squished up against the opposite door. The men had taken the front, leaving the three women and Bryn in the back. "Sun took him out with a single blow. How did you do that?"

"A well-placed kick to his cervical spine, near the base of his skull. It paralyzes them from the neck down and, in some circumstances, causes intercranial hemorrhage."

Jordan hit the brake, bringing the car to a halt along the side of the road. "I need to go back."

Diana gaped at him. "Are you crazy? You can't go back there."

Jordan exchanged a knowing glance with Elam. "If he has the trigger device to detonate all the bombs that have been placed somewhere in DC, then I need to get it before they do."

The realization sank deep. He was right. They had to go back.

She swallowed hard. "Okay, we'll all go."

Jordan did a quick Y-turn and went back the way they came. When he pulled over the second time, he glanced over at them. "I'm going in while the rest of you stay here. If I'm not back in ten minutes, Elam will get you someplace safe."

No! Diana didn't want to let Jordan go alone, but glancing at Bryn and Meira, she couldn't argue. They didn't deserve to be put in danger.

"I'll give you ten minutes," she said hoarsely.

Jordan met her gaze, nodded, and slid from the vehicle. Within seconds, he was out of sight.

SEPTEMBER 10 – 11:19 p.m. – Washington, DC

Jordan approached the safe house from the rear, keeping all senses on alert. He wasn't sure how long the men in the car out front would wait but suspected it wouldn't be long.

Holding his weapon ready, and hearing nothing from inside the place, he silently entered the townhouse. Tariq was lying on the floor where he'd fallen, the stench of death horribly familiar.

Ignoring it, he forced himself to approach the body. He checked for a pulse, thinking they could call 911 if there was a way to save him, but there was no pulse. He then checked Tariq's pockets. He found cash, which he took, and a phone, which he also took. He hesitated, wondering if there was something he was missing. What would the trigger look like? He ran his hands over Tariq's western clothes but didn't find anything hidden in the seams. Tariq wasn't wearing any jewelry either.

No trigger meant that it was still out there, somewhere.

Ready and able to be used by whomever Tariq may have put in charge.

CHAPTER TWENTY-TWO

September 11 – 12:21 a.m. – Washington, DC

Mustaf didn't like being strapped onto the gurney in the back of the ambulance, but of course, he tolerated the bumpy ride without complaint. Waves of pain washed over him, making time irrelevant. He had no idea the day, the hour, or even where he was other than somewhere in DC. The occasional glimpse of houses and buildings visible beyond the two windows located in the back doors of the ambulance were meaningless.

He much preferred the helicopter as a way of being transported from point A to point B.

Better yet, he should never have been captured by his enemies while in Libya in the first place. He wrestled back a flash of anger.

He couldn't think about revenge now. Not until he was safely back in his own country with his own people.

Which needed to happen, soon.

When the ride smoothed out a bit, and he thought it was likely because they'd hit the interstate, he closed his eyes and tried to breathe through the pain.

"Uh-oh." The voice came from the driver.

The pretend paramedic sitting across from him leaned forward. "What's wrong?"

Mustaf tensed and opened his eyes. Was there no part of this rescue that would go smoothly?

"Looks like there are roadblocks set up on the exit ramps."

The man seated across from him waved a hand. "Doesn't matter, they're not going to stop ambulances."

"I guess." The guy was silent for a few miles, then swore loudly. "They are stopping ambulances! The exit I just passed had an ambulance stopped even though the red lights were flashing indicating they had a patient on board." The driver sounded concerned. "Do you think they're looking for us? For our patient?"

There was a long pause before the guy seated across from him replied, "I don't see how they could know about him. The roadblock could be related to something else completely."

"Don't be naive," the driver snapped. "Who else would they set up roadblocks for all along the interstate at this late hour? I'm telling you, they're out there searching for that VIP we have back there."

Mustaf could feel the man's gaze boring into him. He turned to stare back. "You have been paid well for your assistance in getting me out, yes?"

The guy glanced away. "Yeah."

"Then it is your job to get me past the roadblocks, is it not?" Mustaf continued glaring at him until the guy reluctantly nodded.

Idiots, both of them, but he didn't have any choice but to trust they could accomplish their mission.

Being detained at a US federal prison was not an

option.

SEPTEMBER 11 – 12:28 a.m. – Washington, DC

"I think I've found a new place for us to stay for what's left of the night," Sun said. "It's only five minutes from here."

"I need to understand how Tariq found the previous safe house," Jordan said.

"Me too," Diana added. Being crammed in the back seat with Bryn beside her wasn't the worst thing in the world. Having Bryn close was reassuring, especially since she couldn't get the vision of Tariq holding a gun on them out of her mind.

And tiny little Sun had taken him down without a weapon. She really needed Sun to show her how to do that.

"Elam? Any ideas?" Jordan's voice held an underlying note of steel. It took Diana a minute to realize that Jordan suspected Elam had somehow led the terrorist cell to their safe house.

Which was crazy since Elam had gone to great lengths to free his pregnant wife, Meira, and Bryn. He'd blown up a parking structure for Pete's sake.

An action Elam hadn't taken lightly.

"I do not know," Elam said in a low calm tone. "However, it could be that they had someone watching Liberty Bell and, when we drove past the first time, followed us back to the safe house."

"Despite the way we did our best not to be tailed?" Jordan challenged.

Elam shrugged. "With two vehicles, they could easily do such a thing without our noticing."

"I didn't see two cars back at the safe house," Jordan said.

"Tariq may have had one nearby," Diana felt compelled to point out. "It's not like we took the time to search for one."

"Elam did not call them." Meira's voice was soft but firm. "It's insulting of you to think such a thing."

Jordan met Meira's gaze in the rearview mirror. "I almost lost Diana and Bryn. I'll risk being insulting to get to the bottom of what happened."

It warmed her heart to hear Jordan talk about her and Bryn as if he cherished them. "Please, Jordan, you must see Meira is right. If Elam was going to turn us in, he would have had several opportunities long before now. And he wouldn't risk anything happening to Meira."

"I didn't accuse Elam of turning us in," Jordan said curtly. "I was wondering if he had some sort of tracking device on his person that he doesn't know about. After all, we were found at the motel too."

The implication of a hidden tracking device made Diana shiver. That would not be good. And why would the device only be on Elam? Why not Meira or even Bryn?

As if reading her thoughts, Meira said, "I have checked my garments very closely and have found nothing that might be a tracking device."

"For me, as well," Elam said. "The Master always contacted me via phone. I would think any possible tracking would have been done via the device. They knew I would answer at any time, day or night, as they had Meira. I left the phone in the backpack at the store once the child had made her call."

"Jordan? Turn right up ahead," Sun said, interrupting

them. "The motel is only a couple of blocks down from the corner."

"I see it," Jordan said. He made the turn, then glanced at the man seated beside him. "I'm sorry, Elam, but I had to ask."

Elam inclined his head but didn't say anything more.

"Elam, I want to thank you again for rescuing Bryn." Diana felt the need to try to smooth things over. "And I thank you, Meira, for taking good care of Bryn while the two of you were being held in that horrible place."

"I would never abandon a child." A hint of reproach laced Meira's tone.

"I know." Diana thought back to the brief interaction she had with her cousin Tariq. A man who didn't care about anyone, not even the life of a young child.

She should be upset that he was dead, but she wasn't. Deep down, she knew Tariq was responsible for killing other people. How many, she couldn't be sure, but in the twelve years she'd been in hiding from him? Many.

No, she would not mourn Tariq's passing. She hadn't wished him dead, prison would have been fine with her, but she would always do whatever was necessary to protect herself.

The most important thing was for her and Bryn to be safe.

And Jordan too.

SEPTEMBER 11 – 12:58 *a.m.* – *Washington, DC*

The sound of a ringing phone dragged him from sleep. With a muttered curse, he answered it. "What?"

"There are roadblocks preventing the transport of our

VIP off the interstate. We're at a rest stop now because we don't want to be caught."

It took a moment for the news to sink into his sleep-deprived brain. "Roadblocks?"

"They are stopping all vehicles, including ambulances."

He dragged a hand through his hair and resisted the urge to put his fist through the wall. How had this happened? Who had the power to put up that many roadblocks?

His boss, of course.

A fluttery panic hit hard, and his temper snapped. "What am I paying you for? To get our cargo safely to the Richmond airport. The rest is for you to figure out. Create a diversion of some sort or find another way through the roadblock."

There was a pause before the guy muttered, "Yes, sir."

He disconnected from the call and threw the phone aside, rising to his feet and stalking across the room.

Sleep would be impossible now. He couldn't believe Yates had remained one step ahead of him.

Yates knew Mustaf had escaped and had assumed they'd use an ambulance. He mentally kicked himself for not changing the mode of operation, but it was too late now.

Those idiots were wasting time, sitting at a rest stop. He had an idea and spun around to grab the phone. He called his contact back. "Okay, here's how you're going to beat the roadblock."

After explaining what he wanted done, the guy had the audacity to argue. "How are we going to manage that?"

"Find a way!" he shouted, then quickly disconnected the call.

He needed Mustaf to reach his next destination, and soon. Or he wouldn't have the cash transferred into his offshore accounts in time for him to disappear before the big event.

Those idiots better not fail him now.

SEPTEMBER 11 – 2:19 a.m. – Washington, DC

Jordan couldn't sleep. Diana and Bryn were sharing one bed in the motel, leaving him the other. Elam and Meira had requested their own room.

Sun had chosen to sleep in the SUV. He suspected that she was tired of being crammed in with the rest of them.

He couldn't blame her.

Except she had their one and only satellite computer with her, leaving him with nothing but his whirling thoughts for company. He should have grabbed the other one when he'd gone back for the trigger device.

Too late for regrets now.

Tariq's death wasn't at all reassuring. In fact, just the opposite. Now Jordan had no idea who held the trigger for the devices and no idea where the multitude of bombs Elam had made were located.

He also didn't know where Mustaf was and what role his carefully orchestrated escape played in all of this.

And worst of all, he didn't know who inside the multiagency task force was being paid off to allow this to happen.

It all made his head hurt.

Diana had pulled him aside after they'd arrived and let him know she didn't like the way he'd gone at Elam. Easy for her to defend the guy, but he didn't know the first thing about him.

And knowing Diana and Bryn were at Tariq's mercy had shaken him to the core.

He turned to see Diana ease out from beside Bryn.

They'd all taken to sleeping with their clothes on since it made for a quick getaway if needed.

"Is something wrong?" she whispered.

So many things, but that wasn't what she meant. "No, I'm fine. Go back to sleep."

She rested her head against his shoulder, and he pulled her into his arms as if they'd been together for years, instead of reunited for just two days. "I'm glad Tariq is dead."

He'd wondered how she was dealing with seeing her cousin face-to-face after all this time. "Me too."

"Do you think God is upset with us for feeling like this?"

"No." His response was instinctive. "It's not like we're happy he's dead so much as relieved he's no longer a threat."

"Yeah." Her tone sounded uncertain. "Although, I felt a surge of satisfaction the moment Sun kicked him and he went down."

He rested his cheek on her hair. "There is some sort of poetic justice that he was taken down by a woman as small as Sun."

"Exactly. After listening to his wife, Fadia, I know he's hurt so many people, more women than men." She hesitated, then added, "You know how some people are truly evil, all the way through? That was Tariq. A trait he shared with his father, Omar."

He didn't doubt her. "Try not to think about it."

Diana shifted in his arms, tilting her head back so she could see him in the dim light from the moon. "I asked him to spare Bryn because she's innocent, and you know what he said? None are innocent, and he'd kill them all. He would have killed me, Meira, Bryn, and Sun without a second thought."

He tightened his grip, hating that she'd had to face

Tariq like that without his being there to help protect them. "I'm sorry."

She gazed up at him for a long moment. "You know what I regretted the most in those few minutes that I thought I might die?"

He shook his head, unable to answer.

"This." She reached up to draw him down for a kiss.

Her lush mouth tasted sweet, and he wanted nothing more than to steal this time alone with her. To kiss her and hold her the way he hadn't for the past twelve years.

He loved her.

Had actually never stopped loving her. Despite believing she'd betrayed him. The way he'd held on to her obituary all these years confirmed that his heart had always belonged to Diana.

Not that he intended to tell Sloan that what he'd felt for Shari was less than what he had with Diana. Or maybe different was a better word.

"Mommy?"

Bryn's voice drew them apart. He pressed another kiss on Diana's temple before releasing her.

"I'm here, baby." Diana quickly crossed over to the bed.

"Where's Daddy?"

For a moment, he was so shocked to hear Bryn ask about him he couldn't move. "Here." His voice was low and rough, partially from kissing Diana and partially because Bryn had called him Daddy.

Daddy!

He'd never get tired of hearing that. He joined them, hovering behind Diana as she knelt beside the bed, stroking Bryn's hair.

"I thought you left me."

His chest tightened painfully. "Never. We'll never

leave you, Bryn." It was a rash promise, considering so many things were beyond his control, but he made it anyway.

He wasn't going to allow anything to happen to either of them.

"Okay, I'm glad." Her voice sounded faint, as if she were about to fall back asleep. Then she surprised him by adding, "We're going someplace fun when this is over, right?"

He glanced at Diana for help, and she nodded. "Yes, of course we are." He couldn't imagine anywhere else he'd rather be. "Where would you like to go?"

Bryn yawned and blinked groggily. "Maybe we could ride roller coasters."

"I love roller coasters. Disney has plenty of them if you'd like to go there."

Bryn smiled. "I'd like that."

"Me too," Diana added. "Try to get some sleep, okay, baby?"

"'Kay." Their daughter's big brown eyes drifted closed, and soon her breathing deepened.

Jordan stepped back, feeling as if he'd been handed the moon and the stars and everything in between.

Time alone with Diana and Bryn would be the best gift a man could be given. And he wanted that time more than anything.

But first he needed to put a stop to whatever evil plan had been put into motion.

SEPTEMBER 11 – 3:25 *a.m.* – *Washington, DC*

Mustaf must have fallen asleep because he was rudely awoken by someone shaking his shoulder. "Get up."

"What?" He didn't understand. Had he missed something? Had they reached their final destination?

"Get up!" It was the man who had been sitting in the back with him. "You have to crawl under the gurney."

"No." He batted the guy's hand away. Enough was enough. He was recuperating from surgery without the benefit of pain medicine and was fed up with these rude Americans.

He deserved respect. Would *demand* respect.

"Do you want to get out of DC or not? Get under the cot or we'll leave you here to be recaptured."

Once again a wave of helpless fury hit hard. But what choice did he have? It galled him to admit how much he needed them.

The ambulance was stopped. He frowned, wondering where they were. Somewhere along the highway, he assumed, since the roadblocks were covering the exit ramps.

"Where are we?"

"A rest stop, where we've been hiding since we learned of the roadblocks. Now get moving!"

Pushing himself up onto his elbows, he noted the back door of the ambulance was open. Outside, a man was pulling a woman toward the vehicle. It took only a moment to register she was large with child.

"Hurry," the guy said impatiently.

Realization dawned, and he understood the plan. Didn't particularly like it, but understood it. With a grunt, he rolled off the gurney and onto the ambulance floor. Pain sent a red haze over his eyes, and he simply lay there for a moment, unwilling to move.

"Get under the cot."

He pried his eyes open. "There isn't enough room."

"Here." The fake paramedic lifted the side rail, revealing more room underneath.

Moving awkwardly, Mustaf managed to slither beneath it. When the side rail came back down, he felt as if he were trapped in a prison cell.

"No, let me go! Stop! Please, my baby. Let me go!"

The woman's cries were loud enough to attract attention, and the idiot who had her must have realized it too.

"Shut up or I'll shoot you in the belly right now."

The woman stopped crying.

There were more jostling movements as the two men negotiated her up and into the back of the ambulance. Mustaf could feel the gurney move as she was set on top of it.

"Do as you're told and you'll live. Continue fighting and we'll kill you and the kid you're carrying. Understand?"

"Yes." The woman's voice was a mere whisper.

There was a loud noise as the back of the ambulance was shut, and within minutes, the vehicle was moving again.

Despite his discomfort, Mustaf smiled.

The pregnant woman would assist them in getting through the roadblock without a problem.

Maybe these men weren't as useless as he'd thought. He might make it back to Syria after all.

CHAPTER TWENTY-THREE

September 11 – 5:30 a.m. – Washington, DC

Jordan awoke when his cell phone rang. He felt around for his phone, then squinted at the number.

Yates. This couldn't be good.

"Rashid," he whispered so as not to wake Diana and Bryn.

"A pregnant woman was taken from a rest station roughly two hours ago." Yates got straight to the point. "When we sent out the word to the checkpoints, one of the cops admitted to letting an ambulance through carrying a pregnant woman who was unusually silent as they checked the vehicle."

Jordan felt a wave of helplessness wash over him. "Mustaf got away."

"I believe so." Yates paused, then added, "Not only did we let an innocent woman and her unborn child get kidnapped, I'm very much afraid we'll never find him."

He glanced over to where Diana and Bryn were sleeping. Easing away, he made his way into the bathroom where he could talk without disturbing them. "They have to be taking him to an airport."

"I already have them all on high alert," Yates said wearily. "But that hasn't stopped them so far, has it? You were right about the ambulance, but they got through anyway. Who knows what tactics they'll use to fly him out of here?"

"Only because they're heartless enough to use a pregnant woman." He felt sick at the thought of the poor woman being found dead when she was no longer needed. "How could we have anticipated something like that?"

Yates didn't answer. Jordan sighed, knowing it was Yates's job to do just that. Anticipate every possibility. He felt bad for the guy, knowing how much pressure he must be under.

"Any idea where the strike will take place?" Yates asked.

Jordan sighed. "No. Any or all of the monuments could be potential targets."

"There has to be a way to stop this." Yates sounded desperate. Jordan could relate.

"We're trying our best." He thought back to the bombs Elam had made, the one with the odd row of flowers design that stuck out as different from the rest. "You should know that Sun took out a man named Tariq Omar Haram Shekau at our last safe house. He is high up on your terrorists watch list."

"When and where?" Yates asked with sharp interest.

He filled the FBI director in on the details of how Sun had taken out Tariq. "I went back to search for the trigger for the bombs but didn't find it."

"Which means it's still out there," Yates said in a grim tone. "You need to find it."

"I know." Too bad he didn't have a single workable clue.

"Getting Tariq might be the only bright spot in this whole fiasco. Call me as soon as you know something."

"I will." Jordan disconnected from the call. Since he was up, he quickly used the facilities and showered, feeling slightly more human when he emerged fifteen minutes later.

Diana and Bryn hadn't moved. For a moment he gazed down, watching them sleep. He thought about what Tariq had said about none were innocent and he'd kill them all.

But he was wrong. Kids were innocent. They didn't deserve to be used as bait, or worse, murdered. He thought of his mother, the way she'd taken him to the amusement park when he was young. The same way he'd planned to take Bryn.

In that moment it clicked. The row of flowers bomb Elam had made was something he'd seen before at the carousel in the amusement park.

No. Was that really possible? Would Tariq have cold-bloodedly planted bombs at a local amusement park?

He pulled out his phone and called Sun. "Bring the sat computer in ASAP."

"Okay." She sounded sleepy.

He paced the length of the room, waiting impatiently until Sun tapped lightly at the door. He pulled it open and gestured for Sun to come inside.

"What time is it?" Diana asked groggily from the bed.

"Early." He took the computer and waited impatiently for the device to pick up a signal. Then he typed in amusement parks in DC, and his heart dropped to the soles of his feet when he realized there were several.

"What are you looking for?" Sun asked, leaning over his shoulder.

"That row of flowers design Elam made might be something from one of those merry-go-round rides." He pulled up each amusement park's website until he found two of them that had carousel rides. "Like a border that might be on the sit-down section or on one of the horses."

At least there were only two parks with merry-go-rounds. He glanced up at Sun. "Get Elam, hurry. We need him to tell us which one of these is the target."

Sun nodded and slipped out of the hotel room. Diana crossed over to him, running her fingers through her tousled hair. "You found something?"

"Maybe." He couldn't say for sure, but it all seemed to make sense.

Diana glanced at the image on the screen and paled. "No. He wouldn't."

"Why not? Didn't he tell you none are innocent and he'd kill them all?" Jordan felt certain he was on the right track. "What would the country see as a worse attack than nine eleven? Killing our children. That's what."

"Dear Lord in Heaven," Diana whispered.

He silently agreed.

"Wait, though," Diana said with a frown. "I thought we were working with a timeline that indicated the attack would take place at eight thirty-nine in the morning, about the same time as when the first plane hit the tower? These parks don't open until eleven a.m. on weekdays."

She had a point. "But they open at ten on Saturdays." Today was a Saturday. He felt a flash of excitement. "The plane that was headed for Washington, DC, the one the passengers caused to crash in Pennsylvania. What time was that?"

"I don't remember."

He'd already googled the information. "The plane crashed at 10:07 a.m."

Diana sucked in a harsh breath, and they both stared at each other for a long moment. The good news was they had a lead and possibly extra time to work with. They'd find a way to convince Yates to shut it down.

The bad news was that if they were wrong about the amusement park location, or didn't find the bombs in time, far too many young innocent lives would be lost.

SEPTEMBER 11 – 6:17 a.m. – Richmond, VA

"Let her go, we don't need her anymore."

Mustaf had remained lying beneath the gurney for far too long. Pain was his constant companion, and listening to the woman silently weeping for the past few hours hadn't helped.

"Kill her," he said.

The two fake paramedics ignored him. The ambulance had come to a halt, and he heard the back door open. The vehicle moved as someone jumped out the back.

"Please don't hurt me or my baby," the woman begged.

"Get out here, now."

More movement of the vehicle as she was taken out through the back. Mustaf struggled to extricate himself from beneath the gurney, no easy feat as there wasn't a lot of room to work with.

And wave over wave of pain made his vision blurry.

"Where do you think you're going?"

Mustaf looked up at the fake paramedic looming over him. Had he blacked out? He seemed to have lost a few minutes. "Did you kill her?"

"Get up, old man." The paramedic sat back without

offering to help. "We're late for our appointment at the airport."

The driver slid behind the wheel and started the ambulance. Within seconds, they were headed back on the interstate.

Mustaf managed to get up off the floor and back onto the gurney. He tried to look through the back window but couldn't see any sign of the woman.

"If you didn't kill her, she'll point you out to the police."

The fake paramedic shook his head. "I don't think so. I took her driver's license and told her I know where she and her husband live."

Mustaf closed his eyes, finding some comfort in being on the gurney compared to the ambulance floor.

He would have preferred no witness left at all, but it wouldn't matter. By the time the police found these two idiots, he'd be safely in the air on his way back to Syria.

Where he belonged.

SEPTEMBER 11 – 6:46 a.m. – Washington, DC

"Which one is it?" Jordan asked impatiently.

Diana put a warning hand on his arm, knowing that Elam was doing his best. The poor guy looked scared to death at the way Jordan was glaring at him.

Elam had gone back and forth between the two websites, zooming in on the photos to get a better look. It seemed to be taking forever, so she understood Jordan's impatience.

Still, it was better to get the right answer than a forced guess.

"I believe this one." He lightly tapped the screen over

the first website Jordan had pulled up. From what Diana could tell, it was the larger of the two amusement parks.

"You believe or you know?" Jordan asked in a testy tone.

Elam regarded him steadily. "I believe. I cannot say for sure without seeing the carousel up close. The flowers need to be exact, yes? If they're not exactly right, it could be the wrong one."

"Jordan, maybe we just have both parks closed as a precaution," Diana said softly. "At least there wouldn't be casualties."

"If I can convince Yates one or both of these are the actual targets." Jordan sighed.

Diana felt a warning chill skip down her spine. "Why wouldn't he?"

"Because we need proof." Jordan waved at Elam. "And all we have is a definite maybe."

"Let's get over there and see if we can find any of the devices ourselves," Diana suggested. "If we find one, then it's a no-brainer that Yates will close the parks."

"It's going to take time to get there, and what if we've picked the wrong one?" Jordan's voice was tense with the weight of responsibility he carried. "Not to mention the places are huge. We could look for hours and not find one of the devices."

"Then stop wasting time," Sun said. "Let's go. You can contact Yates along the way, warn him of the danger. He may just go ahead and shut them down."

"Bryn and I are ready to go." Diana glanced over as Bryn emerged from the bathroom.

"Can we get something to eat on the way?" her daughter asked. "I'm hungry."

Diana was relieved that Bryn had gotten some sleep and was feeling hungry again. She didn't delude herself that the effects of the kidnapping had already faded, but maybe Bryn was finding a way to move forward.

"I'd rather you and Bryn stay here." Jordan glanced at Sun. "You could stay with them again."

"Jordan, you need more than two people to search the park," Diana protested. "And we're going to get Yates to shut them down, so the danger will be minimal."

Jordan's gaze clashed with hers, naked fear in his eyes. "If something happens to you or Bryn . . ."

"It won't." She hoped.

"She's right in that we need all the help we can get," Sun pointed out. "Maybe we can get the local authorities to assist as well."

Jordan sighed. "Fine, let's hit the road."

Diana caught one last glimpse of the amusement park website before Sun closed the satellite computer. She shivered, thinking of the dire possibilities.

Giving herself a mental shake, she silently prayed to God for wisdom and guidance so that no children would die today.

Please, God, not children.

SEPTEMBER 11 – 6:58 a.m. – Washington, DC

His plan was to arrive at the airport early, hoping to get word on Mustaf's reaching his destination so that the money would be transferred into his offshore account. He wanted to be on his flight and out of DC for good.

If traffic wasn't so awful, he'd already be at the airport. But thanks to the roadblocks, things were moving even slower than usual.

What was taking so long anyway? Mustaf should have

arrived in Richmond, Virginia, by now. He'd expected a call confirming his arrival before now.

But he hadn't heard a thing from either of his contacts. Not the one paying him for making Mustaf's travel arrangements or the other contact, keeping him informed of the impending terrorist attack.

He smacked the steering wheel with frustration. Soon, very soon, his absence at the task force meetings would be noticed. And while he'd booked his travel arrangements under a false identity, he needed to be long gone before they began looking for him.

If Yates really had suspected him, it wouldn't take them long to flash his photograph all over the news. And Yates had the power to get his photo into the hands of every blasted TSA agent of every airport within a one-hundred-mile radius.

Another reason he'd hoped to get to the airport early. If he didn't get there soon, there was a stronger risk that his photo ID would be flagged.

His phone rang, startling him. It was one of his contacts. "Yes?"

"I need you to meet me at the amusement park."

What? That wasn't part of the plan. "Why? I thought you had everything under control."

"Yes, but there has been an unanticipated problem. I need you here, now."

No way. He wasn't going. "That's impossible. I'm needed elsewhere."

"Oh, I think you will come. Mustaf hasn't reached his destination yet and won't unless you do as I say. I need you here. Do not disappoint." His contact ended the call.

His grip tightened on the steering wheel with a rare flash of panic. He didn't like it. Mustaf should have been at his destination, and things should be progressing as planned. He'd done his part, hadn't he?

But if he ignored his directive, he'd never get the rest of his money. And he didn't trust these creeps not to turn him in.

This detour would be cutting things close, but there was still time. He'd have to find a way to make time. Cursing under his breath, he exited the freeway so he could turn and head in the opposite direction.

This thing needed to be finished once and for all.

SEPTEMBER 11 – 7:02 a.m. – Washington, DC

"The president would like to see you." Yates had just returned from the bathroom and eyed the Secret Service agent standing in front of him through red bloodshot eyes. After spending the entire night in the office, he was in no condition to meet with the president, but then again, saying no wasn't an option.

"Of course." He ran a hand over his stubbly chin. At least he looked as if he'd been working hard.

Too bad he didn't have much of anything to show for it. A missing and likely dead pregnant woman, Mustaf's escape, and no location for the terrorist attack.

He glanced down at the conference room where the task force was beginning to assemble. He paused and poked his head inside. "I'm meeting with the president, stay here until I'm finished."

The task force members eyed each other warily. "Sure thing," Geoff North said. "Sounds like you have updates for us."

Not enough of an update, Yates thought sourly as he left the building with his detail. Not nearly enough to prevent another terrorist attack from taking place right under their noses.

SEPTEMBER 11 – 7:13 a.m. – Washington, DC

"Yates isn't answering his phone." Jordan couldn't believe Yates wasn't answering his calls, even though he'd used the guy's personal cell phone. The number only five people had, including the president. He hoped that this was only temporary and that Yates would respond as soon as he was able.

If someone within the task force had gotten to Yates, they were in deep, deep trouble.

"Did you leave a message?" Diana asked.

"Two of them." He slid the phone into his pocket, trying to calm his racing heart. There was still time. The amusement park wouldn't open for a while yet.

He bowed his head and prayed that God would show them the way. They had to get there in time to find what they needed and to shut the place down.

They just had to.

"Traffic's worse than usual," Sun said from behind the wheel. She'd insisted on driving as she claimed she'd gotten more sleep than he had and that he needed to focus on getting in touch with Yates.

Usually he preferred to drive, maybe going back twelve years to the car crash that had occurred when Diana was driving them away from the explosion. The crash that had sent him to the hospital and had taken Diana from him forever. Or so he'd been told.

It was a testament to how exhausted he was that he simply didn't care about letting Sun drive. All he wanted was for Yates to respond to his calls.

"Don't forget to get us something to eat," Bryn reminded him.

He managed a crooked smile. "I won't. Sun? When you find a fast-food restaurant close to the exit, we'll need to grab something."

"There's one up ahead about three miles. I'd prefer to use the drive-through."

"Fine." Normally Jordan wouldn't stop at all, but traveling with an eleven-year-old meant you couldn't ignore basic needs.

And he wouldn't mind coffee. Lots and lots of coffee.

Elam, Meira, Diana, and Bryn were all crammed into the back seat. Elam and Meira were unusually quiet. He knew he'd been rude to Elam yet again but ignored the flash of guilt.

They needed to find these bombs Elam had created and get rid of them as soon as possible. If that meant being rude, then so be it.

He pulled his phone out and stared at the blank screen with a sense of frustration.

Come on, Yates, call me back!

As if reading his mind, Diana leaned forward. "How are we going to get inside if we don't hear from Yates?"

"We'll find a way." He wasn't about to let a locked park prevent him from getting inside. Abruptly, he straightened and glanced at her. "What time do you think the employees arrive?"

Diana lifted a brow. "I have no idea, but I would imagine at least a half hour before it's time to open. I assume they have to set up stuff, like in the food areas, so they're ready to go."

"Yeah, maybe even an hour or two before, depending on

what they're doing. There might be groundskeepers there by now. If so, we can convince them to let us in."

"Let's just hope one of the groundskeepers, or any of the employees for that matter, doesn't have the trigger."

Dread congealed in his chest at the thought. She was right. The person with the trigger could be a groundskeeper, an employee, or a guest.

It could be anyone.

CHAPTER TWENTY-FOUR

September 11 – 7:53 a.m. – Washington, DC

Yates left his meeting with the president feeling lower than a worm, as if he'd let the man and their entire country down.

He had missed several calls and had a couple of messages on both his personal cell and his work phone, but before he could begin returning them, his work phone rang once again. A glance at the screen confirmed the call was his contact within the police department. He desperately needed to get back to the task force but answered as he walked. "Yates."

"Richmond cops picked up a pregnant woman at the side of the interstate," his contact said. "She claims she was kidnapped just outside of DC and forced into the back of an ambulance."

Finally, a badly needed break! "She able to provide a description of the men who kidnapped her?"

"No, says she couldn't see their faces." The guy hesitated, then added, "I'm not sure that's entirely true though. She's a mess. States they have her driver's license and threatened to come back and kill her, the baby in her belly, and her husband. She's been crying uncontrollably through most of the interview."

"Get a cop stationed outside her house, just in case. And keep working with her on those descriptions. Nothing would make me happier than to get the men responsible for getting Mustaf out of the city."

"Done. Anything else?"

"No, I'll take it from here. Good work, thanks." Yates disconnected, then called his Virginia field office. "Ahmed Mustaf is in the Richmond area, likely already in the airport. Shut down all flights and have every available person scouting the place for him. He's likely with one man at a minimum, maybe two."

"We have his photo up on all TSA stations," Special Agent in Charge Dirksmeyer said. "And they're all on high alert. So far, no sightings have been reported."

"Then you're missing something because we know for sure Mustaf is in Richmond." At least, Mustaf had once been in Richmond. That didn't mean the ambulance hadn't taken him elsewhere. But Yates didn't think so. They would want to get him in the air and out of the area as soon as possible. He thought fast. "What about private chartered flights? Have you checked all of those as well?"

"We've put the entire airport on alert, but I'll make certain no private charter flights leave until further notice. I'll call you back if I find something."

"You do that." Yates disconnected from the call, thinking there was still a chance to apprehend Mustaf. A slim chance if the guy hadn't already managed to escape on some small charter flight out of Virginia, but still a chance.

He needed every sliver of positive news he could get.

. . .

SEPTEMBER 11 – 7:59 a.m. – Richmond, VA

Mustaf was happy to be out of the ambulance, even if that meant being pushed in a wheelchair into the private charter hangar located across the street from the main airport hub. He'd been told that a private plane had been arranged for him. The man who took over for the fake paramedic had seemed irritated he had arrived so late.

"Where have you been? We were due to take off an hour ago."

"Hey, we ran into problems. Here, take him. Not sure he was worth the effort." Mustaf's wheelchair was shoved forward with enough force to make his head snap.

"Whatever." The man took his wheelchair and pulled it forward. "We will be ready to take off in roughly twenty minutes per the flight deck, our destination is Chicago. There isn't any time to waste." He'd raked a gaze over Mustaf's hunched figure slumped in the wheelchair. "Can you get inside on your own? You're no lightweight, I'm not sure I can carry you up there without dropping you."

"Yes." Drop him? He wanted to spit in this man's face but managed to hang on to his temper. It was hardly his fault they were late, and again these people were being paid very well to help him. It was inconceivable they treated him with such disrespect.

Biting back a groan, he stood and managed to take the few steps necessary to reach the bottom rung of the stairs leading up and into the private plane. Gritting his teeth, he forced himself to climb. His vision blurred again, but he clung to the rail and pulled himself up each step until he'd reached the top. He sagged against the doorframe for a moment, then lurched inside, finding and dropping into the closest seat.

He'd made it! The man who'd told him to get up and

inside had followed behind him, closing and locking the door. Mustaf imagined the stair ramp being moved back and out of the way.

He closed his eyes and listened to the brief conversation between the two men, before the pilot turned on the twin engines.

The taste of freedom was sweet. Oh, so very sweet.

SEPTEMBER 11 – 8:06 a.m. – *Marlboro, MD*

Reining in his anger, he arrived at the amusement park as ordered. The parking lot was empty except for a few cars off to one side, which he assumed must be owned by park employees.

He didn't like being out in the open like this. For a moment he considered turning around and heading back to the airport, but without the money, what was the point? He needed the rest of the promised payment in order to disappear. As it was, his phone was buzzing constantly, indicating the rest of the task force members were indeed looking for him.

After deciding to park next to the other employees, he pulled out his phone and sent off a quick text to his boss.

Overslept, will be there shortly.

It was a lame excuse and likely wouldn't be believed, but he needed to try to buy some time. As soon as he put whatever this issue was to rest, he'd get to the airport. Maybe he should detour to the Baltimore airport. It might be closer, and he could still use his fake ID to get out on the first available flight to anywhere that wasn't here.

He slid out from behind the wheel and glanced around for his contact, a man he only knew as Amar.

There was no one in the area. Where in the world was he?

As if on cue, his phone buzzed. He answered it. "I'm here."

"I see. Come through the employee entrance, you will not need a key."

The call disconnected before he could say anything more. Cursing under his breath, he made his way toward a small doorway labeled employees only. As promised, the door was unlocked, so entering the park wasn't difficult.

Still, he didn't see any sign of his contact.

Then something hard crashed down on the back of his head, and he saw nothing at all as he crumpled to the ground.

SEPTEMBER 11 – 8:18 a.m. – Marlboro, MD

"Yates still hasn't called you back?" Sun asked as they climbed out of the vehicle.

Jordan shook his head. "No, but let's get inside the park and see if we even have the right place. If so, we'll have more to tell him."

Diana stayed close to his side, as did Bryn. Jordan hated knowing they were here and in the middle of the danger but couldn't deny he felt better having them close at hand.

Look at what had happened the last time he'd left them alone? Tariq had found them and, if not for Sun's martial arts expertise, would have killed them.

No, better to have them close by. He could always get them out of here well before the ten o'clock hour.

"There's the employee entrance," Sun said, gesturing to the left. "Let's check it out."

"Okay. Elam? I'll need you to get over to the carousel as

soon as possible to verify if the flower design you created is a match."

"Yes. I would ask Diana to keep Meira safe as I do that."

"Not a problem," Diana assured him. "Meira can stay with me and Bryn."

Jordan led the way across the asphalt parking lot to the employee entrance. He was surprised but glad to find the door unlocked. He paused for a moment, realizing he was bringing his family into a place that was very likely the source of many explosive devices. Glancing at his watch, he grimaced.

They had to move fast.

"Jordan?"

He paused, glancing impatiently back at Sun. "What?"

"Does this look like fresh blood?"

He turned so fast he nearly smacked head-on into Diana. Easing her aside, he went over to where Sun was crouched down, staring at the ground.

The dark splotches could have been anything, but then he noticed the bright crimson smear on the pad of Sun's index finger.

Definitely looked like blood. And whatever had happened here had been recent if the blood hadn't dried yet.

"What do you think happened?" Sun asked, looking up at him with concern.

"I don't know." He swept his gaze around the area but didn't see anyone lurking nearby. In fact, there was no sign of any employees who had shown up for work as indicated by the cars in the parking lot near the staff-only entrance.

"I don't have a good feeling about this," Sun said in a low voice.

He didn't either. "Let's just check the carousel and then

get out of here. We still have time to reach Yates and to shut this place down."

Sun slowly rose. "Maybe we should just go ahead and shut them all down, even those without merry-go-rounds."

It was a valid point. Still, he felt certain they needed some kind of proof. Something to indicate this was actually the potential source of a terrorist attack.

If they'd guessed wrong and the target was one or more of the monuments scattered around Washington, DC, one that had some sort of hidden flower design, the consequences would be dire. Innocent lives would be lost. He needed to be sure they were on the right track. Before they ran out of time.

As they made their way across the park to the carousel, he noticed there were hundreds of places where the other bombs could be tucked away without being seen. Maybe if they got a bomb-sniffing K-9 in here, they could find them before the park opened.

Why hadn't Yates called him back?

"Hey! You can't be in here!" Jordan swung around to see a park security guard standing there with his hands on his hips, glaring at them. "The park doesn't open until ten o'clock, and you can't just waltz in without paying."

"I'm here on behalf of the FBI," Jordan said, pasting a smile on his face. "We have permission to be here."

"FBI?" The security guard scoffed. "Yeah, right. As if the Feds would give you permission to come into the amusement park early."

From the corner of his eye, he noticed Elam edging away from the group. To give him time to slip away, he approached the security guard doing his best to distract the guy.

"I'm not kidding about working with the FBI," Jordan

said, missing the credentials and badge that normally got him out of tight spots like this. "Here's my phone, I have a direct line to Clarence Yates, the Director of the FBI. I'll call him right now for you, okay?"

"Give me a break. As if I'm going to listen to some guy pretending to be the director of the FBI." The security guard was getting wound up now. "You all need to leave right this minute or I'm calling the police to have you arrested."

Jordan considered the fact that having the police here might not be such a bad thing. But before he could respond, Sun sneaked up behind the guy and used a trigger point hold that made the guy sink to his knees.

"Sun," he protested.

"We need to hurry. Go on ahead, I'll take care of him."

He hesitated, but Diana tugged on his arm. "Come on, let's catch up to Elam."

Trusting Sun wouldn't hurt the guard, he allowed Diana to pull him away. They quickened their pace, trying to find the carousel or Elam for that matter.

"There it is," Bryn said, waving to the right.

Trust his daughter to find it. Breaking into a slow jog, he headed over, searching for Elam. He saw Elam up on the platform of the merry-go-round, his expression grim.

When Jordan approached, Elam held something up in his hand. Jordan abruptly stopped as his brain registered the row of flowers design running along the bench seat of the carousel. It was the exact same pattern as what Elam had crudely drawn.

"This is the correct place," Elam said solemnly. "This is my work."

Overwhelmed with a mixture of relief and dread,

Jordan grabbed his phone and called Yates for what seemed like the tenth time.

The director had to answer, and soon.

Before it was too late.

SEPTEMBER 11 – 8:30 *a.m. – Richmond, VA*

Mustaf opened his eyes, doing his best to focus on the interior of the plane. Why had they stopped moving? They should have been in the air ten minutes ago.

What was going on?

"The tower has shut down all flights," the pilot said over the loudspeaker.

What? Mustaf straightened in his seat, grimacing as a stab of pain slashed through his abdomen. "I don't understand."

The guy who was acting as the cabin steward reached up to grab the radio. "What seems to be the problem?"

"I'm not sure," the pilot replied. "At first I was told there would be a slight delay, now they're telling me all flights are to remain grounded."

No. This couldn't be happening. "Just go," Mustaf barked. "There is nothing they can do to stop us once we are in the air."

There was a long silence as neither the pilot nor the crew member spoke. Finally, the pilot said, "I'm not risking my pilot's license for this guy."

"What are we going to do, then?" the crew member asked. "Just sit here and wait?"

"Yes. Until I know what's going on, that's all I can do. All flights have been grounded, there's no other option."

"Yes, there is another option. Fly the plane as you've

been paid to do." Mustaf worked hard to make his voice sound demanding.

The crewman scowled at him. "Shut up, old man. We'll go when we're good and ready."

"I'll double whatever you've been paid," Mustaf said through gritted teeth. "I'm worth millions if you get me out of here."

More silence and he could tell the two infidels were considering his proposition. If they were smart, they'd take him up on it.

Well, if they were really smart, they'd know he had no intention of paying them anything, much less double their original fee. Once he'd gotten where he needed to be, they could easily be disposed of.

His only priority was getting out of Virginia, to Chicago, and ultimately to Syria.

It didn't matter how many lives were lost along the way.

SEPTEMBER 11 – 8:32 *a.m.* – *Marlboro, MD*

His head pounded painfully, but he forced himself to wake up and think past the horrific throbbing that mirrored the beat of his heart.

Where was he?

He tried to move his arms, but they were tied tightly behind his back. Darkness surrounded him, but there were a few slivers of light shining through what appeared to be cracks in the wall.

He vaguely remembered coming into the amusement park to meet his contact when he was hit from behind. What was this all about? He'd held up his end of the bargain, hadn't he? He'd removed every possible obstacle in order to get Mustaf out of federal custody.

What more did they want from him?

He was sitting next to something firm and hard. Maybe a post of some sort. He must be somewhere in the park but had no idea where.

Straining at the binds, he tried to get his feet underneath him so he could stand. If he could find a way out of here, he could find an employee, maybe even someone from security to help free him.

Other than a bird sitting near the pillar next to him, he was alone.

Then he heard the sound of voices. Several voices. He stopped struggling against his binds and listened intently.

Within seconds, he understood he was in more danger than he could have possibly imagined.

SEPTEMBER 11 – 8:35 a.m. – Marlboro, MD

"Put the phone down or I'll trigger the bombs here and now."

A slender man stepped out from behind the carousel holding something in his hand. Jordan froze in the act of calling Yates a second time. He didn't understand why the director wasn't responding to his calls but suspected it wasn't anything good.

"Amar, I did not think I would see you again," Elam said as he lightly jumped off the platform, still holding the explosive device in his hand. Jordan wanted to yell and scream at him to throw it as far as possible, but then it registered that Elam had called the man by name.

He turned his attention to the slender man, shifting so that Diana and Bryn were somewhat sheltered behind him. The guy holding the trigger wore an employee uniform, exactly the way he'd feared. He found his voice. "Amar, you must know it's over. The FBI is going to have this place crawling with cops at any moment. What good will come of detonating the bomb now? Your big bang and loss of young lives isn't going to happen today."

"And Tariq is dead," Diana added. "So there's no point in pushing forward."

"Put the phone down," Amar repeated in an oddly hoarse voice. There was something . . . off about it. "I won't ask again."

"Did you hit someone before we arrived?" Sun asked, coming up from behind him. He hadn't realized she was beside them and wished there had been a way for Sun to get behind Amar. "We found the blood stains. Rather messy, don't you think?"

"It doesn't matter. He is tied up and left someplace where he can no longer do any harm. He will die today, just like all of you." Amar turned ever so slightly to face Sun. "You believe you outnumber me, but the difference is I don't care if I die. I push the trigger and we will all be blown to bits, including the man who actually believed he would become rich by helping my brother Mustaf escape."

"Your brother?" Jordan echoed. "Is your name Daboor?"

"No." Amar lifted the hand holding the trigger. "Be silent. Today, Allah's will shall be done."

"Fadia? Is that you?" Diana stepped forward, staring openmouthed at the man whom Elam called Amar. "It is! I remember that scar running down from the corner of your left eye. The one you claimed Tariq put there with his knife."

The scarred eye widened in horror. Suddenly it all made sense. Amar wasn't a man, which was why his voice didn't sound deep and his stature was so slight.

This was a woman, pretending to be a man. Fadia was

Tariq's wife and the woman Diana had assisted in her quest to find freedom. She was also Mustaf's sister. His mind reeled as he realized Fadia had betrayed Diana in the worst way possible.

And was soon about to betray them all.

CHAPTER TWENTY-FIVE

September 11 – 8:42 a.m. – Marlboro, MD

Diana couldn't believe helping Fadia escape Tariq was the catalyst for everything that had happened.

Bryn's kidnapping, the death of Chris Wallace, her US Marshal handler, and so many other awful things.

Because of her choice to honor her mother's memory, freeing the women who'd been tortured by the very men who should have honored and protected them.

She stood frozen, unable to move, braced for the inevitable explosion. If Fadia pressed the trigger, they would all be dead.

Even Bryn.

Dear Lord, no. Please. Not my baby. Not Bryn. Please, Lord, help us!

A sense of calm washed over her, and she took a step toward Fadia, hoping and praying that she might be able to get through to the woman. "Tariq is dead, Fadia. Sun killed him. He can never hurt you again."

Fadia's gaze darted toward her, then away as if she couldn't bear to see her up close.

"I know he hurt you, Fadia. I know you fled from him in fear. All you have to do is hand us the trigger and walk away. You will be free of the past, forever."

"I will never be free," Fadia said harshly. "Tariq was a monster, breaking his promise to my brother to treat me well. I spit on him! But when I saw you, I realized there was a way to get even with Tariq. Unfortunately, my brother is not free yet either. I have not received the signal."

Diana thought that Fadia's talking was a good sign. "You don't want to die without knowing your brother is safe. That would make all of this useless, wouldn't it?"

Again, Fadia's dark eyes flickered toward her. "He will be in the air soon."

Diana decided arguing wouldn't get her anywhere. "I'm sure he will, after all, you orchestrated this plan very effectively. I'm impressed. Not once did I suspect you were the mastermind behind this."

"Men are greedy and will do anything for money. And men always underestimate us, yes?" Fadia looked directly at Diana for the first time, maybe sensing a kindred spirit. "He never once recognized me while in disguise because women are nothing to him."

"Men do underestimate us," Diana agreed, wondering if Sun could do her martial arts moves to get the trigger out of Fadia's hand. "But not children, Fadia. Not my Bryn."

This time, Fadia didn't so much as glance toward Bryn. "This is what my brother wants to be done. What my brother paid Tariq to do. Tariq failed thanks in part because he became obsessed with killing you, your daughter, and the FBI agent who killed his father, but I will not."

"No, Fadia, I'm sure your brother wants you alive," Diana pressed. "As I said earlier, you can walk away. Jordan can help you find a way to join your brother in Syria." It was a rash promise, and she hoped Jordan wouldn't give anything away. "Please, Fadia. Let us go."

Fadia hesitated, and for a moment Diana thought she'd gotten through. Then the woman dressed as a man shook her head. "Take a step back, Diana. And the rest of you too." Fadia held the trigger device up higher so they could see it. "Or I'll blow us away now, regardless of where Ahmed is."

A wave of helplessness washed over her. If she couldn't change Fadia's mind, she felt certain they would all die here today.

SEPTEMBER 11 – 8:45 a.m. – Richmond, VA

Mustaf was concerned at the length of time they'd been waiting on the tarmac. He'd repeatedly told these men to simply take off, but they'd stubbornly refused.

If he was physically stronger, he would have forced the issue. But as it was, he could barely keep himself sitting upright.

A glint of light caught the corner of his eye. He turned to stare out the small window. More lights were visible now, red and blue flashing lights.

Police?

"What's going on?" Mustaf did his best to sound authoritative.

The guy stood and looked down at him. "They're coming for you."

No. *No!* Mustaf straightened in his seat. "I already promised to double your fee. If you leave now, I'll triple it. Get me out of here!"

But in a nanosecond he knew it was already too late.

The plane engines died, and he heard the voice outside the plane, coming from some sort of bullhorn.

"Come out with your hands up!"

"Idiots!" Mustaf screamed. "You could have left. We could have been long gone from here!"

The man in the cabin ignored him. He opened the door and lifted his hands. "We didn't know who this man was, and now that we know he's a terrorist, we're happy to turn him over to you."

Infidels! Traitors! This couldn't be happening.

But when the cops swarmed the plane, surrounding him at gunpoint, he knew it was over.

Despite being so close, he'd lost his freedom, forever.

SEPTEMBER 11 – 8:48 a.m. – Washington, DC

"Did you get him?" Yates demanded.

"We got him," his SAC from Virginia confirmed. "But mostly because these guys on the plane decided to turn him in. If they'd just taken off . . ."

"We would have had fighter jets tracking the plane until they were over a wide open space and shot them down," Yates finished. "I'm sure the pilot knew that was a distinct possibility. And it wouldn't be viewed badly, no one would mourn Mustaf's death."

"True. Well, we got him and are using FBI resources to fly him back to DC."

"I want double the amount of protection as before. Heads will roll if he escapes a second time," Yates threatened.

"Trust me, we are well aware of that."

Yates disconnected from the call, then frowned realizing just how many calls from Rashid he'd missed. He quickly tried Rashid's number but to no avail, then listened to the two messages. Something about the terrorist site being that of an amusement park?

A sliver of fear snaked down his spine. He'd gotten Mustaf, but the terrorist threat was all too real. If Rashid needed help, they had to respond.

He swiftly walked down the hallway to the debriefing room where his team was assembled. Raking his gaze over the room, he realized two members of the team were missing.

"Where are Ben Cunningham and Rick Slater?"

The remaining task force members glanced at each other. "We're not sure and have been unable to reach either of them by phone."

Yates scowled. "Track them down, use every single resource you have. One of them has been leaking information outside the task force, and I want to know which one and where they are right now."

The men sat dazed for a long moment.

"Hurry!" Yates snapped. "It's a matter of life and death!"

They jumped into action, digging into computers and muttering between themselves. Yates turned and walked away, dread dogging his steps.

He'd let Rashid down, having been too focused on Mustaf.

If Jordan, Sun, and other innocent lives were lost today, their deaths would rest solely on his shoulders.

SEPTEMBER 11 – 8:51 a.m. – Marlboro, MD

Jordan ignored the sweat dripping down the middle of his back, never taking his gaze from Fadia's hand holding the trigger. His phone vibrated in his pocket, but he didn't dare reach for it. While he appreciated Diana's attempts to get through to the woman, he didn't think there was any way she could talk Fadia out of her plan.

He didn't have Sun's expertise with martial arts and sensed that any attempt to get the trigger from Fadia's hand would result in the bombs being detonated. Bombs plural, even though he felt certain that the one here at the carousel was the only one with the potential to harm them.

And at this range? Kill them.

That other children would be spared was some consolation.

He couldn't bring himself to glance at Bryn. The daughter he'd only just discovered. The daughter he'd barely had time to talk with. To hold.

And then there was Diana. The woman he still loved. If only he'd taken a moment to tell her. Tell her and Bryn both how much they meant to him.

How much he loved them.

He tensed, debating the right time to make his move. If Fadia was going to kill them anyway, he may as well make a last-ditch attempt to retrieve the trigger.

Without detonating it.

A tapping noise reached his ears. He frowned and risked a glance off to his left, the direction from which he'd heard the noise.

There it was again, *tap tap tap*.

Strangely enough, the sound seemed to be coming from somewhere inside the merry-go-round.

"Fadia, it sounds as if the man you attacked is still alive." Sun's voice was conversational, as if she was unconcerned with their impending doom. "Tell me, what was the purpose in that?"

"To torture him with knowing he's going to die, why else?" Fadia responded, glancing at Sun.

He met Sun's gaze and gave a slight nod. Only in working together did they have even a chance of getting out of this.

"Stop! FBI! Drop your weapons!"

The startling command drew Fadia's attention. Jordan didn't hesitate. He launched himself at Fadia, striking the underside of her arm holding the trigger in an attempt to shake it loose, trusting in God and in Sun's graceful ability to grab it.

He hit Fadia hard, feeling only a twinge of regret at decking a woman. He heard Diana shout but ignored the sound as he and Fadia landed on the ground with a bone-rattling thud. He tensed, waiting for the resulting explosion.

It never came.

Jordan lifted his head and looked over his shoulder. Indeed, Sun had the trigger cradled in her hand. She was standing stock-still. Diana and Bryn were too.

It took a long second for them to realize it was over.

They'd managed to successfully disarm Fadia.

"I said, this is the FBI!" the man shouted again.

Jordan rolled off Fadia, grabbing her wrists and forcing them together. "Good for us. Then toss me your cuffs so I can secure this terrorist."

"Terrorist?" The man approached cautiously, staring in confusion at the small group. "What's going on?"

"Toss me your cuffs," Jordan repeated. "Tell me who you are and we'll fill you in."

The man hesitated, then tossed the cuffs toward Jordan. He caught them one-handed and tightly cuffed Fadia's thin wrists.

Then he stood, dragging Fadia upright. "This is Fadia

Mustaf, sister of Ahmed Mustaf. Apparently, she's been working behind the scenes to free her brother and to mastermind this terrorist attack." Jordan stared at the guy for a moment. "And you are?"

"Ben Cunningham. I tracked Rick Slater's cell phone to this area. He's been acting strangely, and I have reason to believe he's a traitor."

Jordan hesitated, glancing at Diana. She shrugged. "I didn't find any red flags in Cunningham's file, but Slater seemed to have more money than he should."

"I believe you'll find him inside the merry-go-round," Sun said, jerking her thumb in the general direction. "Fadia hit him and tied him up in there. We heard him tapping, so he's still alive."

Instead of looking alarmed, Fadia smiled. In that moment he knew.

There was more than one trigger.

SEPTEMBER 11 – 9:09 a.m. – Washington, DC

"Sir? We've found a possible location for Cunningham and Slater."

Yates looked up at Geoff North hovering in the doorway. "Where?"

The guy looked sheepish. "As strange as it sounds, their cell phones are pinging off a tower near an amusement park in Marlboro, Maryland."

Amusement park? Exactly what Rashid had mentioned in his voice message. Yates swallowed hard at the idea of children and families being in harm's way. "We need the park evacuated ASAP, and I want you and I to fly there, immediately. I'll call for the chopper."

"Yes, sir," North agreed. "But you should know the park doesn't officially open until ten a.m."

"Then make sure it doesn't open at all, in fact, I want every single one closed until further notice." He picked up his phone, ordered the chopper, and then joined North. "Let's go."

As he and North ran toward the waiting chopper, Yates hoped they weren't already too late.

SEPTEMBER 11 – 9:11 a.m. – Marlboro, MD

"This way," Elam said, gesturing toward the carousel. "I believe there is a space in the center."

Jordan glanced at Diana, Bryn, and Meira. "The three of you head back to the vehicle. I want you far away from here in case something happens." He hadn't voiced his suspicions of another trigger device, but from the grim expression on Sun's face, she'd had the same thought.

For once, Diana didn't argue. "Come, Bryn, Meira."

Meira hung back, her gaze clinging to Elam's. She whispered, "Come back to me, husband," in Arabic.

Elam nodded. "I will, my love."

Jordan glanced at Cunningham. "Stay here with Fadia and don't let her out of your sight for any reason. She'll sacrifice her life in an effort to take ours."

Cunningham looked uncertain. "Shouldn't I come with you?"

"Just wait here." Jordan tried to temper his impatience. He followed Elam up onto the platform, then around to where they found a door. Opening the door, they carefully went inside.

The interior was dark, and it took a moment for his eyes to adjust. Then he saw the man tied to a post, a gag in his mouth, still using his heels to make the *tap, tap, tapping* noise they'd heard.

"Elam, is that one of yours?" Jordan spied the bird sitting on the ground at the base of a pillar.

"Yes." Elam looked at him with large soulful eyes. "And there are many others hidden in the park I'm sure."

"We'll get a K-9 team here to find every one of them, but I'll need you to take care of that bird. And tell me what to look for as far as a trigger." He stared at the bound man. "I'm afraid to move him."

The bound man grunted and squirmed, clearly anxious to be let loose. Jordan removed the gag first, as it was just a cloth tied around his head without any sign of a trigger.

"Don't you know who I am? Rick Slater with the FBI! Untie me right now!"

"Slater, huh?" Jordan stared down at him, trying to find something, anything that might be a trigger. "You're the one who leaked information from the task force, aren't you?"

"Me? Of course not," Slater snapped. "How dare you accuse me of such a thing?"

"You're here, aren't you?" he countered, still searching for the trigger. "I'm assuming you were planning to meet Amar, AKA Fadia, here before she knocked you unconscious."

Slater struggled against his binds. "Cut the ties around my wrists and ankles, you worthless piece of trash!"

"I'd hold still if I were you, there's a trigger device hidden somewhere on your person that could make us all go boom." There, he saw a tiny wire leading from the bind around his wrist to the guy's back pocket.

Slater froze, the blood draining from his face.

Jordan knelt beside him and traced the wire to a trigger

device that looked similar to the one Fadia had. "Elam? I need your expertise here."

Elam had moved the bird bomb to the other side of the enclosure, then crossed over to help. Less than a minute later, Elam had disconnected the trigger and pulled the device from Slater's pocket.

Jordan breathed a sigh of relief. "Let's get these items out of here."

Elam nodded and went over to retrieve the bird.

"Wait! You can't leave me here," Slater shouted.

"Sure, we can." Jordan didn't bother to look at him. "You're under arrest for treason and plotting a terrorist attack. And that's just for starters." He stopped and glanced back at the man. "Did you pay Frank Carlson to betray Diana too?"

Guilt flashed in his eyes. "No."

"I don't believe you." Jordan wasn't going to trust anything Slater had to say.

Outside, the air never smelled so fresh, the sun never looked so bright, and the breeze never felt so soft. Jordan handed the second trigger over to Sun and rushed over to where Diana, Bryn, and Meira were standing.

They hadn't left the park after all.

In some corner of his mind, he noted that Elam had set the bird bomb off to the side before going over to embrace Meira.

He turned his attention to his family. "Diana, Bryn." He drew them close. "We're safe now. It's over."

"Thanks to God," Diana murmured.

"Yes, absolutely," he agreed.

"I'm glad God was watching over us, but that was really scary," Bryn added, curling her fingers into his T-shirt as if she might never let go. "I don't want to go on a roller coaster ride after all."

That made him laugh. "We'll find something else fun to do, okay?" He eased back so he could look at Diana. "If your mom is okay with that."

Diana smiled. "Very okay with that."

There was no privacy here, but he wasn't going to let that stop him. "Diana, I love you. I've always loved you, even when I thought you were dead. Will you please give me a second chance?"

"Yeah, Mom, please?" Bryn piped up.

"Oh, Jordan." Diana's eyes were bright with unshed tears. "I love you too. But I don't know what my future holds. Our witness protection cover has been blown, and I'm sure they'll want me and Bryn to relocate."

"If they do, I'll give up my company and go with you," he said without hesitation. "But we're not using Frank Carlson from the US Marshals Service. I asked Slater if he paid the guy, and he denied it, but I don't believe him."

She shivered. "I agree."

"I'll make sure Yates takes care of Carlson, but I don't think we'll need the program, Diana. Tariq is gone, and we have Fadia. I'm not sure if Mustaf has been captured or not, but if he managed to escape, I don't think he'll be returning to the US anytime soon."

Hope flickered in her gaze. "You really think so?"

"I do. But it has to be your decision." He wasn't letting her go. Not this time.

Not ever.

"I'll try Yates again." He pulled out his phone and winced when he saw several missed messages. The sound of a helicopter grew louder, and he lifted his head to the sky, unsurprised to see a black chopper with the FBI logo stamped on it landing in the parking lot of the amusement park.

"I'm sure that's Clarence Yates." He smiled wearily at Diana and Bryn. "We have a few loose ends to tie up here."

"Jordan?" Diana surprised him by drawing him down for a kiss. He hauled her close, uncaring that their daughter was grinning at them with a knowing look. When they broke apart to breathe, he had to find a way to draw his scattered thoughts together. "I love you," Diana said before he could speak. "And we choose to stay with you, right, Bryn?"

"Right," Bryn said with an enthusiastic nod. "'Cause you're the best at keeping us safe."

It hurt a bit to know how much fear his daughter had faced since this nightmare began, and he silently vowed to do whatever was necessary to help her get through this. "I love you, Bryn."

"I love you, too, Daddy." Bryn wrapped her arm around his waist and leaned against him.

With the two women he loved the most on either side of him, he waited for Clarence Yates to approach. "Sir? We have Slater in custody along with Fadia Mustaf, Ahmed's sister. We have reason to believe Fadia has orchestrated her brother's release and undermined her husband Tariq with this terrorist attack while disguised as a man. This park and all the others in the area need to stay closed until the K-9 team finds and locates all the bombs, although we have two of them so far."

"Is that so?" Yates offered a rare grin. "Well, Ahmed Mustaf never made it out of the country, we captured him on a private plane in Richmond. This has been a good day all around."

"A good day for Security Specialists, Incorporated too," Sun said, joining them.

"Yes." Yates sobered. "Thanks, Jordan and Sun. There are several threads we'll need to tie up, but you did very good work here. Our country owes you a great debt for the service you provided today."

"That reminds me." Jordan gestured to where Elam and Meira were standing. "Elam and Meira Nagi need immunity and new identities. We wouldn't have been able to do any of this without them." He glanced at Bryn. "I'll fill you in later in more detail on the roles Diana Phillips and our daughter Bryn played in all of this, but Meira and Elam rescued my daughter. Helping them is the least we can do."

"I don't have a problem with that." Yates stared for a moment at Diana and Bryn, then swept his gaze over the amusement park. "Kids," he muttered, shaking his head with disbelief. "It's so wrong they targeted kids. I'm glad you were able to prevent this tragedy."

"Me too." He glanced at Diana and Bryn, humbled to know he had a future with them.

The family God had returned to him.

DEAR READER

I hope you enjoyed *Target For Ransom*, the second book in the Security Specialists, Inc. series. I had a great time writing Jordan, Diana, and Bryn's story, and my goal was to make this book full of action and suspense. I had the wonderful opportunity to tour the FBI and the CIA a few years ago while in Washington, DC, and learned from them how important knowing foreign languages, such as Farsi and Russian, were to the security of our nation. From that moment, the idea for Security Specialists, Inc. was born.

I'm blessed to have such wonderful readers like you! As you know, reviews are very important to authors, and I would very much appreciate you taking the time to leave a review from the vendor where you purchased the book.

If you're wondering about Sun's story, I'm working hard on her story and have included the first chapter for you to preview. I'll provide updates on my website, newsletter, and Facebook as to when *Target For Revenge* might be available.

Lastly, I adore hearing from my readers! I can be contacted through my website at https://laurascottbooks.com. Also on Facebook at https://www.-

facebook.com/laurascottbooks/ and Twitter at https://twitter.com/laurascottbooks. Lastly, please take a moment to sign up for my newsletter, not only do I provide new release information but I offer a free novella exclusive to all subscribers. This free book is not available for purchase on any platform.

Until next time,

Laura Scott

TARGET FOR REVENGE

Chapter One

December 29 – 7:04 p.m. – Washington, DC

"You're up to your pretty eyeballs in danger."

A deep voice from the shadows sent Sun Yin into instant attack mode. She executed a roundhouse kick, aiming high and hitting her mark. A muffled oomph gave her a surge of satisfaction. She danced to the side and kicked again, only this time her foot was deflected away, sending her off-balance. With the grace of a ballet dancer, she spun and found her center before striking again, determined to neutralize the threat.

"Sun! It's me, Mack."

His words came a second too late, her next kick hit him square in the chest. He grunted but didn't strike back, although if the man in the shadows really was Mack Remington, he could have easily held his own against her.

"Stop already! I didn't come here to hurt you."

She went still, every sense on alert. It was impossible to see his face clearly in the darkness. If he hadn't come to harm her, why was he lurking in the shadows outside her house? "Where did we meet?"

"The Mensa roundtable in Geneva, Switzerland."

Sun let out a deep breath and relaxed her guard. No one knew the details of her Mensa group meetings, except those who were there. "Why hide in the shadows? I could have killed you."

"Yeah, right." He stepped forward, revealing his tall, broad-shouldered frame and light blond hair. He dismissed her assertion with a wave of his hand. "We've sparred too many times for you to beat me. I know your tricks."

They'd often fought as teens, verbally and physically, so there was an element of truth to his statement. She stared at him, trying to understand why Mack was here in Washington, DC. The last time she'd seen him was more than five years ago, at her last Mensa roundtable. They'd practically grown up together in the Mensa school they'd both attended, until they'd gone their separate ways.

"Aren't you going to invite me in?" Mack asked.

"No." She and Mack had spent more time fighting than getting along, and she was in the middle of a case. She wasn't in the mood for a trip down memory lane. "Why are you here? What makes you think I'm in danger?" She didn't point out that her job with Security Specialists, Inc. put her in danger every single day.

"Sun, please. Let's go inside." Mack glanced around the area. It was dark and cold, a hint of December snow in the air. "We need to talk."

She didn't move. "About what?"

He blew out his breath, a puff of smoke forming in the crisp air. "You're being targeted. Someone is going to great lengths to find you."

A shiver of apprehension shimmied down her spine. "How do you know?"

"Because they found and attacked me." Mack's voice turned grim. "Thankfully, I managed to get away relatively unscathed. They underestimated my martial arts training. I came here to warn you."

"You played into their hand," Sun said in a rare spurt of anger. "You led them straight to me."

"No, I did not. Give me a little credit, will you? I took precautions to avoid being followed."

She didn't believe him. Oh, sure, he'd tried his best not to be followed, but Mack wasn't an undercover operative the way she was. Her current role within Security Specialists, Inc. had taught her a lot about staying under the radar.

"Thanks for the warning." She was anxious for him to leave. "I'll keep that in mind."

When she moved toward the door, he caught her arm. She could feel the heat of his hand through the sleeve of her coat. It took all her willpower not to toss him over her shoulder like a bag of bricks.

"Sun, please. I'm worried about you." Mack hesitated, then added, "I think they're searching for your mother."

Her heart stopped, her breath froze in her chest. Her mother escaped North Korea long ago. But the current regime maintained lengthy memories and did not tolerate defectors.

If there was the slightest possibility her mother was in danger, Sun needed to be prepared. "Come inside, then."

"Gee, thanks." Mack's sarcasm wasn't lost on her, but she ignored it.

Moving quickly now, she unlocked the door and went inside, Mack following close behind her. As always, she did a quick sweep of her house, looking for anything that may have been disturbed.

Paranoid? Maybe, but if Mack was telling the truth, there was good reason to be. Returning to the kitchen, she flipped on a light and faced Mack.

Oddly enough, he looked older, wiser, and more muscular than she remembered. In her mind, he was always the pesky kid who constantly nagged her. Kind of like an older brother she didn't have.

The way her pulse kicked up proved she wasn't as immune to him as she'd have liked. Brother, remember? She needed to keep him firmly in the annoying friend bucket. Steeling her resolve, she tipped her chin. "Start at the beginning."

Mack pulled out a chair and sat, rubbing the center of his chest where one of her kicks had landed. "You've been practicing."

She stared up at the ceiling for a moment, praying for patience. "If you're not going to tell me what you know, then leave. I'll figure it out on my own."

"Still stubborn, aren't you?" Mack offered a crooked smile. "I've missed your sass." When she scowled, he went on. "I was in Central Park, New York, when two men attacked me. They held me in place, punching and hitting me as they demanded to know where you were. I didn't fight back right away because I wanted to know what they wanted. They used your full name, Sun Yin-lee. When I got as much information as I could, I fought back and got away. Still, I heard enough of their personal conversation to be concerned."

"Like what?" Intrigued, Sun dropped into a seat across from him.

"They mentioned a traitor going by the name of Hana

Yin-lee." Mack's expression turned serious. "I remembered you mentioning your mother's name was Hana."

"Yes." Her voice sounded faint, and she worked hard not to show her deep visceral reaction to the news. "What language were they speaking?"

"A North Korean dialect." Mack leaned forward, resting his elbows on the table. "This is serious stuff, Sun. They're seeking revenge."

The knot of fear in her stomach tightened. "Revenge against my mother? Or me?"

"I don't know," Mack admitted. "Likely both. This must have something to do with those who are devoted to Kim Jong-un."

Her stomach tightened to the point she felt sick. Kim Jong-un was known to be a brutal dictator when it came to finding and executing those he considered traitors. He had no qualms about doing so, even boasting about killing members of his family.

Living here, halfway across the globe in the United States of America, wouldn't protect her if Kim Jong-un wanted her or her mother dead.

"I need to warn her of the danger," Sun murmured, thinking fast. She hadn't seen her mother in years, on purpose to keep her safe. The timing couldn't be worse as the FBI had hired Security Specialists, Inc. to find intel on a potential nuclear threat coming from North Korea.

A coincidence? She didn't believe in them.

"I agree," Mack said. "When do we leave?"

"We?" She gaped at him in surprise, momentarily forgetting he was there. "This is my problem, not yours."

"Wrong answer." Mack's expression tightened, and for the first time, she realized how far he'd come from the prankster he'd once been. He was only two years older but looked very much like a man determined to do what he felt was best. "I was attacked, Sun, which means we're in this together."

Every instinct in her body rebelled against the idea of teaming up with Mack, but there was no denying that he was in danger too.

Because of her.

And the regime's insatiable thirst for revenge.